Penguin Books
STORIES FROM THE WARM ZONE
AND SYDNEY STORIES ·

Jessica Anderson was born in Queensland but she spent
most of her life in Sydney, where she still lives. Her first
novel, *An Ordinary Lunacy,* was published in 1963, and
was followed by *The Last Man's Head* (1970), *The Commandant* (now both published by Penguin) (1975), *Tirra
Lirra by the River* (1978), and *The Impersonators* (1980).
She has written a number of plays and done adaptations for
broadcasting.

Tirra Lirra by the River and *The Impersonators* (both
in Penguin) won the Miles Franklin award in 1978 and
1981 respectively. *The Impersonators* won the New South
Wales Premier's award in 1981. These stories won the
Age Book of the Year Award, 1987. Jessica Anderson is
now working on a novel.

Other books by Jessica Anderson
An Ordinary Lunacy (1963)
The Last Man's Head (1970)
The Commandant (1975)
Tirra Lirra by the River (1978)
The Impersonators (1980)

JESSICA ANDERSON

STORIES FROM
THE WARM ZONE
AND
SYDNEY STORIES •

PENGUIN BOOKS

Penguin Books Australia Ltd,
487 Maroondah Highway, P.O. Box 257
Ringwood, Victoria 3134, Australia
Penguin Books Ltd,
Harmondsworth, Middlesex, England
Viking Penguin Inc.
40 West 23rd Street, New York, N.Y. 10010, U.S.A.
Penguin Books Canada Limited,
2801 John Street, Markham, Ontario, Canada L3R 1B4
Penguin Books (N.Z.) Ltd,
182–190 Wairau Road, Auckland 10, New Zealand

First published by Penguin Books Australia, 1987

Reprinted 1987, 1988

Copyright © Jessica Anderson, 1987

Typeset in Century Old Style by Dudley E. King, Melbourne
Made and printed in Australia by Australian Print Group, Maryborough, Victoria.

CIP

Anderson, Jessica.
Stories from the warm zone; and, Sydney stories.
ISBN 0 14 009708 2.
I. Title. II. Title: Sydney stories.
A823′.3

CONTENTS ·

AUTHOR'S NOTE ·

'Outdoor Friends', 'The Milk', and 'Under the House' were written with the aid of a fellowship from the Literature Board of the Australia Council, whom I wish to thank.
'Under the House' was published, in a slightly different form, in the Literary Supplement of the *Bulletin* in September, 1980.

The first section of this collection is autobiographical fiction. Though I have been true to the characters of my immediate family, and to our circumstances and surroundings, few of the events described occurred as written, but are memories fed by imagination and shaped by the demands of the narrative form. As a reflection of this fictional content, and to put myself at a necessary distance while writing, I changed the names of the characters and of various streets and places.

J.A.

STORIES FROM
THE WARM ZONE·

UNDER THE HOUSE ·

'If you don't wait under the house,' said Rhoda to me, 'she won't come at all.'

Sybil, at Rhoda's side, jumped up and down and said, 'She won't come at all if you don't.'

'And for all we know,' said Rhoda, 'another visitor might come with her. So go on, Bea, wait under the house.'

'Go on, Bea.'

At the foot of the wooden steps, which jutted like a ladder from the verandah of the house, the three of us stood in the solid heat. We all wore dresses of brown and white checked cotton made by our mother. Rhoda, who now took me by the shoulder, was ten, Sybil was six, I was four. I deduce these ages from my knowledge that when I was five we left that house, which, with its land, was known as Mooloolabin, having been called after Mooloolabin Creek, the secreted stream on its northern border, to which our brother Neal, the eldest of us all, was allowed access, and we girls were not.

Rhoda's long greenish eyes, as I pleadingly sought them with my own, did not regard me with her usual love, her almost maternal concern, but were made remote and pale by the projection of herself into her intention, by the heat of her imagination. I had had much delight from my sister Rhoda's imagination, but that day I was resistant. I felt she and Sybil were deserting me. 'I want to wait here,' I said.

3

'Not in the sun,' said Sybil. When Sybil asserted herself, she sought the backing of our mother. 'Mum would be angry if we left you in the sun.'

'And you would go to the gate and peep. I know you,' said Rhoda, turning me by the shoulder. 'You can't peep from under the house.'

Rhoda could be coaxing and implacable at the same time. She kept hold of my shoulder as she and Sybil walked me alongside the cool breath of ferns under the steps, and then beneath the floor of the verandah. In the vertical slats encompassing that area which is still called, in Queensland houses, the under-the-house, there were two gaps, back and front, and through the front gap I was now ushered, or pushed.

'And no coming out and looking down the front paddock,' warned Rhoda, as she and Sybil hurried away.

I could never go alone into the under-the-house at Mooloolabin without an uneasiness, a dogged little depression. Unless it was raining, no lines of washing hung there, and nor did my father use that space for his workbench, as he would do in the suburban house to which we were soon to move, for at Mooloolabin all such needs were filled by the Old Barn, the first shelter my father's parents had put up on their arrival with their family from Ireland.

So, in the under-the-house at Mooloolabin, there was no extension of the busy house above except the meat safe hanging from a rafter, the boxes of wood cut for the stove, and the tins of kerosene used for the lamps. These objects, dull and grey in themselves, left dominant to my eyes the sterile dust at my feet, the rows of tall sombre posts with blackened bases, and the dark vertical slats splintering the sunlight outside. Broken cobwebby flowerpots were piled in one corner. From a nail in a post hung the studded collar of the dog Sancho, who had had to be shot, and from another hung the leg irons dug up by my grandfather, relic of 'some poor fellow' from the days when Brisbane was a penal colony.

Feeling imprisoned, put away, discarded, I stood where Rhoda and Sybil had left me, waiting for them to get too far away to detect me when I ran out and peeped through the garden gate. Above my head, in the big front bedroom where the three of us slept, I heard Thelma crossing the floor, slow as ever in her clumsy boots. Thelma came in from one of the nearby farms to help my mother. By the brief muffling of her footsteps, I knew when she passed over the red rug beside my bed. My discontent with the dust and husks of the under-the-house made the bedroom upstairs seem packed with colour and interest, increasing the attractions of the embroidered bedcovers, the lace valances over the mosquito nets, and that particular red rug, so memorable because of that dawn when Rhoda had plucked it from the floor and flung it over my shoulders.

We had both been wakened by the silence, the cessation, after so many days, of the hammers of rain on the iron roof. Warning me to hold the edges of the rug together, Rhoda took me by the other hand. We crept down the front steps, stealthily opened and shut the gate dividing garden from paddock, and ran splashing down the broad rutted track towards the road. It was a quarter of a mile (my brother Neal has since told me), but memory, woven tight though I know it to be with imagination, insists that it was longer, showing me, beyond correction, a flat extended prospect crossed by those two running figures, one backed with red wool, the other with her long tangled brown hair.

I had no goal in mind. My elation in the expanding daylight was enough. But when we reached the road, a goal was provided. Heard before seen, the gutter was running with water, a miniature torrent, over stones a cascade. Instructed by Rhoda, I squatted beside it. Still holding the edges of the rug together, I put the other hand, cupped, in the torrent. I shouted to find myself holding a ball of live water. I was amazed, enraptured by such resilience, freshness, softness,

5

strength. I had never seen a swiftly running stream, had never seen the sea. Rhoda took no part, but stood at my side, satisfied with my delight, with the rewards of the entertainer, until she judged it time for the scene to change.

'Come on. Come back. Quick. Or they'll catch us.'

Who would? I didn't ask, but gleefully connived, adding my own hints of danger. The sun was prickling the tops of the uncropped grass as we ran back.

Now I heard my mother enter the bedroom above my head, her footsteps also muffled for a moment by the red rug. I could not distinguish the words she said to Thelma, yet could hear the swishes and soft bumps as they gathered up the mosquito nets and tossed them on top of the valance frames, out of the way before mattresses were turned and beds made.

My mother's presence in the bedroom stopped me from running out and peeping through the gate. The bedroom window overlooked the front garden and the paddock beyond, and if she happened to look out and see me peeping, she would call to me in her pleasant commanding voice and ask why I had been left alone. Rhoda, when delegated to mind me, was gravely warned never to leave me alone, because of the creek.

So I fidgeted and waited while her footsteps crossed and recrossed the floor above my head, brisk and staccato above the indecisive steps of Thelma. She wore neat black or brown shoes (polished by Neal) laced over the instep. Her parents had emigrated from England when she was three. Both she and Thelma wore aprons, Thelma's of opened-out sugar bags, hers of checked cotton.

They went at last, together, but left me in indecision by standing talking in the corridor near Neal's room. I would feel safe once they were in there, working. Neal's room, like the creek, was forbidden to me, though in this case the risk was to him. I had drawn a margin of red crayon round a page in one of his exercise books, in emulation of his own neat margins ruled in red ink. The consequent hullaballoo he raised is my strongest memory of Neal at Mooloolabin. Visually, all that reaches me is the misty outline of a thin figure, not much less than man-sized, standing in profile, with the hump of a school satchel on his back.

Neal and Rhoda went to the local school, where the teaching was deplorable and they were likely to get nits in their hair. 'Are we to bring up our children among ignorant cow cockies?' my mother sorrowfully asked my father, by lamplight. They owned half an acre of suburban land, near a 'good' school. They could sell here and build there. But my father, though agreeing about the teaching and the nits, was reluctant to leave his father's meagre acres. From an office in Brisbane he instructed others how to farm, how to treat disease in stock and crops, but still hankered to return to farming himself, so that sometimes he would respond to my mother; 'Better a cow cocky than an office johnny.'

As soon as I heard my mother and Thelma go into Neal's room and begin work, I ran out from under the house and stood at the gate, looking through the palings. But no visitors were approaching, neither by the track across the paddock nor through the long grass from the clump of she-oaks to one side.

But suddenly, under the she-oaks, I caught a movement, a flash of shining blue. I jumped to the bottom bar to get an unimpeded glimpse between the pointed tops of two pickets, eager to see again the exotic high gloss of that blue.

Instead, I saw a boy emerge, in grey and white. For a moment he stood uncertainly in the sun, then ran back into the she-oaks. As he was about the size of Curly Moxon, from the adjacent farm, who was moreover the only child within range, I thought that Rhoda and Sybil had been diverted, the game of visitors abandoned, myself forgotten.

The sun beat on my back and penetrated my green-lined sunhat. I went back under the house and wandered drearily about. In Neal's room work was still going on. I passed beneath our parents' bedroom (which I remember only as white, starchy, insipid, and often locked) and wandered about beneath the other side of the house, longing for solace and company, tempted by the red and blue medallions on the kitchen linoleum, the blue and white crockery on the dresser. In the windowless living room, dimness would make magnetic the forbidden objects – the dark books on the higher shelves, the shining violin in its red velvet nest, the revolving top of the music stand. But the books on the lower shelves were permitted, and beyond the glass doors, on the verandah, stood canvas chairs with sagging mildewed seats wide enough to contain entirely my curled body.

Thelma and my mother crossed the corridor into the kitchen. I saw myself standing at the table (spoken to, tended, receiving something on a plate) and considered wandering out to the foot of the back steps and having a fit of coughing. Yet when I heard Thelma come out of the back door and embark on the stairs, I instantly took off my hat and slipped behind the nearest post, my heart beating in that manner so interesting when Rhoda was with me.

Thelma took a plate of meat from the hanging safe. I was much thinner than the post I stood behind, and I held my hat crushed against my chest, but I must have moved; she must have glimpsed me as I had glimpsed that flash of blue under the she-oaks.

'Hey, who's that?' she called out. 'Beatie? Syb?'

Behind my post, I did not move.

'One of you, anyway,' concluded Thelma.

She turned and started up the steps. With one eye, I watched her feet rising between the treads. Then I ran over and seized the tennis ball lying among the boxes of wood and, by the time my mother's feet appeared between the treads, I seemed engrossed in bouncing the ball against a rafter, and catching it and bouncing it again.

'Beatie?'

My mother stood in the gap in the dark slats, behind her an expanse of sun-yellowed green and the weathered silvery timber of the Old Barn. The horse Pickwick was moving into the gap with his usual slow intent, cropping grass.

'Beatie, where are Rhoda and Syb?'

I resumed my game, saying they had just gone off for a while.

She came and took the ball from my hand. 'Gone off where?'

'You'll spoil it.'

'Spoil what?'

'It's a game.'

'What kind of game?'

Did she know about our visitors? She had sometimes stunned Rhoda and me (though not Sybil) with her knowledge of our secrets. 'I have to wait here,' I said with crafty vagueness, 'till they come.'

She looked dubious, but gave me back the ball. 'You *will* wait here?'

'I promise.'

'And not go wandering off to the creek?'

'I promise. God's honour.'

'Your promise is quite enough,' she said with a tartness I noted but did not yet understand. She twitched straight the hat I had put on in such a hurry. 'And that sandal is loose. Here.'

As she had crouched, I extended a foot and submitted to this service I could have done for myself. Her hair was already grey, making her olive skin look fresh and polished, and kindling her eyes beneath their dark brows. At that time she must have been in her early forties, about the age at which Rhoda died. She rose to her feet to go. 'Mum?' I said.

'Yes, dear?'

'Ro won't get into trouble for leaving me?'

'Rhoda has been told again and again.' My mother turned

9

and started back up the stairs, adding, 'We will have to see.'

'We will have to see' meant that it was important enough to consult my father. I crushed the tennis ball between my palms, hoping that Rhoda would get off with a reprimand, chastisement being the alternative. As soon as my mother's feet disappeared, I dropped the ball and ran towards the front of the house. Warnings must be carried. But when I reached the ferns under the steps I heard the high affected voice of a visitor, and I stepped back under the house and waited.

Rhoda and Sybil came in from the sunlight. Rhoda wore a floppy-brimmed hat of shining blue crinoline and carried a little petit-point bag. Her cheeks and lips were pink with cochineal and her face white with what could only have been talcum, for our house was as unprovided with face powder as it was with lipstick and rouge. She held the bag at a dainty distance and swung her hipless body from side to side, while Sybil, dressed as a boy in grey pants, white shirt, and a tweed cap, tried to trudge.

'You are Beatrice, I believe?' said Rhoda, in a high, bored drawl.

But I could not rise to my part. I was distracted not only because I had betrayed Rhoda's dereliction to our mother, but also by the evidence which Rhoda and Sybil presented of other punishable acts. It did not matter that the clothes Sybil wore were Neal's, made to fit by many pins and tucks, nor that the tweed cap was my father's. Forgivable also were Rhoda's apricot silk dress, court shoes stuffed with paper, and little handbag; all were play property, donated by my mother's youngest sister, who was modern. And Rhoda's hair was not really cut, but looped and pinned to the top of her head, so that beneath the crown of the blue hat it approximated the look of the bobbed hair she longed for, but which was denied to her though granted to Sybil and me.

No, it was the hat itself that alarmed me, the hat, the hat. Not even the modern aunt would have worn it. It was the type called by Rhoda a 'see-through' or 'actress' hat. It was in fact by these descriptions of hers that I recognised it as utterly foreign, and certain to fall into the category of the forbidden. It looked brand new, too, and attached to its band was a bright pink rose of stiffened cloth. And then, to divert my attention (if anything could) from the scandal and mystery of the hat, were the military medals and regimental colours pinned to Sybil's shirt.

Rhoda's body was moving from side to side in a stationary sashay. 'The little girl must be shy,' she remarked to Sybil.

'Why don't you answer, little girl?' gruffly demanded Sybil.

I cried out at Rhoda, 'Where did you get that hat? It's brand new. And those are Neal's medals.'

'Oh, no, no, no,' said Rhoda with a laugh. 'Those are Johnny's father's medals. But goodness, I quite forgot to introduce us. I am your sister Rhoda's rich friend Maisie Lemon. And this is Johnny Pumper.'

Overhead, Thelma clanked a bucket down on the bathroom floor. By my mother's footsteps I could locate her in the kitchen. Under compulsion not to shout, I wailed instead. 'It's not Johnny Pumper. It can't be. And where did the hat come from? It's *new*. And those are *Neal's medals.*'

On my forbidden forays into Neal's room I had seen how he kept those Anzac decorations in little separate boxes, each laid out on a piece of card, with a border ruled in red ink. I was aghast at Rhoda's sheer nerve in having gone in there and simply grabbed them.

But Rhoda was looking at me with mild adult surprise. 'Who is Neal, little girl?' she asked. Sybil frowned and folded her arms.

'You'll get into awful trouble,' I said.

'What a silly little girl,' remarked Rhoda to Sybil. Sybil shook her head in wonder at my silliness. Rhoda turned again to me.

'Johnny's father was a war hero, killed at Gallipoli.'

11

For a moment I was arrested. At the nitty school there were many fatherless children. But the attraction of the word 'hero' could not conquer my distress, my confusion at having been presented with too many problems at once, so that I did not know which to tackle first. I said, trying to be calm, 'That is not Johnny Pumper. And how will you know the right boxes to put the medals back into?'

Sybil gave a gasp and turned shocked eyes on Rhoda. For a moment Rhoda's eyes responded in kind, but in the next moment she had converted her shock into the energy with which she patted her hair and thrust forward her painted face.

'Little girl,' she said with clarity, 'you are not very polite. I introduce Johnny and myself, and instead of saying how-do-you-do, you go on with all that bunkum. I will give you one last chance.' She indicated Sybil, who again folded her arms and set her feet apart. 'This is Johnny Pumper, and I am your sister's great friend, Maisie Lemon.'

Also with my feet apart, I flailed my arms around like a windmill. This reduced my impotence and anxiety, and enabled me to say, 'Those are stupid *stupid* names.'

Rhoda did not move nor speak. The hand with which she had indicated herself remained suspended in graceful limpness near her chest, a hostage to the game behind which she could withdraw into brief consultation with herself. For of course I was right. The names were stupid. Rhoda had reached that point in her creation where her characters had slipped away from her first flippant choice of names and now needed rechristening.

'It is true,' she said at last, 'that I am not Maisie Lemon.'

I pointed vehemently. 'And that is not Johnny Pumper.'

For very near the heart of my offendedness was Sybil's impersonation, which deprived me of the original Johnny Pumper, a foolish pigeon-toed redhead who resided in the sky and was often in serious trouble with his father. Whenever it thundered Rhoda said that Mr Pumper was roaring at Johnny, and demonstrated the terrified tumbling gait at which Johnny tried to escape his father.

'No,' admitted Rhoda, 'it's not Johnny. That's true, too.'

'Then why did you say it was?'

Rhoda's eyes were narrowing, her tone becoming threatening. 'I had an important private reason. It is something to do with the government. And now, dear—'

'And the hat!'

'And now, dear,' said Rhoda, in steady and overt threat, 'I have a little present for you.'

I was silent at once. After giving me a glare of warning, she opened the petit-point bag and took out a small parcel. Unwrapped, it disclosed three big lollies, tenderly pink, perfectly globular. We were seldom allowed sweets, and these looked as desirable as the kind bought in shops. I put my hands behind my back and stared at them. Sybil shuffled closer, licking her lips. I said, through my watering mouth, 'Where did you get the hat?'

'You may take one, little girl.'

Suddenly Sybil and I both plucked with greedy little hands at Rhoda's palm. Rhoda took the remaining sweet, raised her eyebrows as she examined it, then slowly and fastidiously put it into her mouth. With my own sweet still melting in my mouth, I flung both arms round Rhoda and clutched her tight.

'Ro! Tell me about the hat.'

'I shall never tell you about the hat,' said Rhoda blithely.

'Ro!'

'I shall carry the secret of the hat to my grave.'

One of Rhoda's eyes had a cast. It was extremely elusive. Like that flash of blue under the she-oaks, or the movement Thelma glimpsed of the child behind the post, you saw it, then doubted that you had. Even at her photographs I must look closely to detect it.

She can't have been physically punished – chastised – for leaving me unguarded, or I would have remembered it. At that time illness was taking hold of my father, stiffening and hollowing out his big frame, and sometimes, after he had made the long journey home from Brisbane, his coughing and exhaustion left my mother room for no other concern. In any case, it was certainly not one of those occasions when Rhoda, her face wet with tears, would hug me and whisper that she was going to run away, and would give me as a memento her cinnamon brown handkerchief with the clown embroidered in one corner. How we bawled and clung! The next day she would take the handkerchief back.

As for the medals, I recall only my mother saying, with absent-minded benignity, that no great harm had been done, and Neal could put the medals back himself, though Rhoda must promise not to take them again.

Maisie Lemon evaporated, as characters will when untimely exposed, and so did both Johnny Pumpers, the fake drawing the original with him. Rhoda's attempt to reinstate the original during the next thunderstorm met with my absolute stubborn and insulted resistance. Later, an attempt was made to bring on a Christabel Someone and a Cyril Somebody-else, but before they could take hold, we moved to the suburban house.

As soon as we moved from Mooloolabin it became Old Mooloolabin, by the same process as, when our paternal grandparents moved from their first stout unornamented shelter, it became the Old Barn. At the new house we had less need of outright fables. Relations and our parents' friends could easily visit, other children lived nearby and could be asked home, and we could see, passing in the street or standing behind counters in shops, persons of sufficient familiarity, yet sufficiently strange, for Rhoda and I to graft upon their lives our frequently outrageous speculations.

And in a bush gully at the straggling end of the street ran a creek frequented by children my mother would have called rough or even undesirable. We did not have that child-tracking device, the telephone; I would say I was going to Betty's or Clare's and would go instead to hang around at the creek, keeping a slight distance, shy yet fascinated. I kept the creek secret even from Rhoda, feeling that it would lose value if it were not all my own. Rhoda, now that she had friends of her own age, also had her secrets, but in spite of our different preoccupations a special fidelity to each other remained, and for me, the hat remained a marvellous apparition, ever blue, shining, and brand new. At first I continued to beg Rhoda to tell me where she got it, losing my temper and pummelling her when she wouldn't; but she would only give her former answer, or would smile as if at private knowledge as she fended off my fists. And after a few months, though I continued to ask, my question – Where did you get the hat? – became cabalistic, something to sing into a silence, to murmur for the mystification of cousins, or to whisper for reassurance if we found ourselves isolated in uncongenial company.

Only once did the ground of our tacit deceit shift a little. Now that we lived near shops we managed to get more manufactured sweets than before, but I continued to remember as so excellent those three pink lollies that one Saturday afternoon, when my mother was out visiting, attended by Sybil, and Neal was helping my father in the garden, I persuaded Rhoda to show me how to make them. I watched closely as she mixed icing sugar, milk, coconut and cochineal, and as she rounded the mixture between sugared palms. She covered it briefly – a magician's gesture – before presenting it. And I saw that it was imperfectly round and slightly grey with handling. Yet there was Rhoda's face, as confident and triumphant as at Old Mooloolabin.

I took the lolly, put it in my mouth, and twirled away through the house until I reached the front verandah. Here I rotated quickly and silently, the better to meditate on what I had just learned. Rhoda came out and twirled nearby. The wide verandahs and smooth boards of the new house had set us dancing, and a Christmas play had given us our models.

Coming to a stop beside Rhoda, my speculation complete, my decision made, I advanced my right foot, curved my right arm above my head, and gazed upward at my hand. Rhoda, the backs of her hands forward, bowed low to the audience. Beneath our feet, in the under-the-house, the leg irons hanging from one nail, and Sancho's collar from another, were seldom noticed among all the stuff from the Old Barn. Outside in the garden Neal, now clearly defined as a tall youth with dark curls and a meritorious frown, walked in a strenuous slope behind a lawnmower. Gazing upward at my primped hand, I said to Rhoda, 'That hat wasn't new.'

'It's true,' she said, 'it wasn't *new*.'

Undefeated, she contrived to imply, by that slight inflection, that its lack of newness was a distinction, adding mystery, extending possibilities. Filled with delight, I flung myself twirling away down the length of the verandah. Once again, as when we ran back from the marvellous torrent, I fully connived, this time by silence, so that together, twirling at different parts of the verandah, we put my new-found cleverness in its place.

THE APPEARANCE OF THINGS ·

'Rhoda wants to go to church,' said my mother.

'Now why?' said my father. 'Why should Rhoda want to do that?'

'She has become friendly with Helen Scott.'

My father postponed his reply by picking up his newspaper or magazine and starting the browsing that accompanied his evening talks with my mother. When he came home from work, my mother, hearing him mount the side steps and cross the verandah, would go to the door of the dining room. They would kiss and murmur each other's names – 'Charlie', 'Iris' – then he would hang his hat on the rack just inside the door and take his seat at the big table. While he sat in silence, getting his breath, my mother quickly made him tea, or, if he were very pallid and exhausted, would first bring him a tablespoon of brandy mixed with water.

If he failed to recover his breath, he would get up and go at his swinging, stiff, defeated gait to lie propped on pillows, coughing dreadfully, in their bedroom; but usually, at that stage of our lives, he would recover, and drink his tea, and then pick up the *Courier* or the *Bulletin* or one of his foreign magazines, and talk to my mother as she came and went from the kitchen. He sat sideways at the table so that he would face the kitchen door.

At these times I liked to come and loll behind or beside his chair. If I was, say, eight, he was fifty-eight. I read over his shoulder and asked the meaning of words. I would take his

free hand and pinch the skin along the knuckles into a ridge
that remained until I wiped it away. If he had loosened his
collar and tie I might ask him to shrug so that I could examine
the huge hollows behind his collar bone. I also liked to turn
inside-out the upper folds of his ears and smooth his back hair,
which was not grey, but that dun colour left by the retreat of a
blond brightness.

He was a man of unreliable temper, but under these inspections he was always patient and humorous. I don't recall my
sisters Rhoda and Sybil often being present, and my brother
Neal had started work in Brisbane, and as Neal loved to yarn,
and was easily waylaid, he was likely to reach home long after
my father.

By these inspections I hurried to the dining room to make, I
vented an anxiety about my father I was not allowed to
express, but there was also an attraction in my parents' conversation, which often had the tantalizing significance of
something I felt I was on the very verge of understanding.

I knew that Rhoda wanted to go to church, because she had
told me, but when my father said, 'So she wants to follow the
sheep', I was attentive to the sharpness of his tone, church
not having been presented to me before as one of the banned
or scorned places, like the creek or the picture show.

'I don't suppose church would hurt her,' said my mother.

'Isn't it enough, by Jove, that they have compulsory religious instruction in their schools?'

'Not for Rhoda, apparently.'

My father lowered his newspaper and looked directly at my
mother. 'Which church does she want to go to?'

'Well, Charlie, if it's to be any church—'

'Of course! She wants to hear the Anglican bleat. Well,
next week it will be something else. Next week she will want
to play the banjo.'

My mother laughed. I sprang to the rung of his chair and
cried, 'What is a banjo?' and my father raised his paper with a

satisfied crack and said, 'Give her a week. See if she doesn't get over it.'

My interrogation of Rhoda ended by her taking me to see the church. Sybil came too. Sybil and I, close in age, were still dressed in identical gingham or Fuji silk dresses made by our mother, but Rhoda, fourteen, had started high school, and by helping to make her clothes, had achieved a wobbling approximation of the modern styles she demanded. In this and in other ways she and I had moved apart since we had come into the suburbs of Brisbane. When we had lived on the outskirts, on Old Mooloolabin, the land once farmed by our paternal grandfather, that rural monotony had found out our natural affinity and had closely bonded us; and even now, when we lived among houses and shops and tramcars, and had each made other alliances, an invisible ligament remained, and it was always to Rhoda I went for information withheld from me.

The three of us walked across the park. 'I've seen the church before, you know,' I said.

'Not the inside,' said Rhoda.

'Everyone else goes to church,' said Sybil. 'And it's not far to walk. Only over the park and down Murdoch Street.'

Pictures from books were amassing in my mind. 'What does Notre Dame mean in English?' I asked Rhoda.

'We're not up to that yet.'

On the rough beige expanse of the park, both earth and grass being that colour, rectangles had been made smooth here and there, and on these, brilliant green or clayey pink, tennis and bowls and croquet were played, in all the sub-tropical seasons except the stormy end of summer, by adults dressed in cream or white. We walked down Honour Avenue, between the two rows of trees running from the little concrete cenotaph, which was behind us, to the big gates of the park. At the foot of each tree was a white-painted post, to which a plate of some alloy was nailed, and on each plate was engraved LEST WE FORGET, and beneath it, a man's name.

'Imagine thinking those trees would do well there,' my mother would say. 'Imagine the ignorance.' Many of the trees were stunted, and some were dead, and in the rows of posts there were also spaces, where the white ants had been busy. 'I see McCulloch is down,' said Rhoda blithely as we passed.

'Ooooo,' said Sybil and I, shocked. On Anzac Day she and I were among the hundreds who marched from the school down Honour Avenue to the stained concrete cenotaph, each carrying a wreath. Our wreaths, assembled with impatient help from our pacifist mother, were among the worst, but all the same, the ceremony, or the bloody legend of the war itself, did touch some awe in us.

It was a Saturday afternoon, and not hot. To reach the park gates we had to pass the school. When I hung my head and pulled paspalum grass, and diverged to kick the little russet stones off anthills, Rhoda dropped a hand to the nape of my neck, holding me lovingly, keeping me walking. The school stood (I am still convinced) raised above its surroundings on a wide low mound. Although the buildings were on stilts, and had verandahs, they were not pleasantly domestic, nor shaded by trees. There were no jacarandas, figs or eucalypts, not even a military palm. Moreover, the buildings were painted khaki, with brown railings, while the posts on which they stood were grey, as was the concrete area beneath, where we played on rainy days. I was at present assigned to the newest of these buildings, around which hung a smell of damp concrete.

I hated this school quite as much as it deserved. When told to answer a question in class, I stammered. But when I leapt away from it on Friday afternoons, I could forget it completely until the very hour of my return on Monday, a respite which relied, however, on my keeping the school itself out of sight. As we walked alongside its fence, Rhoda tightened her grip on my neck, and shook me slightly.

'If we go to church,' she said, 'we won't walk. Helen Scott's father will pick us up in his car and take us round by the road.'

This was too facile; I did not believe it. She was more successful in diverting me when, without releasing me, she cried, 'Why do I have to fight for every single thing I want? Look at the way I had to fight to get my hair cut!' For I also felt our parents' edicts as too final, their explanations not enough. At the park gates, Rhoda released me and tossed her head very fast from side to side, so that the cut ends of hair flicked in triumph on her cheeks.

The church was built only a few feet above the ground, which was not trodden and dusty like the school ground, but simply weedy and unkempt. It was built of brick, with a stucco exterior painted cream. Wishing to be impressed, I looked up at the small tower.

'The inside is best,' said Rhoda. 'Come on.'

'Don't we have to ask?' I said.

'Churches are always open,' said Sybil with sudden authority.

'Yes,' said Rhoda. 'Criminals can seek sanctuary in churches. Even if you murder someone, you can go and lie at the altar, and no one can touch you, not even the police.'

'That was only in the olden days,' I said.

'And only in Catholic churches,' said Sybil.

Rhoda took my hand. 'You go home, Syb, if you like.'

'No, I'll come,' said Sybil.

I shrank back, rolling my eyes. 'What if there's a murderer in there?'

'You're not supposed to make jokes on holy ground,' said Sybil.

'That's right,' said Rhoda.

The concrete floor of the porch was stained like the steps of the cenotaph. Inside, in her hailstone muslin, Rhoda decorously spread her arms. 'See?'

I saw that the two rows of seats were more interesting than those at the school, being deeper, darker, shinier, and having carved uprights at each end. On the carpeted aisle between I could not imagine Miss Rickard's dogmatic sauntering, nor Mr Alpin's strolling pace as he kept his cane in practice on the palm of his own hand. I rather liked the look of polished brass and flowers at the other end, too, and the stained glass reminded me of our front door.

'They've made a man in the stained glass,' I said to Rhoda.

'Jesus Christ.'

'He looks different from his pictures.'

'It's the black lines.'

'There are no statues,' said Sybil.

'I should hope not,' said Rhoda, in our mother's tone.

'Josie Carr let me look in the door of her church. They have statues.'

'They worship idols,' said Rhoda.

'And graven images,' I intoned, from some deep place in my mind.

'*You* like it, anyway,' said Rhoda to me.

'Yes,' I said kindly.

'Why don't you?' accused Rhoda.

I looked at the altar, where I could not imagine a murderer lying, then up at the ceiling. 'It's not spooky enough.'

'What's this thing?' said Sybil, at a slight distance.

'Don't touch that,' said Rhoda, running to her on tip-toe.

Sybil gasped, and pulled her hand away. 'That's the *font*,' said Rhoda sternly.

'Where babies get baptized?' panted Sybil.

'Of course.'

'Is that all? Josie Carr's is big and black, with gold on it, and steps all round it.'

I joined them. 'It looks like a bird bath,' I said.

We all suddenly giggled, then Rhoda said, 'Sh,' and pushed us both on the shoulder.

'Where were we baptized?' asked Sybil.

'In the different towns we were born in,' said Rhoda, 'when dad was a stock inspector. Which means I was baptized in mum's old church, up in Toowoomba.'

'Let's go and do something else,' I said; but Rhoda said, 'Sh, here's Mr Gilliard.'

I recognized the man who had opened the vestry door. I had seen him at a distance, at the school. But as he came down the aisle towards us, I saw that although his church was disappointing, he himself was a genuine storybook clergyman: tall, thin, light-boned, with a narrow head, shining silver hair, unused hands, and the smile appropriate to that sort of collar. He inclined his head to all of us before speaking to Rhoda.

'I thought it might be you, Rhoda.'

'Yes,' said Rhoda breathlessly. 'This is Sybil, and this is Beatie.'

Sybil, to the amazement, I am sure, of all of us, suddenly slipped into a pew, dropped to her knees, shut her eyes, and raised her hands in prayer. Mr Gilliard looked at her with an unexpected expression, curious and rather hard, before turning on me his benign smile.

'What do you think of our church, Beatie?'

I stepped behind Rhoda and hid my face in her folds of muslin. Rhoda said, 'She thinks it's not spooky enough.'

Mr Gilliard's laugh sounded very bold in the silent church. Rhoda was also laughing: I felt it with my forehead. Looking sideways at Sybil, I saw that she had bowed her head lower and was moving her lips.

'I understand very well what Beatie means,' said Mr Gilliard.

I came out from behind Rhoda and instead leaned against

her. 'Only,' said Mr Gilliard, 'we must remember that God is everywhere.'

Rhoda absent-mindedly put an arm round my shoulders. 'But that's what dad says.'

'Oh?' said Mr Gilliard. 'Then you are mistaken about your father, Rhoda. He isn't an atheist, nor even an agnostic.'

'No, wait,' said Rhoda, with amazing familiarity, 'what he says is that if God exists – you see, he always says *if – if* he exists, he exists everywhere, and not only in churches.'

'Except that there is no *if* about it,' said Mr Gilliard with his peaceful amusement, 'he is quite right. But some of us like to build a meeting place, where we can gather together and raise our voices to the Lord.'

'Oh *yes*, Mr Gilliard.'

It was so unlike Rhoda's usual voice that I twisted my head to look up at her. I had never seen her long greenish eyes so rapturously fixed. Mr Gilliard was smiling down at her.

'I hope you and Helen will come and have tea again soon, Rhoda, with Mrs Gilliard and me.'

Sybil slipped out of the pew and joined us, with her hands folded in front, looking modest.

'Oh yes, please, Mr Gilliard,' said Rhoda, 'we will.'

Rhoda did not speak to either of us until we were out of Murdoch Street and through the park gates. Then she turned on Sybil and pushed her shoulder. 'You were showing off.'

'I was praying,' said Sybil.

'Praying!'

'I was. When he laughed, I prayed for him.'

'*You*,' said Rhoda, laughing angrily, 'you prayed for *him*?'

'Yes, because it's a sin to laugh in church. And I'll tell mum you've been having tea with the Gilliards.'

'Ha. Mum knows. I told her.'

Foreseeing that we would dawdle past the school, cavilling,

I shouted that I hated the church, and ran away. I didn't stop when Rhoda called me, but ran as fast as I could, cutting out of Honour Avenue, passing the tennis courts, crossing the bleached grass, and slowing down only when I came to the row of houses, among them ours, which abutted on the park. I did not go home, but went through the back gate of my friend Clare's house. On their lawn, which was fresh and dewy, Clare and I raised our arms and twirled. We twirled until our heads were emptied, then were filled with such bliss that we fell on our backs, panting like dogs, on the freshly watered grass.

My father's opposition to church-going must have lasted some months, because on the day of the trumpery rubbish, the mild spring or winter weather had passed, and it was hot enough for me to be sitting, as I often did in summer, on the cool linoleum under the dining room table. I had some non-sensical homework with me. It is possible that I was learning by heart the imports and exports of Chile. My father sat with crossed legs so that one boot was suspended beside the table, and as I read I regularly tapped the toe and kept his foot at a gentle jog.

My mother's footsteps passed to and fro from the kitchen, my father's newspaper rustled, and they spoke of politics. They did not speak of the old days, or of their former hopes, or of imperialist wars, or of the yellow men who would take the white men's jobs. They spoke of Theodore and Gillies, which I had only recently understood was not the name of a shop. Without heat, my father called Theodore a blackguard, and my mother mechanically asked what else he had ever been. But when my father went on to call Gillies a turncoat, and my mother said, 'So much for his early ideals,' my father's tone changed.

'And how much for ours, sweetheart? Bit by bit, we fall

back. Do we want the whole shebang to fall down?'

My mother advanced from the kitchen. 'It wouldn't take much, when it's been so undermined.'

I saw her feet halt at the table, her narrow laced-up shoes set together. And now her tone also changed. 'Look, Charlie. Just look at this trumpery rubbish.'

That tone, so intense with disgust, disturbed me as little else could do. I knew that her mouth was turned down as if she were truly tasting some disgusting substance, and that her eyes would be accusing. I heard my father say, in soft astonishment, 'Where the blazes did they come from?'

'Sybil's bag. Sybil has been going with Josephine Carr to their instruction, after school. That's how they induct them. Oh, it is! And you know yourself how they got control of the party. Just look at this. Saints, if you please. And these. And there's something else.'

But now the sudden silence told me my father had remembered my presence. He was pointing, I guessed, at the table top. I bent assiduously to the imports and exports of Chile. The table cloth was lifted, and my mother appeared in a curtsy, raising with both hands the white starched cloth that yet passed straight across her forehead.

She smiled. 'What a little possum you are. The places you get to.'

My mother was twelve years younger than my father. Her brown skin, dark brows, and broad high cheekbones were cited by my brother Neal as evidence of Spanish blood, one of Neal's current enthusiasms being the story of the castaways from the Spanish Armada. He said some of my father's family looked Spanish, too, in a quick nimble way, but my father was one of the tall fair sort.

My mother looked at my book. 'Good girl. But go and do that somewhere else.'

'It's cool here.'

'It's cool in the room under the house.'

26

'Neal says we can't use his desk any more.'

'I will speak to Neal. Run along, dear.'

In Neal's room under the house, Sybil was doing a heading in Old English lettering in one of her exercise books.

'Mum's got your holy medals,' I said.

'I know,' said Sybil. 'They fell out of my school bag. But she wasn't a bit angry. She asked to borrow them. So I took off my rosary and gave her that too.'

The next day, Rhoda came dancing down the verandah, singing, 'We're allowed to go, we're allowed to go.' And I, thinking for one ecstatic moment that at last we were allowed to go to the pictures, jumped up asking, 'When?'

'This Sunday. To morning service.'

Her hug lifted me from my feet. I did not want to spoil her joy, yet had to express my own unwillingness. 'But,' I wailed, 'what will I wear?'

'Your Fuji, I suppose. I'm going to run down and tell Mr Gilliard.'

And now Rhoda hugged herself instead of me, and her eyes took on that rapturous look I had observed in the church. 'Mum says she will buy you and Syb gloves,' she murmured.

'Does this mean I'll have to do all the weeding?' Neal asked our father.

Moths and big beetles hurled themselves at the white table cloth, the suspended light. When they came in numbers, we were squeamish, and put saucers over our cups and glasses, and waxed paper over the sliced paw-paw.

'As well as cut the grass and do the hedges?' asked Neal.

'I would help you if I could, son,' said my father. Though he still did much gardening, his spine was fixed, and he could not bend.

'You girls can do your weeding,' said my mother, 'before you go to church.'

'All right,' said Rhoda and Sybil.

Their assent was taken to include mine. 'Three reformed characters already,' remarked my father.

Neal, his father's acolyte, flung back his head and gave one of his long rolling laughs. Rhoda said with disdain that she could see the food in his mouth. Between her and Neal was strung the same kind of discord as between Sybil and me.

I said that I wouldn't mind staying home from church to do the weeding, but my mother, with the haphazard propriety she could make sound so logical, said that if two went to church, three must go.

Helen Scott's father did drive us to and from the church. My father, who conceded that Scott was a decent enough little fellow, gave him a curt nod as the car drew up, but Neal, working beside my father in the garden, and in equally disgraceful clothes, did not repress his derisive grin.

In church I was hit by a desire to sleep. I was quite alert as the congregation was settling down. I was interested in their clothes, and in their prayer books, some of which had white celluloid covers decorated with gold crosses; but the ceremony had hardly started when I began to glide in and out of those dozes I found so delicious at home, when curled into a chair or under the table while the voices of my parents' group purled and washed and receded around me. These tides advanced on me also at the school, where they were not delicious, but there I had my enemies to keep me awake. I looked at Rhoda, and at Sybil beyond her, but both were as engrossed as at a play. I picked at a hailstone on Rhoda's muslin dress, but she did not notice. In desperation I told myself that if I went to sleep, a tiger would jump on my head and start eating me. His glaring yellow eyes, his bared teeth, his twitching whiskers, kept me awake during the sermon. Perhaps there was some other event before we were told to rise. I lumbered to my feet. Rhoda pointed in my utility hymn book to the words we were to sing. Miss Thurlow took her place at the organ.

I had never heard an organ before, and thought it would sound something like a piano. As the echo resounded from its first fulsome notes, the tiger jumped, his body huge, and soft as ashes. I was thought to have fainted, and was carried out. 'The little one,' said Mr Gilliard later, in the porch, 'may be too young for church.' He put a hand beneath my chin and raised my face to his benevolent curiosity, which, as our eyes met, was touched by that slight hardness I had noticed when he had glanced at Sybil praying alone in the church.

'Perhaps,' he said, 'for this one, Sunday school would be better.'

Mr Scott was displeased with me. I was the last one to get out of his car, but was not slow. 'Go on,' he said. 'Out you get.'

On Sundays we had a hot midday dinner. White curtains with faded blue borders moved at the open windows. My mother looked puzzled. 'Too young? But Sybil is only nineteen months older. Did you like it, Sybil?'

'Oh, *yes*,' said Sybil. She looked round the table. 'There is no hell fire,' she announced.

'What idiot told you there was?' demanded my father.

Owing to his inflexible spine, he could direct a question sideways only by turning his head and torso as one, and this, when combined with the angry blue blaze of his eyes, had a very intimidating effect. Sybil sank low in her chair and mumbled that she had forgotten.

'Charlie,' said my mother. It was some kind of warning, or reminder.

'There is no hell,' proclaimed Neal, 'and no heaven either.'

'Heaven exists for true seekers,' said Rhoda serenely. 'Mr Gilliard explained it.'

Neal gave his laugh. 'Did he tell you how to walk on water?'

'Much is metaphor,' said Rhoda.

I did not know what metaphor was, but could see that Rhoda was having one of her successes, and did not want to spoil it by asking. But Neal first flushed red and then broke the respectful silence by saying that metaphor was what people used when they wanted to get out of speaking the truth.

'Tell old Gilliard to read Shaw,' he shouted.

'That's enough, son,' said our mother.

'Mr Gilliard may even be a saint.'

'That's enough, Rhoda.'

'Quite enough.' My father pushed away his plate and leaned back in his chair. 'Let them sink into superstition,' he said in a faint tired voice, 'if that's what they want.'

Neal reached across and patted my head. 'The only one with a bit of commonsense.'

'I'm not going to Sunday school,' I took this chance to say.

'If one goes to Sunday school,' said my mother, 'three go to Sunday school.'

'No, no,' cried Rhoda and Sybil. 'Church! Church!' they begged.

'This beats Bannaher,' said my father, in weary affront.

'But I don't have to do their weeding, do I?' I asked, 'as well as my own?'

At first, when I saw Rhoda and Sybil climb importantly into the Scotts' car, I did not feel much excluded. After my weeding I could take a book and lie on top of the bags of feed in Pickwick's stable, while the ageing horse snuffled and tramped in his yard below. Or I could go to see Clare, free after early Mass, or Betty, who went only at Christmas and Easter. Or I could wander down to the creek where the poor kids hung out. These children of vagrants, boys and girls, who lived in tin shacks and humpies or any old bit of bush, beat the school system by the sheer admirable persistence of their truancy. They were forbidden company, yet were to be pitied, both for reasons unexplained, except by their classification as Undesirables.

I did not like all of them, but attached myself to a few. A display of the genitals, by both boys and girls, was one of the rites of admission to this society. It was called a 'showing', and was referred for 'passing' to a boy named Les. I have wondered since from what official Les derived his glance of inspection and peremptory nod of approval. 'Pass.' As he was Scottish, he may have remembered passing through Customs. These boys and girls taught me how to catch yabbies, and to roll cigarettes of tobacco mixed with grass. I brought them matches and tinned peaches I stole from our pantry. As I approached down the slope, through the scrub and thin saplings, they would call out, 'What you got?'

I did not mention them to Rhoda, as I would once have done. She had retreated into her own age group, which at that time consisted of three other girls equally devoted to Mr Gilliard. They quietly talked about him as they sat on our verandah or in our living room, each embroidering a small square with some heathenish design, such as a fairy or an elf on a toadstool, which were then to be made into a quilt for the Children's Hospital. Towards the end of these sessions, they brought Neal's portable gramophone upstairs and sang along with Richard Crooks, or they talked about John Gilbert. Secured by this company, Rhoda was now allowed to go to the pictures once a month.

I don't remember Sybil working on these squares, but she knelt each night by her bed to pray, which Rhoda did not.

Sybil and I shared a room, or, on hot nights, slept side by side on the verandah, and as I watched her rise from prayer, briskly dust down the knees of her pyjamas, and get into bed, her look of adult satisfaction, of repletion, made me shy before her. Nor did she talk any longer about demons and bats and pitchforks (which, instead, found a repository in my dreams) but went straight to sleep.

One night I was wakened by my father's cough, and heard my mother moving about, and I jumped out of bed and turned on the light in a panic, sure that the dreaded moment had come, and that this time his frame must be broken by those terrible convulsions. Sybil was kneeling by her bed, praying with closed eyes. I ran weeping into the kitchen, where my mother was preparing an inhalation. 'Stop that crying *at once*,' she said, 'and go back to bed.' To Neal, who came upstairs as I ran out, I heard her say, 'It's no use, son. He won't allow it.' I ran to Rhoda's room, and though the dreadful cough was much less audible from here, found her sitting up banging the bed with both fists. 'Oh, why won't he get a doctor, like everyone else?'

'Because they're all blackguards,' I sobbed.

'Of course they're not. That's just silly. Oh, all right, you can get in with me.'

My father reduced his smoking to one pipe a day. At his chair in the evenings, he taught me how to roll tobacco in the hollow of my left hand with the heel of my right, how to fill and tamp his pipe, then solemnly to light it. By both of us, the solemnity was maintained because it gave the right emphasis to the next moment, in which, after a few puffs, he would turn his eyes to my expectant face and say, 'Best pipe I ever smoked.'

Passing Rhoda's room one day, I heard her weeping. I went in and put my face against the mosquito net under which she was lying, like a runner in profile, blinding her eyes with her hands. I said her name, and asked what was wrong. She turned on her back, still crying, and began to pull up the net. I helped her, begging her to say what was wrong, and by the time she was clear of its folds, and sat upright on the edge of the bed, and had prepared the drama of her reply, she had stopped crying.

'We have never been baptized.'

'But you said we had.'

'That's what I *thought*,' she said bitterly. 'That's what *any*-one would think. And now, because I haven't been baptized, I can't be confirmed.'

'Can't you still be baptized?'

'It would look stupid. I'm too big.'

'I'll go and ask mum.'

She gripped my arms. 'Don't you tell a *soul* we haven't been baptized.'

I was confused. 'But mum must know.'

'Oh of course. I don't mean her. But don't you tell a *soul* outside this house.'

My mother did not, as might have been expected, proclaim that if two were baptized, three must be baptized. This supports my belief that she never did manage to coax or argue my father into agreement, but that to avoid presenting a disunited front, they came to a compromise, which demanded of her that I was not to be included unless I asked to be, and of him, that he would remain silent. Neal may have been commanded to the same silence, but if so, it was asking too much.

Neal would tickle Rhoda and Sybil on the shoulder blades. 'No wings yet?' And Rhoda would not hit him, nor Sybil run to tell, but both would merely collect themselves, draw themselves inward with a determination just too dignified to be called prim.

My mother, too, in those weeks before the baptism, bore herself in rather the same way, though to her demeanour was added a touch of uneasy defiance, which made her march rather than walk. One day I saw her put on her hat, pick up her handbag, and leave the house. I assumed she was going to the shops, and when looking out of the kitchen window a little later, did not immediately, because of that assumption, recognise the small sturdy dark figure walking down Honour Avenue as my mother. There had been rain; the park was green, the playing fields almost indistinguishable, and only the rutted track of the avenue beige. When I saw the figure twitch the right arm in a gesture unmistakably my mother's, I was filled with alarm. If she was crossing the park, it could only be to the school, to receive some complaint about me. But it was a Saturday. I ran to ask Rhoda, and learned that she was going to see Mr Gilliard, to ask his advice, and to explain why Rhoda and Sybil could not be baptized in his church.

'Because if we were, everyone would know we hadn't been baptized before. Mum says it would not look well, so the ceremony will be at one of the big churches, somewhere else.'

I began to be jealous of Sybil and Rhoda. I would not let Neal teach me greetings in Esperanto, nor laugh when he sprinkled me with water from the kitchen tap and told me I had just been baptized by Saint Neal. Rhoda was always sitting now with her head bent, spreading her hair on her fingers and muttering words from a small dark blue book. When I went to read beside her, she put an arm round me, but did not stop muttering. One night, when Sybil and I were in bed, I heard Sybil say slowly, in the dark, with intense satisfaction, 'We are going to be baptized in a big – stone – church.'

I felt lonely, but did not want to lose the approval of my father. Thoughtfully I wiped away the ridge I had made across his knuckles; regretfully I stroked the back of his head. In the words he spoke after those first few puffs of his pipe, I heard a new confidentiality, a comradely intonation.

I may have continued to resist had it not been for the naming. We had all been given only one name, but now Rhoda and

Sybil were each allowed to choose a second name. The
Women's Mirror, novels, volumes of poetry, the *Girl's Own
Annual*, and Shakespeare's plays, lay open on Rhoda's bed,
where the sight of them would not irk my father. Rhoda and
Sybil asked each other, What about Georgia? Isobel? Katherine? I hung round the doorway, pretending to be interested
only in practising the dance steps Clare had taught me. Film
actresses were evoked. Bonita? Greta? Marion? I sidled in at
last, and looked over their shoulders.

'As long as it isn't just one of your fads,' said my mother.

'It isn't, is it?' said Rhoda, my sponsor on this occasion.
'You'll make a new start at church, won't you?'

'Oh yes,' I said.

I knew my father had learned of my defection when,
instead of saying this was the best pipe he had ever smoked,
he patted my shoulder, sympathetic, yet to my guilty mind,
dismissive too. I left him quickly, skipping through the house
and along the verandah to Rhoda's room, where the books
now lay open on the floor. I flopped to my knees, and with
tearful resolution, considered Marguerite. And though on
many evenings afterwards I read over my father's shoulder,
and filled and lit his pipe, I never resumed my inspection of his
person, nor sat beneath the table while keeping his foot at a
gentle jog.

When I was older and crueller, I used to copy that curious
twitch of my mother's upper right arm, but now that I am far
older still, I wonder if by that quick indignant pumping movement she was obeying an instinct to send energy into some
reluctant part of her, to shake some laggard nerve or gland.
Nowadays I find it easy to imagine her, with just that movement of the wing, marching out of her mother's house to

marry my father; but then, as she supervised our dressing for the baptism, and ushered us down the side steps towards the gate, I had no idea that anyone had ever dared to disapprove of my father, nor that she had ever been imperfect enough boldly to defy her mother. I trusted the example they showed me, though doubted if I could attain it.

My father and Neal stood at some distance to the side gate, converting a vegetable bed into grass. I expected Neal to laugh at our cavalcade, and my father to give a humorously exaggerated wave. I did not expect that they would simply stand and exchange what looked like amused adult remarks, and then wave quite casually, and that, even as we waved back, they should resume their work.

The church was big, and built of very pale stone, and was so new that blocks of used or spoilt stone were still heaped nearby, and the earth was still turned and trampled by the builders. Inside, I saw that it was lofty and had many complicated arches, with sharp new edges, and much strong light from the windows. From somewhere near the font I could faintly smell damp concrete.

I scarcely remember the ceremony, except that it was a calm mumbling affair. I was not much disappointed. As we left I saw that my mother and Sybil looked satisfied, and that Rhoda had that exalted expression with which I had become familiar. My mother had been given our certificates of baptism, and at the tram stop we made her unroll them. I gaped at my name written there. It suggested a thrilling and inescapable fate. On the way home, dangling my legs from the tram seat and rolling my ticket into a cylinder, I looked out of the window and saw it again, written in well-formed, slightly shaky copperplate, among scrolls and flourishes of the palest sepia.

But the name was all. Church was no less anaesthetizing. The hats during the brief winter period were brown or black or dun felt, and for the rest of the year brown or black or natural straw; the hair of the boys and men was greased. The smells of sweat and scented grease, the rustlings, the responses, the weighted singing, the pleading organ, the wandering echoes – all were soporific. Mr Gilliard moved along the altar rail, his head bent to the communicants, his hair like a medallion of polished silver, while I called up my new assailants, creatures from my dreams, with bat wings and black talons. At the creek the light foliage of the trees would be stirring, the kids would be watching intently as the yabby rose to the bait, or would be rolling on the ground in fights or curled like cats asleep in the stippled shade.

It seemed useless to try to get out of going to church. Both our parents, and our mother especially, greatly valued what she called stickatability, a virtue we could only attain by absolutely persisting in any practice we had begun. Misery, however, made me try.

'What? When only two months ago you were begging to be baptized?'

It was what I had expected. But then she said reflectively, 'It would not look well to stop so soon. Do keep on for a little longer, dear.'

This was as good as a promise to let me off. I was mystified. What would become of my stickatability? But as the weeks passed, it became apparent that my mother had cooled towards the church. My father maintained his silence, but when Neal's teasing became more frequent, she hardly rebuked him. Soon, even I understood that she was worried by Rhoda's excessive devotion to Mr Gilliard. No extremes were acceptable to her; Rhoda's present stickatability was exempt from her admiration.

'The Rushton girls are joining the tennis club in the park, Rhoda. Why don't you join?'

'There is the dress,' said Rhoda vaguely. 'Fees ... the racquet ...'

'We would manage those.'

'And they can only get the court on Sunday mornings.'

'You could go to evening service.'

Tears sprang to Rhoda's eyes. 'You know perfectly well we all go together, all the ones who are to be confirmed.'

My mother found no reply, but in her evening conversations with my father, I heard her energetic praise of tennis.

'It is a good wholesome game. And splendid exercise.'

'Some of those dresses are darned indecent.'

'Rhoda's need not be so short.'

Sybil did not share Rhoda's devotion to Mr Gilliard, though she said he was very nice, or lovely. From the start, she attended church in the same settled spirit with which I had seen her dust down her knees after praying. It was much more puzzling to me than Rhoda's ardour.

My father was seized by his sickness, and for a week had to stay in bed, coughing and raging. When this happened, my mother was always tired and dispirited, and licence was possible. On Sunday morning I said at breakfast, 'I'll sweep both verandahs if I don't have to go to church.'

Rhoda gripped the edge of the table. 'No, *come*. Come to church.'

My mother looked at neither of us. 'Nobody need go to church unless they want to.'

Neal (who was to become a Roman Catholic in his thirties) gave his laugh. 'Wild horses wouldn't keep Ro from Saint Silly Gilliard.'

Rhoda jumped up and ran from the room. 'I wish you wouldn't, son,' said our weary mother. I said, 'I'll do the verandahs,' and Sybil said that Rhoda and she would have to walk to church today, because Mr Scott's car was being mended again.

•

Soon after Rhoda was confirmed the news was given out that Mr Gilliard was to be moved to a parish in Northern Queensland. He asked Rhoda and her three friends – those Neal called the Gilliard Gang – to the rectory one afternoon and talked to them with a seriousness that was reflected on Rhoda's face when she came home. I think he was trying to ensure their loyalty to the new man, Mr Alyard. In the few weeks before Mr Gilliard's departure, Rhoda was sweet, composed and distant.

We all allowed her her distance, Sybil cheerfully, my mother and father gently, and myself with timidity. Neal stopped teasing her and addressed her in such a low voice that with a flash of her former spirit she turned on him and cried that he needn't treat her as if she were just about to be burned at the stake. Neal abbreviated his laugh.

Sybil said to me, 'Mr Scott says Mr Alyard's name is Martin.'

I went eagerly to Rhoda. 'Martin Alyard is like a name from a book.'

'Yes it is. And Mr Scott says he is young and dark. But what really matters,' she added, 'is that he is ordained.'

On the day of Mr Alyard's first service, Mr Scott's car was in trouble again. I was lying with a book on the stacks of feed in the stable, and through a crack in the wall I saw Rhoda and Sybil walking home with the Scotts along the beige track.

By the time they got home I was hanging about in the dining room. My mother came from the kitchen when she heard them cross the side verandah.

'Well,' she said, vivacious and perhaps rather nervous, 'how was it?'

'I would rather have Mr Gilliard,' said Sybil, 'but he is very nice.'

'I'm going to put my hat away,' said Rhoda.

'You put yours away, too, Sybil,' said my mother resignedly. 'Then both of you come out and give me a hand with the dinner. And you,' she said to me, 'I've been looking for you. You may set the table.'

In the distance, at the school, I saw Mr Alyard as a tall young burly man who crossed the ground with boisterous and uncoordinated strides. I did not see him lunge, as demonstrated by Rhoda for my benefit.

'When he wants to emphasize a point, he bowls a sort of underarm. Look.'

She stamped a foot forward, drew her right arm back, and bowled an imaginary ball.

'And he spits. Come here and I'll show you.'

'No thanks,' I would say, running away. If she caught me, I would cover my head with my hands, giggling, while she showered me with spittle.

Sybil came across us one day. 'Ro, you're not fair,' she said. 'Mr Alyard is really sincere.'

'Oh yes,' said Rhoda, 'he is sincere.'

She continued to go to church until the day when Mr Scott's car broke down on the road through the gully. She told the others she felt sick, and walked back home. 'It was too late to go anyway,' she said to me. In a hurry to finish my weeding, I merely nodded at her shining shoes on the grass beside my working hands, and wondered why she lingered.

All of us, with a diplomacy that often went awry, would make a bid for what we wanted at the table, where one parent might catch a mood of approval from the other. Here, that Sunday night, Rhoda announced that she would join the tennis club.

Stung by her daughter's presumption, my mother said, 'Will you indeed?' before catching, from the other end of the table, the required mood. 'Well, I know it was my suggestion.'

'Yes,' said Rhoda.

'You won't wear a downright indecent dress,' said my father.

'Dad,' said Neal, 'they can't wear them down to the ankles.'

'Trust *you*!' said Rhoda with fury. 'As if there's nothing in between.'

'She doesn't like Alyard, that's it,' said Neal.

'What's he like, this fellow Alyard?' asked my father.

'A bit like Neal, in fact,' said Rhoda coolly.

'You will make your own tennis dress, Rhoda,' said my mother.

'Make it out of your confirmation outfit,' said Neal.

Neal so seldom got my father's stiff-backed blue glare that he withered beneath it. My mother spoke calmly to Rhoda. 'You could ask Gwen or Helen to lend you a pattern, dear. And you can go to evening service.'

'You said no one need go to church unless they want to.'

'Fair enough, mum' said Neal.

I sat next to my father at the table, and perhaps it was only I who caught (such a fine shade it was) his mood of assent.

Next Sunday, dressed for tennis, Rhoda said to me, 'Come out to the front. I want to see Mr Scott looking more hurt than angry.'

When Mr Scott fulfilled this prediction, Rhoda brazenly waved to him with her racquet. '*Oh, Ro!*' said Helen Scott, standing by the open door of the car protectively to usher Sybil in. When Rhoda and I were adults we were still mournfully breathing it out. '*Oh, Ro!*'

Rhoda told me that if I could contrive a good alibi, she would take me to the pictures. As our local picture theatre was fobbed off with films the more powerful operators would not accept, the first film I saw was a German *Faust*. We sat in canvas seats, our upturned eyes reflecting the light as it pounced and retreated. I was fascinated as by my parents' evening conversations, in which plain patches were interspersed with enigmas I felt I was soon to understand. This Faust, about to be claimed by Mephistopheles, was saved, or so it seemed to me, by a vision of Gretchen – a vision which incorporated, anyway, a feminine face, and which came in a burst of silver to the screen, flowering fast, then lingering, then nailed by the subtitle, LOVE.

We had to let everyone go out first at interval, because Rhoda was crying. She sidled with her head down past the ice-cream and lolly stall, letting me scuttle behind her. When we reached the street and she turned for home, I realized she had really meant it when she had said we wouldn't stay for the second half, because she had seen it in the city.

'But *I* haven't,' I said.

'It was what we agreed. You have to keep promises. Oh, it was a sad ending.'

She was walking fast; I skipped indignantly beside her. 'I was never really religious at all,' she said in a burst. 'I feel ashamed, as if it was all a pose. But *honestly*, it felt so real.' She began to cry again. 'Oh, it was sad.'

Mr Scott's car broke down completely, and as he could not afford a new one, Sybil walked with the Scott family down Honour Avenue to church. I saw them come and go from the kitchen window, from the stacked bags of feed in the stable, from the boughs of Clare's mango tree. When they passed the tennis courts Rhoda would give them an exuberant wave, and later would show me how neatly they waved back.

'Still,' she would say, 'you can't deny that Syb really means it. I don't know why, and neither does she.'

At high school Rhoda played on the tennis team, joined the choir, and was sometimes home as late as my father, or even Neal. More and more, now, she belonged with those who dressed every weekday with dutiful care, who wore serge or worsted even in heat of a hundred degrees or more, and whose footsteps could be heard morning and evening as they walked between the two rows of timber houses to the tram stop at the top of the street. From the broad road set with shining tram-lines the street dropped sharply down, then flattened out. If my father and Rhoda came home on the same tram, they would walk down the street together, Rhoda smilingly responding to neighbours' greetings, my father giving his stiff halfturn and lifting his hat. If Neal and Rhoda came home on the same tram, they might start down the street together, but when Neal stopped to yarn about this or that, Esperanto, the plaiting of stockwhips, or the League of Nations, Rhoda would impatiently cross to the other side of the street, our side, behind which lay the park. Going across the park to school, Sybil and I would start off together, but would drift apart as if by instinct, to walk each alone or in separate groups. On the trodden dusty ground, in front of the ugly school, beneath the Union Jack and the Southern Cross, we hundreds fell in at first bell into soldierly lines, were commanded to stand straight, to stand still, were inspected, and at second bell were marched in to shouts of *Lep*-ri! *Lep*-ri! From these ranks occasionally broke one of the poor kids, always a boy, pounding away, showing his hardened heels, his spirit crying *Enough*! resounding in my heart, while from the ranks of the good kids rose that soft shocked feminine sycophantic Oooooooo! On the verandah, Mr Alpin, with his flexible cane, very lightly, and all in good sport, hit the calves of the girls' legs as they passed. It was said to be one of the best state schools in Queensland, and so it may have been, in that society where brutality and gentleness rested so easily side by side.

I wept long and hard when Rhoda died. I was in my thirties, she in her early forties. Later, speaking to her widower, I mentioned the religious feelings of her girlhood.

'I thought perhaps when she knew she was to die,' I said, 'she may have asked for a clergyman to visit her.'

'We talked about that,' he said. 'She said only if it could be Mr Gilliard. You know how I feel about these things, but I rang and enquired, and it turns out he's dead. They told me he became a bishop.'

'He would become a bishop.'

'That's what she said. She had hardly even mentioned his name before. What was he like? Do you remember?'

'Oh yes,' I said. And I went on to describe him – his manner of bending, his fine light bones, his narrow head, his unused hands, his silver hair, never once pausing to reflect that that was not what Rhoda's widower had asked me. He had not asked me what Mr Gilliard looked like.

AGAINST THE WALL ·

F's and S's were the worst, but I was sure I remembered a time when even they came unimpeded from my mouth.

My stammer was one of the many things not mentioned in our family, but I often pondered it in my mind. It baffled me so much that at last I went to Rhoda, who was six years my senior, and asked if it had begun after I had that f-f-fall from the ladder propped against the wire enclosure of the half-built tennis court in the park.

Rhoda said she was pretty sure I used to stammer a bit at Old Mooloolabin, before we moved into the suburbs and became acquainted with such things as tennis courts and parks. I asked Sybil, but she, close to my own age, remembered no more than I did. But when I asked Neal, the eldest of us all, he replied reluctantly that yes, if I must know, I was already stammering a bit before we moved into the new house, and that the best thing to do was just to ignore it.

I went and asked my mother if I had been born with it. 'Indeed you were not,' she indignantly replied. She always resisted any suggestion that any of her four children had not come perfect into the world. In a Church of England upbringing she must have heard of the sins of the fathers, but perhaps she was required to stifle all such ignorance and superstition when she became active in the Queensland labour movement in which she met my father.

'It's not a stammer at all,' she said. 'It's only a little hesitation. Ignore it, and it will pass.'

I imagine us both standing in the radiation from the wood stove. I often approached her as she worked there, because I did not want her undivided attention. We employed no farm girl now to come in daily to help her, but only Mrs Hanly on Mondays. I fiddled with the row of ladles and spoons and said, 'Then why isn't it passing?'

'Did you stammer just then?'

'No,' I admitted.

'Well, you see?'

'But I do other times.'

'That's because you dwell on it. Stop thinking about it, and it will pass.'

But I couldn't stop. It was so mysterious. I was puzzled especially by its long remissions. It would be absent for hours, even for days, and then suddenly, there it would be, in response, I felt, to some emanation, either from inside myself, or issuing from those I was speaking to. *What is it?* I would inwardly cry, while outfacing mimicry or commiseration.

What *is* it? There was no reply. I tried to settle for the family attitude: ignore it and it will pass. At home and with my friends this was fairly easy, but at the ugly school across the park it was considerably less easy, and when a new teacher, Miss Rickard, came into the classroom one day and took charge, it became impossible.

Miss Rickard did not like teaching us.

'Oh, you po-or barbarians. Or, as you yourselves would say, *pore*.'

Sometimes she would take the class into her confidence. 'I have travelled,' she once loudly announced, 'in realms of gold.' She let her glance move slowly over us, showing incredulity at her own presence before us. She was short and slender, about forty, and wore interesting embroidered blouses and short, dark knife-pleated skirts.

When I mentioned the realms of gold at the table at home, my father remarked that she must have been quoting, Sybil said that Miss Rickard had spent two years in Europe, and Neal said, indistinctly but forcefully, 'Much *have* I travelled in *the* realms of gold.'

He had not been quite able to finish one of his huge mouthfuls before speaking. 'Neal makes me sick,' cried Rhoda with equal force.

'That's enough,' said our parents together.

'Keats,' said Neal contentedly.

The word-blocking emanation issued very strongly from Miss Rickard, or from myself in her presence. When called on to answer a question, I held up the class and diverted everyone's attention, so was excused from answering until, one afternoon, Miss Rickard happened to follow in the footsteps of myself and my friends, Betty and Clare, across the park.

'You,' she said the next day. 'You can speak perfectly well when it pleases you. Now, stand up.'

I stood, the hinged seat clacking against the desk behind mine. I knew I was not innocent of provocation. It was likely that she had heard me asking Betty and Clare just to look at that pooh-ah little bird.

'Now,' said Miss Rickard, 'you will kindly answer this.'

As I struggled and hissed, the class grew restless. Some giggled. 'Very well,' said Miss Rickard. 'Perhaps tomorrow you will change your mind. Now please go and stand against the wall.'

Miss Rickard did not give cuts, but used her cane only as a pointer. She told us she would not demean herself by giving us cuts.

For a week or so Miss Rickard would challenge me to answer a question, and a few minutes later, there I would be, against the wall, wiping with the sole of one sandal the timber on which the feet of trouble makers had left a row of marks like the shadow of darkened teeth. Then, for days, perhaps for a whole week, she would suspend the challenge, and I would hope that she had understood, or had forgotten me. Now I think it likely that she herself was sick of it, worried by it, and wanted a rest. In any case, she would always return to the attack.

'Come along now. Stand up and give us the answer. We all know that you know it.'

I can't imagine why Miss Rickard believed I had devised this torment for myself, nor why she persisted in her belief, and kept us locked in a struggle she was doomed to lose, for as I stood and struggled to speak, the former emanation came to seem like a substance, visualised by me as a tangled mass of some sort, spiny, prickly, or a forward-inclining jagged rock which blocked at last even the contorted sounds I had managed before. I think she did suspect then that speech was truly beyond my control, because she spoke to me, less curtly, of will power, but that exhortation did not help either.

Somewhere in Australia in the twenties there may have been parents' associations, but I have heard of none in Brisbane. On the contrary, parental intervention was considered very eccentric, and was dreaded by the children themselves. At the nitty school Neal and Rhoda had attended when we lived on Old Mooloolabin, our father's intercession in school affairs had resulted in daily taunts from the other children that Rhoda and Neal had a mad father. The nitty school was one of the reasons my mother had advanced for moving from my father's childhood home, and I now often heard her commend the ugly school across the park, saying with the utmost confidence that it was one of the best schools in Queensland, and my father would agree, replying that in that respect at least, the move had been a success. Sybil, two classes above mine, did not complain, and Rhoda had had an uneventful attendance there before going on to high school. So that left me, only me – my troubles must be my own fault, in accord with my other transgressions, such as arriving in class late, going to play with the poor kids at the creek, smoking Betty's father's cigarettes, and stealing threepences to buy pies from the pieman who came to the school in his painted cart, ringing his bell, every lunch hour.

I am not sure how my parents came to hear of my trouble, but as it was only a few days after the headmaster came into the classroom and found me against the wall, I think he must have summoned my mother, by letter, to the school. I heard of it only when Betty and Clare, as we set off one day for home, whispered that they had just seen my mother going with Miss Rickard into the headmaster's office. I gasped, and we all three tried to think what I had done. I could think only of the pies, which my mother said were nasty unhygienic things, on no account to be touched.

At home, I said nothing to Sybil (I always thought of Sybil as 'on the other side') but waited with anxiety until I heard Rhoda's tread on the side steps.

I trailed after her to her room. 'Ro, do you know what? Mum's over at the school.'

Rhoda put her panama hat on the bed, upside down, to let the sweat band dry out. 'You've been dawdling across the park again, I bet, Bea, and getting there half an hour late.'

'I haven't. Not si-si-si-'

'Since Miss Rickard?' Rhoda sat on the edge of her bed staring at me while she unlaced her shoes. 'Do you do that much there?'

'I told you about it,' I said angrily.

'Then that's it. Holding up the class.'

'You forgot I told you.'

'I have things on my mind.'

'What things?'

'It's too hard to explain.'

'I wish I could run away.'

'Don't worry. If they go after school, hardly anyone sees them. Not like dad that time. When I think of it!'

'It can't be only for holding up the class.'

'You could ask mum when she comes home.'

'You know she won't tell me. They never tell us anything.'

'Well, it will come out in the end.'

Rhoda took off her school tie and hung it on the end of the bed to dry out. In spite of daily baths in the cold hard tap water, and an occasional sluice with the precious rain water from the tank, all the older ones must often have smelled of sweat. Rhoda took off her navy blue skirt and held it up to see if the pleats were sharp enough, or if she would have to light the petrol iron and press the sweat back into the serge. I still wore my gingham dresses, which Mrs Hanly washed every Monday, and hung, with Sybil's, in a row on a line across the back yard, or, if it rained, under the house.

When my mother came home from the school, she put a kindly hand on my shoulder, but I saw that she was smouldering and taciturn, and when my father arrived home from work, and I lolled about his chair, she told me to leave the room; she wished to speak to him privately.

I went to pester Rhoda again, but she was cleaning the bath, and was in high declamation.

'It's not my turn, it's Syb's turn. Why does mum always say it's my turn? And anyway, why can't Neal have a turn? He's the biggest and dirtiest. Just because he's a boy. Or man, according to him.'

At the table that night it was apparent that my mother's taciturn mood had been dispelled by her talk with my father. Both were noticeably gentle and attentive towards me, and towards each other were rather humorous and conspiratorial. My reading of these signs gave me nothing specific; it was not until I went to the school next day that I got a glimmering of what had happened in the headmaster's office.

Miss Rickard, after asking me a question, told me not to bother to stand. She explained to the class that I was to be excused from standing, but would stay seated, just as I was, and they would see how nicely and promptly I answered. And in the weariness and irony with which she soon passed the question to another child, I heard her addressing my mother.

When I reached home that afternoon, my mother was on the side verandah to greet me.

'How was school today, dear?'

'Good.' I ran past her, through the dining room, into the kitchen – her footsteps following – and took the lid from the bread crock.

'I hoped it would be,' she said.

My side vision caught a nervous gesture of hers, patting or smoothing the dress over her thighs. 'Bread rolls!' I said joyfully.

'I was sure,' she said, 'that that little hesitation became worse in class because of the psychological effect of having to stand and to draw attention to yourself. I explained to your teacher that if you answered sitting down, it would be just like speaking at the table with us.'

'Yes,' I said. I sliced a bread roll, trying to sound like Sybil. 'Oooo, I love these bread rolls. I'm terribly hungry.'

My mother could always be distracted by our appreciation of food. It gave her intense satisfaction to feed us well. It expressed both her love for us and her triumph over the shortages of an immigrant childhood. Hovering, wishing to share the ritual, she removed the gauze dome from the butter and cheese, reminded me that there were plenty of tomatoes, and suggested that there might be ripe bananas on the hand hanging under the house.

The next morning, I stole a packet of dates from the pantry, and instead of going to the school, took my satchel and lunch to the forbidden territory of the creek.

A few months before, among the children of vagrants I met at the creek on Sundays, two new ones had appeared, a twin brother and sister, the Kellaways, both very thin and knuckly and narrow, almost albino. Everything about these two interested me. I was fascinated to observe the way their joints moved, their forearms scaled by the sun, the blinking made conspicuous by their whitish lashes, the set of their hand-me-down felt hats, their professional way with the yabbies. And they were so good-tempered with me, almost condescending as they put their heads back and squinted drolly at me down their cheeks. I always felt joyous after seeing them, and would run home waving my arms point-lessly about. When they disappeared, without warning, as such children did, I felt so deprived that I had to convince myself they would soon return; and now, while my expecta-tion was still high, there they were, as if in reward for my first truancy, in their unmistakable grasshopper crouch by the creek.

Shouting their names – Peggy! Des! – I ran recklessly down the slope, vaulting the low scrub, yelling and halloo-ing, my satchel flying and thumping, until I saw that Peggy was running softly towards me, tapping her lips. As I slowed down I heard Des say, 'Damn and blast it.'

'There,' said Peggy. 'That's all your noise. It was a big one, too.'

'Ar, well,' said Des, with the cadence of resignation.

Des and Peggy took their yabbies home for food. If I caught any, they took those too. 'Gee,' I said, 'I'm sorry.'

'Ar well,' said Peggy.

'I've got a packet of dates.'

'Never mind,' said Des. 'I'll get him yet.'

'He didn't take the meat,' said Peggy. 'That's one thing.'

'I've got dates.'

'We heard you,' said Des. 'Now shut up till I get him.'

'I'm so sorry,' I said again.

'Ar, well, never mind,' they said together, with their lilting resignation.

I took off my sandals, lay on the rough ground, and rubbed the soles of my feet luxuriously against the trunk of a she-oak. Holding aloft *The Last of the Mohicans*, first in one hand and then in the other, I read, mechanically waving away the mosquitoes and wiping ants off my legs with my feet. Peggy and Des murmured and fished, the thin foliage shifted against the bright sky, the print blurred, and I lay on my side and slept. At that time I often slept in the day because my nights were disturbed by the dark angel in his various forms. I was wakened by Peggy and Des wiping the ants off me and asking me 'What about those dates?' A sustained distant aerial hubbub told me that school was out for lunch. I could have worried, but would have been ashamed to show concern before the Kellaways. The yabby tin was full, and for a while after lunch we ran around in the heat, flinging ourselves violently to the ground and shooting our enemies with sticks. Practised in being an enemy, I was admired for the loosened knees and head wobble with which I went down. I already knew that their father had shot many people during the war, and today, as we cooled off with our feet in the clayey mud, I also learned that their mother was the most beautiful woman in Queensland, and that they lived in the best camp on Budjerra Heights.

'If anyone moves into that camp while we're away,' said Des, 'they know they got to get out the minute we get back. No fight, no roaring, they just got to go.'

Peggy was nodding, seeming to share a musing pride and happiness in their camp. And I was suddenly begging them to take me to see it. I begged desperately, but they would not promise. I told them about *The Last of the Mohicans*, but they knew all that, because they often went to the pictures. I told them about *Treasure Island*, and they listened intently, and asked for a loan of the book.

'If I can come to your camp,' I said.

'Righto,' said Des.

'We'll have to ask first,' said Peggy.

The word-blocking emanation seldom came between us, and when it did, they were able to dispel it by giving me that droll squint down their cheeks. They went off with their tin of yabbies, and I went on with the Mohicans, until once again the aerial hubbub reached me, and I knew I had to go home.

In the kitchen, Sybil was taking bread from the crock. She excitedly told me her class was going to be allowed to use the school tennis court. She jumped up and down and said, 'Isn't it marvellous!' She had not noticed my absence. The next day, afraid to go to the school without a note of explanation for Miss Rickard, I took extra sandwiches, and three bananas, and went to the creek again.

The Kellaways were not there, but except when the miniature pandemonium of lunchtime stirred my anxiety, I passed the day contentedly enough, reading, eating, paddling, and in the afternoon becoming absorbed in searching the ground for treasure. I had never looked for treasure at the creek before, and was surprised by what I found. How did all those little pieces of patterned china, those smoothed fragments of bubbly glass, like petrified water, come to be in this little bit of bush between two suburbs? The little rubber bag I found being too small for a balloon, I decided it was a toy titty bottle. I washed all these treasures in the creek, set them out on a log to dry, and at three o'clock wrapped them in my lunch napkin and set off for home.

Hoping for a miracle, but feeling doomed, I dawdled, indulging in a daydream in which Peggy and Des were old enough to adopt me. When I got home, after four, I saw Sybil in the back yard practising serves with Rhoda's racquet. My mother was sitting at the dining room table, writing a letter. She said without looking up, 'Come here.'

I stood at her side. She did not stop writing. My eyes gathered the words from her page ... *interested to know if you grow roses there* ... She was writing to the Indian woman from Penfriends for Peace. 'You weren't at school,' she said.

... *as you are on the cooler highlands* ... 'Who told you?' I asked.

'That's beside the point.'

... *where I have heard that even daffodils* ... 'What are you going to do, mum?'

'Speak to your father. Where were you?'

... *and other English* ... 'At the creek', I said.

She stopped writing. 'Who else was there?'

'Nobody.'

'Then what did you do all day?'

'Nothing. I read *Owd Bob*. I made a collection.'

Recalling how warmly she commended Neal's various collections, I swooped into my satchel, which smelled, as always, of banana skins, and rose unfolding the napkin. 'Look, this glass. And this china with tiny perfect fl-fl-flowers on it. And look, a toy—'

She was on her feet. I had already seen her face set in its lines of frightening disgust. She seized my collection, went into the kitchen, lifted the lid of the stove, and dropped it in. I ran after her, babbling about the beautiful glass. She drew me by the wrists to the sink, scrubbed my hands, then her own, and dried them on the roller towel. She walked away from me, with a firm pressure of her heels, sat down and continued vigorously to write. I ran to her, crying. The shape of the toy titty bottle, as it dropped into the flames, had made in my mind a lightning connection. I believed I had kept my attendance at the creek secret from my family because it was all my own, and because to reveal it would be to end it, but now I admitted as another reason that ritualistic 'showing' of the genitals. I put my head against my mother's arm. 'Mum,' I said.

'Go away.'

I wouldn't move. Her hand sped across the page.

... *surprises many people that in this sub-tropical climate we grow splendid roses. Here I have a clay sub-soil* ... 'Go away,' she said.

In the back yard, Sybil was just about to serve. I rushed her, twisted the racquet from her grasp, and threw it over the orange tree. 'Pimp,' I said.

'I had to. Miss Rickard told me to.'

'You could have warned me. You saw me come in. Pimp, pimp, pimp.'

'You see,' said Sybil, 'you can talk if you want to. It's true – you do just put it on. Dad will thrash you, and it serves you right.'

Girls at the school had told me I would be hanged if I killed anyone, and of all the deaths that occupied me, hanging was the one I currently feared most. I took my fury away, running up the side steps three at a time. Through the door to the dining room I saw that my mother still sat, one foot advanced as when she played the violin, engrossed in her letter. I went to the front of the house and took the Gladstone bag from the hall cupboard. I was in the room I shared with Sybil, stuffing the bag with books and clothes, when Rhoda came in, carrying her heavy school case and her panama hat.

'Mum says you played the wag.'

'Excuse me. I am running away.'

Rhoda at fifteen had only recently stopped packing the Gladstone bag herself. 'Where will you go?' she asked calmly.

'I know places. There are little camps, where anyone can live.'

'Camps? Humpies. You mean humpies. Who would live in a humpy?'

'People.'

'Yes, the sort of people who go to the creek. That's what made mum really wild. You went to the creek. She says you put yourself in danger.'

'Nobody in this house knows anything.'

'Why did you *tell* her you went there?'

'She asked straight-out. You know how hard it is when they ask straight-out.'

Rhoda stuck her hat on top of her head, set down her school case, and sat astride it. 'If all this is because of that trouble at school, you should listen to yourself now, Beatie. You *can* talk.'

I burst into tears. When tears came into her eyes, and she reached out to hug me, I punched her away. I shut the Gladstone bag and picked it up. She tried to wrench it from me. Screams of rage would have brought my mother. Instead, I kicked her school case, then seized her panama hat and threw it into the furthest corner of the room. 'The *expense* of those panamas!' my mother often said. I knew it would draw Rhoda after it.

All the same, she wasn't far behind me as I lurched and staggered along the verandah and down the front steps. It was my first experience of the weight of books. On the front lawn Rhoda caught me, and we stood and fought. Mr Mead and Mr Greenlees passed, on their way home from work, but were too discreet to look. Young Mrs Cookson ran past on her high heels, carrying her little white parcel of chops, and called out a careless admonishment. 'Now then, girls!' 'It's all right, Mrs Cookson,' called Rhoda in reply. 'It *is not*,' I furiously gasped. I was beginning to be appeased, but did not want to show it yet. I knew that no matter what I pretended, I could trust Rhoda not to let me go, and in the end I allowed myself to be led back, exaggerating my exhaustion, feeling less debased than before. Rhoda carried the Gladstone bag. 'Golly, what have you got *in* it?'

Sitting on the edge of the bath while Rhoda washed my face, I told her about the china and glass I had found at the creek.

'How did it come to be there? It's a real mystery. And I f-f-found a rubber thing too, with a teat on it, like a toy titty bottle.'

'I know those things,' said Rhoda.

'What are they?'

'Men put them on their dongs.'

'Yes, but why?'

'Gwen and I think so that if they leak a bit, they won't wet themselves.'

'Boys don't put them on.'

'No,' said Rhoda dubiously.

'Are they expensive?'

'How would I know? I'll comb your hair. Bea. You look awful.'

But now I recalled my mother's face as she seized my treasure, and as Rhoda combed my hair I said calmly, 'I think they're for something worse than wetting.'

'That's what two girls in our form say. These two say they know, but they won't tell Gwen and me. But don't worry, we'll get it out of them.'

'Will you tell me when you do?'

She stood back and looked at my hair. 'Your hair's hopeless,' she said absently, and added in the same tone, 'I can't tell you everything, Bea. There isn't time, or something.'

On the edge of the bath, I let my shoulders droop and my hands dangle between my legs. 'Ar, well,' I said, like Peggy and Des. 'Ar, well, never mind.'

'I've got to go,' said Rhoda, unwilling at the door. 'I've got to go and do my bloody homework.'

She was trying to divert me, but her curse failed to make me give my usual joyous shout. 'Wait,' I said. 'Ro, Syb says dad will thrash me.'

'Bea, if it were only playing the wag, you might get out of it. But the creek. Nothing will get you out of that. I would only make it worse. "Is it a matter of indifference to you," asked

Rhoda in our mother's voice "that the child puts herself in danger?" No, Bea, your only hope is if dad comes home sick.'

'I hope he does,' I said

'Don't say that,' said Rhoda, worried.

'I hope he comes home terribly sick. I hope—'

Rhoda sprang from the door and put a hand across my mouth. 'Don't say that. You can't hope that. It's terribly unlucky.'

But the flood of guilt was a relief. I needed it, it seemed, to match my rising anger. When Rhoda ran away with her hands over her ears, I shouted after her, 'I can hope it. I do! I do!'

From under the frangipani tree, I watched my father come down the street from the tram stop with Neal. Two thin men in dark suits, both over six foot, they walked into the red light from the setting sun. I stood on the bottom rail of the fence, holding two palings. My father's fixed spine made him seem to walk slightly backwards. Beside him Neal moved fluidly. I could hear Neal unloose his laughter when they were still a long way off, and when they drew closer I heard my father's fainter laugh in response.

It must have been one of those times when the western sky was red every evening, when the park was parched, our lawn only prickled with green, and most of the rungs of the tank resonant under the sounding stick. My father was always better then; the droughty weather eased his tortured lungs. When Neal and he were close enough to see me, and to expect me to respond to a wave, I jumped down from the rail and went indoors.

Rhoda was doing her homework in her room. Sybil was cleaning the bath and sobbing because it gave her a stomach-ache. Restless and defiant, I waited to be summoned. I knew that in the dining room most of the usual rituals would be suspended, and dinner delayed, until the matter of my truancy had been dealt with. Waiting, I dared to say aloud, 'Just let him try. I will kill him. They don't hang children.'

Neal came to fetch me. I knocked his hand from my shoulder but walked at his side with seeming meekness. At these hearings, only the culprit and the parents were allowed, but Neal, since wearing a suit and working in the city, had become rather officious, and after bringing me in, he took a chair at the table. But he had not yet developed a shell over his natural tenderness, and when my father turned on him with a glare, he got up and went away blushing like a child.

My father was sitting, my mother standing beside his chair, as if for a photograph. I saw them with an exaggerated clarity, noticed my father's look of being thinly wrapped in his skin, his veins and bones apparent, and the contrast of my mother's smooth swaddling. Both were looking solemn and perturbed, and were giving me their undivided attention.

I knew there was some ideal of justice at work here, and that I was supposed to respect it, but I was too angry; my inner voice was still saying with furious concentration, *Just you try*! I was ready to jump at my father's face and to strike his wan cheeks.

But at his first question – 'Why didn't you go to school?' – my rage drained out of me. Nobody else had thought to ask it. My taut shoulders settled, and I was left with only my guilt. I had said those words; I had spoken my intention to murder. It was from inside myself, this time, that the word-blocking emanation came. I tried to speak, but could not get one word across that barrier. I blushed with shame at the sound I was making. My shoulders tensed again. My parents watched with wonder.

'Is it like this at school?' suddenly asked my father.

I violently shook my head, then gulped and nodded.

'Still?' asked my mother.

I nodded.

'Child,' she cried, in ringing perplexity, 'why didn't you tell us?'

I managed to say I didn't know why. 'Well, run along now,' said my father curtly. 'Charlie,' said my mother in distress, 'there is still the matter of the creek.' *'Run along',* repeated my father with force. And when my mother asked, then, if I would like my dinner on a tray in bed (as when I was sick) I knew I was not to be chastised. Exhausted, I shook my head.

Neal was the only talkative one at the table that night. Feeling the pensive weight of my parents' glances, I bent my head to my plate. When Rhoda reached out gently to put my hanging hair behind my ears, I winced away like a nervous horse. When Neal asked my father a question about the great flood of '93, and I realised how my treasure came to be on the ground at the creek, I almost sat up and cried out my discovery, but the reminders, the allusions, my treasure bore, made me sink back again.

At that time the front or dormitory part of the house was left unlocked at night, the doors wide open and hooked back against a wall. The lavatory was under the house, and if I wanted to go there at night, I would slip out of bed and waft in my pale pyjamas through the house, through the open door, across the side verandah and down the steps.

I was the one, through restlessness or need, who made this journey most often. Sometimes, when I passed the door, always shut, of my parents' room, hearing in full force one of my father's attacks of coughing, I would leap and run out of its range, and would rush my passage back. At other times, from behind that door, I heard the low chatter of simple conversation, often interrupted by laughter, and then I would not change my pace and would raise my arms high on the steps as if I were a bird about to rise in flight. But when those voices sounded intense and sibilant, I would walk quickly past their door and be glad to reach the stone path at the foot of the steps, not because such conversation made me fearful, as did the coughing, but because I did not wish to seem to be spying on them in a state of disagreement. As discreet and respectable as Mr Mead and Mr Greenlees, I would glide swiftly past their door and neatly down the steps.

It was this kind of low intense conversation I heard on my way to the lavatory on the night after the truancy hearing. Sybil was on the lavatory seat. I had not noticed her absence from her bed under its mosquito netting. 'Wait for me, Bea,' she said. 'Leave it open and keep guard.'

The guard was against the nightman. We never knew what time the new man would come. I sat on the step and looked up at the stars. In permitting the lavatory to be put under the house, the council had anticipated their own sewerage plan. The perfumes of the garden contending with the power of phenol made acceptable, or perhaps only familiar, the smell of our excrement. Sybil got up from the seat and said, 'Now I'll keep guard for you.'

She sat on the step. 'Mum and dad are talking about you,' she said.

'They are not.'

'They are so. I heard them.'

'I heard them too. They were talking about money.'

'I thought it was you.'

'No, money. I heard them distinctly.'

I don't know why I told this lie; it was quite spontaneous. After I had finished, Sybil and I wandered about the grass, putting our heads back to look at the stars. We put our arms round each other's shoulders and pretended to be falling over backwards. Our animosity was always in abeyance out of doors at night, perhaps impossible to maintain under that rich hypnotic sky. Sybil went to the laundry, also under the house, to wash her hands, while I, who thought this practice silly when I had touched nothing but my pyjama pants, continued to stagger about beneath the stars.

All was silent as we glided past our parents' door.

'They must have decided,' whispered Sybil as we reached our beds.

'About the money, I mean,' she added in quick appeasement, as we slipped under the white nets.

For the next two days I was kept home from school while my mother went out on conferences.

'We will do all we can,' she assured me before she left on the first day, so that when, a little later, I saw her from the kitchen window, crossing the park towards the school, walking down Honour Avenue and twitching her arm in that familiar way, I did not feel my usual apprehension, but calmly continued to iron all the household handkerchiefs and table napkins. I loved this task, which I had only recently learned to do. I felt deeply complacent as I watched the flawless white swathes appear across the damp linen and pressed the squares exactly. 'Aren't you afraid she'll blow herself up with that petrol iron?' one of my father's cousins had asked. 'Indeed I am not,' replied my mother.

'Well done, dear,' she said when she came home from the school. She picked up one of the handkerchiefs. 'Miss Rickard had a handkerchief arranged in her top pocket in such a novel way.'

But she had a trace of her brooding look. 'All my girls are good with their hands,' she then said sharply. And at that moment an image settled into my mind (and has remained with me) of her and Miss Rickard, two small affronted women, standing face to face on Miss Rickard's dais. Miss Rickard puts one hand flat on the table and leans forward from the waist to address my mother with her insulting clarity. My mother stands upright, listening, her eyes flashing and her right upper-arm twitching once before she replies.

On the second day my mother dressed to go to the city.

'I am meeting your father, Bea. We have an appointment with someone we know in the department.'

I was given no tasks, and was free to revel in the rare sensation of being alone in the house. In this treasured privacy I did nothing forbidden, but did even the most usual things with a rapturous deliberation. When I sat in my father's big chair, I listened to the leather cushion hiss slowly beneath me. When I pulled a carrot from the garden and gave it to the horse, I watched intently his top lip retract from his long teeth, and heard his chomping, and his breath on my hands as he nuzzled for more, as if I had not heard both a hundred times before. When heat collected in the house, and I took my book and searched for cool spots, I found, among the currents of air at floor level, some I had not discovered before. (Later, when we had a dog, he would lie in those same spots). I did not give a thought to my trouble at the school. My faith in my parents' ability to do, to act, to make changes, which had wavered lately, had been fully restored by their present energy and determination, and by their appeal to someone they knew in the department.

'Someone we know in the department.' I reconstruct the scene in the city. Though there was bitterness in their retreat from Labor politics, many of the friends with whom they had shared opinions (radical in that time and place) were now in government. I see them entering one of the big polished hollow-sounding offices, the secretary shutting the door behind her, the man rising from his chair. The handshakes. The naming. 'Charlie'. 'Iris.' The arm extended for a moment across my father's shoulders. The swivelling chair, the leisurely talk. Some laughter. Always some laughter. Then the cocked head, the raised brow. 'What can I do for you?'

My father, who had taken time off from work, did not go back, but came home with my mother into my silence. Again I was summoned before them, but this time they were both sitting, my mother, looking tired, with an elbow on the table and one hand, still gloved, under her chin.

'This is the best we can do,' said my father. 'You are to stay home from school for a year. You will have correspondence lessons sent each week from the department.'

'As country children do,' interposed my mother.

'Your mother will supervise your lessons, and you will go once a week to a teacher of speech in the city, to correct that hesitation.'

I wanted to ask if at last I was to be allowed to travel to the city alone, but felt again the speech-blocking emanation rising between us. My malign passion of the day before, when I had wished to fly at his face, had laid down a most regrettable pattern, which he and I were never to be free of until his death. But as neither of us knew this yet, I patiently struggled, and he and my mother watched with equal patience, until my mother told me to stop and take a deep breath, and by doing that, and then addressing her instead of him, I was able to speak. When I learned that I was to be allowed to go to the city alone, I gave a whoop and a twirl of joy, watched with relief and indulgence by them both.

'Sometimes you will have to stay home alone, too,' declared my mother. 'I can't take you everywhere.'

I knew she could not, for example, take me when she visited her own mother, to whose house my father's children were not admitted. I foresaw a repetition of the hours just past, the long long stretches of luxurious privacy. When Rhoda came home I ran to her room.

'No school! No school! No school! And I'm allowed to go to the city alone. And learn speech.'

'As if you need to,' said Rhoda. 'Did they make you promise not to go to the creek?'

'No.'

'They will.'

'They mightn't. They might forget.'

'You've no chance.'

I knew I hadn't. I knew I would be made ceremoniously to promise, and that kind of promise I had never broken. I now perceived, however, that there may be ways of dodging round it, and already, before I had been required to take the vow, I was devising ways of doing this. At the edge of my calculations I could see my father's blue glare turned on my dishonesty, but the lure was too strong, and even through this discomfort, I went on. To see Peggy and Des at the creek would be to break the promise, but to see them at their camp at Budjerra Heights would not. Would there be time, when I was left at home alone, to make my way to Budjerra Heights? And where, exactly, was Budjerra Heights? I could point in the right direction. I could say, 'Over there.' But that was not enough.

Sybil was delighted by my news. She saw it as distinguishing me, setting me apart. She had a talent for transforming facts, the Irish ability that had missed my father, or had been conscientiously repressed in him, but which had burst out in different ways in his three daughters. When I went down the street to tell Clare, Sybil insisted on coming with me, hugging my arm, giggling, and calling out to anyone we met, 'My sister is to have private lessons.'

In Sybil's hugging, and in the mild responses of our amiable neighbours, I felt myself imprisoned in a region from which I would never again escape to the sharper air of insubordination. With an inventiveness sharpened by this sudden desperate suffocation, I realized that I would only have to say to Neal, 'Budjerra Heights is near the river,' to make him indignantly refute it. I would persist, and so would he. Of all Neal's collections, he took most pride in his collection of facts. Neal was eager in dispensing his facts, and could not bear the contradiction of the ignorant. As I submitted to Sybil's hugging, and listened to her talking to Mrs Mead, I could see Neal angrily drawing me a map.

THE WAY TO BUDJERRA HEIGHTS·

I did not succeed in tricking Neal into telling me the way to Budjerra Heights. My plan was craftily laid, my groundwork firm, but (in a process which was gradually to disclose itself as usual) I failed in its execution.

Since Neal had found jam in his dictionary, Sybil and I had been forbidden to use the desk in his room and were told to knock before entering. I went to make my attempt in the first week of the year I was kept home from school. Finding him looking through a magnifying glass at fragments of rock, I automatically reached out for one of them before his roar made me drop it.

'Learn to leave things alone,' he told me.

'Let me do some rubbings then.'

He found me paper, an English crown, and a soft pencil. I made rubbings for a while, with especial attention to the milled edges, then said, 'A girl I know has Chinese coins. She lives near the river at Bud-budjerra Heights.'

'Budjerra Heights isn't near the river,' murmured Neal, dreamy over his stones.

'It is so. This girl lives there.'

Slowly, still holding the magnifying glass, Neal turned his face to me. My face was downcast to my rubbings, but feeling his gaze upon me, I could not help taking a nervous peep which I knew, even as I did it, was a mistake.

He said, 'Why, exactly, do you want to go to Budjerra Heights?'

I had often found myself 'reading' people. All children have this ability, and I had as well a sister capable of bringing it to a conscious level. It was Rhoda who had called it our 'reading'. It was also Rhoda who set the block in my imagination which prevented me from suspecting that Neal could do this kind of reading too. I had been infected by her animosity towards him, and her low opinion of him, so often expressed, had become my own.

Neal's eyes, like Rhoda's, were long, large, and pale in colour. When I gathered my courage and met them at last, he gave a small triumphant smile, 'Come on. Tell me why you want to go there.'

I pushed the rubbings aside and said scornfully, 'I don't. You're mad.'

'Look here,' he said, 'if it's anything to do with those children you used to meet at the creek, forget it. Just you drop that whole thing. I'm not saying the people who live at Budjerra Heights are bad. They're unfortunate, that's all. But a kid your age oughtn't to go hanging around there. Now, dad and mum have fixed it so that you can have lessons at home because of your stammer, so just you concentrate on that, and forget the creek.'

I rolled my eyes and gave a theatrically patient sigh. He said, 'I think I ought to mention this to dad and mum.'

This alarmed me into putting on a better show. 'Mention *what*?' I shouted.

I saw the doubt cross his eyes, as doubt so often came to me after a 'reading', common sense creeping upon and enervating the uncommon. I grabbed up one of his fragments of rock and ran through the door into the garden. He followed, letting forth his roar, which became a laugh when he caught me, and I would not unclench my fist, but would only stand giggling until he seized my other forearm.

'I don't want to twist your arm, kid.'

'Here's your mad old gibber,' I said.

'There's opal in it. See? When I hold it up to the sun like this?'

My first lesson did not arrive from the department for a week. During that time, when my mother went to the shops or down the street to see Aunt Jean (we called my mother's girlhood friends Aunt), I would go to my parents' bedroom to stand in front of the full length mirror scratching a forearm and setting my head back to squint down my cheeks. But I did not look at all like Peggy and Des Kellaway. I looked silly and insignificant and retreated ashamed of my effort. I craved for Peggy and Des not only for the excitement of their forbidden company, but for that other sensation they often gave me, of settlement, of comfort, of having arrived at exactly the right place.

Mooning about, I wondered if they still went to the creek, or if I could find my way to their camp at Budjerra Heights from others of the creek society. My promise not to go to the creek had been extracted from me with such ceremony and solemnity that I was superstitious about breaking it, but on Sunday, when Sybil was at church and Rhoda at tennis, I said I was going to Clare's place and went instead to sit on the sliprail fence on one boundary of the bush reserve through which the creek ran.

Presently Hec and Ian came into sight, both carrying billy cans. I jumped down and said, 'Hey!'

Their pause had a provisional look about it. They asked me What? or What was up? I replied to Hec because I did not like to look at Ian. Ian's beauty was almost incredible. He had dirty yellow curls, bright blue eyes, a golden skin, and the correctly chiselled features of his story-book stereotype, the princeling or angel. But mucus ran continuously from his nostrils and now and again his tongue would dart out and catch it between his pink lips. So, not to betray the sooky squeamishness that would get me debarred, I addressed Hec, a brave high-shouldered boy whose short-sighted stare I could mistake for interest.

'Have you s-s-seen Peggy and Des?'

'Yeh,' said Hec; and Ian said, 'Sorm yesdee.'

We were all said to mutilate the language, but there were degrees, and Ian was often unintelligible. 'When are they coming to the creek?' I asked Hec.

'They go down the river now,' said Hec; and Ian said something which Hec endorsed by saying, 'Yeh, or go rabbitting.'

They were already getting through the sliprails. I climbed quickly to the top of the fence and jumped down after them. 'Wait,' I begged.

'Aw kimmon,' said Ian to Hec, but Hec stopped and said, 'What?'

'How do you get to Budjerra Heights?'

'You know Soden's Corner?'

'Yes.'

'Aw cripes Hec kimmon.'

'You turn in there and keep on for a couple of miles. You see a cement pipe on the right and a bit past that there's a track leads into the bush.'

'Is there only one?'

'There's a few.'

'Aw kimmon Hec.'

'How can you tell which one?'

'You just get to know it.'

'Describe it.'

'It's the one leads up. Hey, Ian,' shouted Hec after his friend, 'wait on.'

But Ian went on running down the slope to the creek. 'Hooray,' called Hec to me as he ran after him.

'Those unfortunate children must have pink eyes,' said my mother.

She and I were in the tram going to the city, I was in the window seat, and had turned my head and was leaning out to catch every last glimpse of Peggy and Des Kellaway. Barefoot even on this cold day, they were walking under the awnings of the shops at The Junction. Des carried a sugar bag, full of lumpy things, over one shoulder, and Peggy was weighted sideways by another, lumpy but less full. Even with these burdens they were walking with the lanky springing undeviating step I so admired, and with that look of cool disregard for passers-by I often tried to copy. I wore white knee-length socks, black laced-up shoes, and a prickly tartan jacket.

'Pumpkins,' murmured my mother. 'I don't like to see children of that age weighted down.'

I could no longer see Peggy and Des. We had left the shops behind and were passing the big flat ramshackle facade of the local picture theatre. I turned back to the cabin of the tram and vented my thwarted longing in sullenness.

'Who says they have pink eyes?'

'You saw their hair. They are albino.'

'I don't care, they have blue eyes.'

Without looking, I felt my mother's sharpened attention, so that when she said, lightly and carefully, 'Then you've seen them before?' I knew she was thinking of the creek, and my disgrace of two months ago. I couldn't claim to have seen the Kellaways at the school, because they attended (technically) another school, and my mother might bother to check with my sister Sybil. So I said, 'Yes, up the sh-shops, when I go messages.'

'Ah yes. Well, I hope they usually wear good shady hats. Imagine allowing children with that colouring out without hats.'

Unable to say that at the creek Peggy and Des had always worn men's old felt hats, I was about to claim that they always wore hats when I saw them at the shops, when my mother remarked, 'But by the look of those children, their parents would know no better.'

I was angered by this casual derogation of the most beautiful woman in Queensland and of her husband the war hero, king of the camp at Budjerra Heights, land of freedom. I started a furious stammer.

'But there's no s-s-s-s-'

'Deep breath, dear.'

'It's *cloudy* today.'

'Well, some people may think the sun can't burn through clouds. What ignorance!'

I had rolled my penny tram ticket into a cylinder and now began to chew it. My mother gently took my hand in hers and lowered it from my mouth. 'Suppose a ticket inspector got on.'

I thrust my chin towards her and demanded, 'How do you know they were pumpkins, anyway?'

My mother laughed. Neal had inherited her free melodious laugh, but unlike him, she used it seldom, so that I always heard it with a startled pleasure. Several passengers turned their heads, and the conductor swinging down the aisle smiled.

'Goodness, child,' she said, on her declining mirth, 'don't you think I've seen enough sacks of pumpkins in my life?'

Little wise adult smiles flitted round the cabin and were returned by my mother merrily, almost flirtatiously. Since being kept home from school, and in her company every weekday, I had glimpsed many new aspects of her character. Even when I liked these, they disturbed me slightly. I raised my eyebrows, as Rhoda did when she disapproved of our mother, and looked out of the window.

In Barry and Robert's basement grocery we encountered Aunt Eliza. She was one of my father's many nieces, but as all of these were close to my mother's age, we addressed these, too, as Aunt.

Aunt Eliza was thin, dark, quick, voluble, and wore complicated clothes. I would have liked to admire her. She immediately tried to grab my arm.

'Syb! Sybil, you wicked thing. Why aren't you at school?'

But I had dodged round behind her so that I could stroke the golden fox's tail hanging down her back, and look up at its small beseeching eyes beside her coils of black hair. My mother was saying, 'It's not Sybil, Liz.'

'Ah, stop that, will you? You naughty girl. You'll be having it off me.'

My mother took my arm and drew me back to her side. Aunt Eliza twitched her fur into a new position and said, 'Can't I see for myself that it's Beatie? What are you doing home from school, Beatie?'

'I—' I said.

'Ah, that stutter. Ah that's nothing. Just tell it to go away, like Siddy. Siddy talked to her gall stones. "Go away, you bad things. Get out from inside me."'

Hearing my own opinion, or feeling, expressed for the first time by another, I gaped; but my mother said sharply, 'Don't talk nonsense to the child, Liz. There's nothing bad inside her.'

'Ah, by bad I don't mean wicked, Iris. I am sorry for her in her affliction.'

'There is no need to be,' said my mother. 'It is only a habit formed by some early psychological difficulty.'

Aunt Eliza drew in her chin and said with suspicion, 'The things they are finding out!'

'She is taking speech lessons once a week,' said my mother, 'from Mr Clarence in the Colonial Mutual Building.'

'Who used to be an actor? Clarence Clarence, is it?'

'William M.'

'Ah, William *Mmmm*.'

Aunt Eliza, pretending to be impressed, reminded me of Rhoda. I laughed. My mother laughed, too, and drew my head against her body, and stroked my hair. Aunt Eliza looked at me closely, and smiled without friendliness. Every moment, I felt something different for her; now I was afraid of her.

She said, 'One day she will grow into her face, Iris,' and then immediately blocked my mother's challenge by embarking on one of her bursts of social intensity, leaning forward from the waist to look into my mother's eyes.

'And how is the rest of the family, Iris? How is my Sybil? Syb,' she declared, as my mother began to answer, 'is my favourite.'

My mother replied that in that case, Eliza should know Sybil when she saw her, but Aunt Eliza drowned this remark with her next enquiry.

'And Rhoda? I saw Rhoda, Iris. I *saw* her. In Vulture Street, in her uniform. She looked so *clean*.'

And while my mother murmured that she should hope so, Aunt Eliza cried, 'And Neal? Did Neal tell you I met him in Adelaide Street, when I was in to pick up my pearls? And so happy in the Justice Department? And working with Horrie Martin from down our street? Ah, but wouldn't you be proud if you could hear Horrie on Neal, Iris.'

And now Aunt Eliza, without pausing, abandoned her vehement social enquiry for a respectful, almost a mourning tone. 'Ah, Iris, he has Charlie's gentlemanly ways.'

'He could not have a better model,' said my mother crisply.

'And how is the dear man, Iris?' enquired Aunt Eliza with her greedy mourning. 'How is dear Charlie's health?'

'He has felt better lately, Liz.'

'Then there you are!' Eliza tossed her head backwards. 'He'll whop it yet. Papa believes he'll whop it, Iris.'

'Eliza,' said my mother, 'I hope you have stopped saying Charlie has consumption.'

'Consumption? Why I never—'

'Then I was misinformed. As I am tired of telling you, Eliza, it is nothing contagious.'

'Ah,' crooned Eliza, 'if he won't see a doctor—'

'He saw a doctor at first. If he chooses not to see another, that's his business and mine. There is no blood, Eliza.'

'Whoever said there was?' asked Eliza with indignation. 'But some people will say anything. Why, I was just about to tell you, Iris, that Papa says – that Papa still tells – you've heard him – how Gran claimed that of all her twelve, Charlie was the strongest. Born of old parents – ' Aunt Eliza transferred to me her black gaze of which the golden lights leapt and danced about my face – 'yet the strongest of the lot.'

My mother tightened the arm about my shoulders. 'That's what we say about this one, Liz.'

Aunt Eliza, still looking into my face, said absent-mindedly, 'He will whop it, Iris. Charlie will make old bones yet.'

'Thank you,' said my mother. 'But I hope you will keep that opinion to yourself, Eliza, when you visit us next.'

'Ah, that must be soon, dear.'

'You have only to drop us a note.'

'You've still no telephone, Iris?'

'What do we need with a telephone?'

'Once you get it, you wouldn't be without it. I'll write the minute this cold snap ends.'

'You're always welcome, Eliza. Come along, Beatie.'

'I suppose you are going to buy your wholemeal flour,' teased Aunt Eliza.

'Call me a crank if you like, Liz.'

'I'm surprised you still bother to make your own bread.'

'I haven't made bread since we left the old place. This is for my gem scones.'

As soon as we were out of Aunt Eliza's sight, my mother allowed herself to be brooding and silent. As we stood at the tram stop in Queen Street I felt, several times, her eyes resting on my face as if trying to see what Aunt Eliza had seen. I, who had once overheard myself described as 'one of those skinny little kids with an old face', had known at once what Aunt Eliza meant, and had not expected the fact to be news to my mother.

But very soon her worry was displaced by anxiety about the tram. It was my task (because my eyes were younger than hers) to tell her the moment it came into sight, so that we would have plenty of time to walk from the footpath to the passenger zone beside the rails. A fear of being late could always shake her composure, and as soon as I announced the tram, she would grip my hand and hurry me across to the zone. 'It's all right, dear, it's all right, we'll get it, no need to rush.' Then as we stood waiting in the zone she would say, with stately contentment, 'We are in good time.'

After we had settled into the tram that day, she began to tap her fingers on the bag in her lap. Rhoda said this habit drove her mad, but since being alone with my mother every weekday, I had learned it usually preceded an abrupt remark.

'Cold snap indeed,' she presently said. 'Eliza simply says the first thing that comes into her head.'

'Dad likes the way she does that,' I said.

'Nonsense, dear.'

'I mean,' I said, 'it makes him laugh.'

'We might as well laugh, I suppose,' said my mother soberly. 'They are a downright strange lot, that whole family, the way they split clear into two. You could draw a line down the middle, and put the rational ones on one side and the rattlepates on the other. Siddy is a clever woman – what a tarrydiddle that was about the gallstones – and I'm really fond of Vivvy and Cousin Fitz. And Vernon is a fine man, of the same stamp as your father. But oh, Lou and Liz and Francis and the rest ... '

I was flattered. I had heard my mother speak in this tone to my father, to Neal and sometimes to Rhoda, but never before had she used with me this simple conversational tone, devoid of a component of instruction. I felt important. I said, 'What about Uncle Conor?'

'I suppose there must be one in between.'

But my question had broken her mood; she spoke with reserve. My father dearly loved this elder brother, the mendacious charmer who was Aunt Eliza's Papa, and would allow no word to be said against him. I said, in an effort to return to our former tone, but truthful too, 'I don't exactly like them.'

'There's a lot to be said for them,' she instantly told me. 'For one thing, there's not a lazy bone among them. Some of the families who emigrated—well, it was pitiful. By the waters of Babylon they sat down and wept. But not that lot. From the moment they landed they were busy. Oh yes,' she rather grimly concluded, 'in one way or another.'

'I'll tell you what,' I said, 'when they visit I always have to run in quickly to hear what they're talking about.'

'Oh, they can be depended upon to dress everything up, I don't dispute that.'

'So do the rational ones. What about dad and the bee-hives?'

'Ah, but the rational ones know they're doing it, you see.'

'Yes, but I'll tell you what—' 'I had forgotten my wish to please in my wish to seek the truth in what I was saying—'I like the others because they always make you think something exciting's just going to happen.'

'Do they? Well, that's enough of them, I think, for one day.'

Her dryness told me that that was enough of the simple conversational tone for one day, too. I think she had been irritated by Eliza into talking so freely, thus—unintentionally—coercing me into revealing my lack of interest in her own family. She must have observed it before, must have noticed how, when her brothers and sisters visited, I would come laggingly in, stand restless under the regard from those handsome and reticent faces, and take my first chance of escape. She may even have noticed how, when her family was under discussion, I would continue to read, or would pass indifferently from the room, whereas at the litany of those other names – Sidney – Vernon – Conor – Louisa – Francis and Cousin Fitz – I would linger, swinging on a chair, finding some reason, any reason, to hang around.

My mother was tapping her bag. 'One day,' she said, 'you and Rhoda will learn that excitement is not enough.'

We were passing the picture theatre again. On the billboards I saw blonde curls and cowboy hats and guns. Except to Charlie Chaplin, I was still not allowed to go, and these days Rhoda was too engrossed in school friendships to take me secretly. My mother, as if to entice me back from these temptations, took my nearer hand and rubbed it in hers.

'I could see that little hand was cold. Here, put on your mittens.'

She was getting the hated blue knitted mittens from her bag. I raised my chin and said, 'I won't.'

With a sound of exasperation, she picked up the cold hand and slapped it sharply, twice. I had not been hit since being kept home from school. The only passenger facing us, a woman in a cardigan with a basket on her lap, looked away. I retrieved the hand with what I intended to be dignity, stretched my neck high, and lowered my eyelids. I was now copying Sybil, who did this to snub people. Beneath the awnings of The Junction shops, the comatose accord of housewives, small children, and old men was no longer disrupted by the passage of Peggy and Des. I said to myself, You just wait till I find the way to Budjerra Heights.

Then, because lately I had heard, from Mr Clarence and others, so much about will power, I whispered, 'I *will* find the way to Budjerra Heights.'

'What was that you said?' crossly enquired my mother.

'It is private,' I said with scorn.

Presently she forgot me, gave a low laugh, and said she supposed Eliza would make a fine yarn about their meeting, especially the telephone and the wholemeal flour. I think she made a fine yarn of it herself. As I passed, still too proud to pause, through the dining room that evening, she was saying to my father, with energetic mirth ' . . . and she *looked so clean*,' while he, leaning back in his chair, was laughing beneath his long moustache.

I see my mother going about the resounding house and the fruitful garden and talking to herself. I hear her mounting the back steps announcing that the marmalade must be done, opening the door to the darkish kitchen, blinking as light motes drop and float before her eyes, and remarking that you can always tell, you don't need clocks, it is like a call that comes and makes you put down the secateurs or turn off the hose.

I hear her advancing from the front of the house while I walk from the back, and before we come into sight of one another I hear her lonely conversational murmur. We meet. She starts. 'Oh. Oh.' And gives an abashed laugh. 'Oh, it's you, Beatie.'

But when I hear her whispering alone in her bed at night, I know that the woman in her eighties, walking about that house and garden, threatens to absorb the vigorous middle-aged woman who supervised my lessons that year, and whose sick husband still lay beside her at night. In our lives, there were two spans of time when she and I were alone in the house together every weekday, the first lasting for a school year, the second for only a month. They have become ravelled together, and deliberation is needed to untangle them.

In the first span, my mother would have walked about the house and the garden mostly in silence, her thoughts forming behind her clear grey eyes. But sometimes (simply because I was there) she would speak them aloud, and more and more often, she spoke in the simple conversational tone she had first used in the tram on the day we met Aunt Eliza.

Each day, when I began my lessons, she would come and sit beside me, her brown hands beside mine, her nails almost invariably earth-stained. We seldom began at once.

'My goodness,' she might say as she sat down, 'Aunt Jean just passed on her way to a day's bridge. A whole day! She says it keeps her brain sharp, and I must say it does seem to work – with Jean, anyway. Now let's see what we have to do with our brains today.'

She was the best of teachers, lively, patient, and herself interested. My simple lessons did not tax the education she had received from the small Church of England school where her father had taught music.

'You would think they would set you something harder than this. But they must know what they're about. Their standard is known to be high.'

She clung to this notion of the high standard, perhaps not daring to do otherwise, and face changes she and my father could not afford either financially or ideologically. It usually took me no more than two hours to finish the day's lessons, and even those she allowed to be interrupted. At the sound of an aeroplane I would seize the white cloth kept for these occasions and run down into the back yard to wave, never losing hope that one day, someone up there would wave back. When we heard 'Pineapples two a bob!' or 'Fiji bananas!' cried from a passing cart, I was allowed to run into the street with a basket and the money. And when the postman whistled at the front gate, it was always I who raced down for the mail. There were magazines from England and America, there were my lessons, bills, notes dropped to arrange visits, and sometimes letters with big exotic stamps from such places as India, Honduras, and Jamaica. These were for Neal and my mother, both members of Penfriends for Peace.

'Look,' my mother said one day, interrupting my lessons to proffer me a letter, 'see what you make of this.'

Did she show such comradely deference simply because I was there? Or was it an effort to build my confidence? The letter was from the Indian woman who, in those days of easy racism, my father called Mrs Unpronounceable.

'Here, read it and see what you think.'

Between the stilted beginning, and the stilted ending, the letter was nothing but a request for the botanical names of certain flowers and shrubs.

'I think the woman is making a fool of me,' said my mother.

'When you got me that penfriend in Africa,' I said, 'I couldn't think of one thing to put.'

'But this is a grown woman. And supposed to be educated. Your father says she is bored with the correspondence, but is embarrassed to stop.'

'That girl in Africa just st-st-st-'

'Deep breath.'

'Oooo, I was glad when she did.'

'I can't just stop. It would be rude. Besides, we mustn't pick things up and drop them just as we please. I suppose there's nothing for it but to get down the botanical dictionary again. And to think I was foolish enough to hope for interesting discussions.'

Some afternoons later, I would come in from Clare's or Betty's house and find her sitting at the head of the table, her writing pad and the botanical dictionary before her. Rhoda, home from school, paused to look over her shoulder.

'Mum, you know she will just chuck it away and wander off laughing in her sari.'

'I know no such thing, girl.'

'Then why doesn't she tell you something interesting? Ask her to tell you about her family. There were enough of them in that photo. Ask her to tell you about the fat son with his mouth hanging open.'

'Please don't interrupt, Rhoda. This is harder than it looks.'

Not long after this, I would overhear, with pride, my mother saying to Aunt Jean or another friend, 'It was Beatie who spotted it, you know. It was Bea who noticed the alphabetical order. The woman had got careless, you see, in copying them from an English gardening catalogue, and she just put down four in a row. I didn't notice it, but Bea did. What the woman's motive was I cannot imagine. Charlie still says embarrassment, but I can't see it. In any case, I wrote, politely, of course, Jean, and said that changed circumstances necessitated ... something like that. And to think that only for Bea I would still be copying out those dratted lists.'

Occasionally, when my mother sat beside me to help me with my lessons, when we took the two places set at the table for our lunch, or when she taught me how to use the sewing machine, I had something of that same sensation of comfort, of having arrived at exactly the right place, which I had experienced in the company of Peggy and Des. Though I still harboured the resolve to find my way to Budjerra Creek, I was now willing to postpone it. Yet I was angry with myself for this, for allowing myself to become, as I sometimes felt, trapped, and one day, when my mother went out and left me alone in the house, I ran across the park, in the opposite way to the school, crossed the broad macadam road to Soden's Corner, and turned into the road Hec had told me to take. There were no ruts in this road, which rose in the middle and was of pale yellowish dust. On its margins quartz-like stones made little glinting peaks. The cement pipe was not easy to find; it started a few yards into the scrub and ran over a gully. There were no houses in sight, though I could still hear the trucks and cars on the macadam road and the slow regular clanging from Soden's forge. In the hot scrub, I searched the ground for some objects foreign enough to the rest to count as treasure, and at last found two smooth pebbles, one pink and one grey. I spat on them, rubbed them on my dress, and put them in my pocket. Now, I told myself as I turned for home, I had taken the first step: I had spied out the land. I ceremoniously wrapped the pebbles in tissue paper, laid them in the French cachou tin coveted by Sybil, and hid it in the back of my handkerchief drawer.

When my mother left me at home alone, it was often to visit her own mother, to whom my father's children were not welcome. I saw her (my one surviving grandparent) only once. On the day my mother first took me to Mr Clarence's rooms, we encountered in Queen Street a small stiff old woman to whom my mother stopped and talked in a bold yet worried way. As the old woman responded she looked not at my mother but at me. She looked amused, as if it were I who was under discussion and not repairs to her roof and verandah railings. The old woman asked my mother where we were going, and when my mother replied vaguely, 'Oh, we have an errand,' I understood that this was one of those persons with whom my stammer was not discussed. When we parted I said, in the grizzling tone I seemed to reserve for walking at my mother's side in a crowded street, 'Who was that?'

My mother's reply was prompt and grim. 'Your grandmother.'

'*That* was her?'

'What did you think she would look like? Her photograph at twenty-five?'

'But she didn't look angry or anything.'

'Oh, she wouldn't, not in Queen Street.'

'She looked as if she wanted to laugh.'

'Not from amusement, child, I assure you.'

'*Why* don't we visit her?'

'Do stop that grizzling. I have told you why.'

'Yes bu-bu-but we could *tell* her, just because dad is *Irish*—'

'He is no such thing. He was born here. The only one. The others are Irish.'

'Well then, we could *tell* her—'

'Child, child,' said my mother, 'I have had enough heart-break over the thing. It will never be different. She is an ignorant and prejudiced woman, incapable of change. She is to be pitied. Now please concentrate on remembering the way. This is Edward Street. When you come alone to see Mr Clarence, this is where you will turn. Observe, on this corner is Stewart Dawsons . . . It may be a good idea if Neal were to draw you a map.'

So instead of the map showing the way to Budjerra Heights I had plotted to get, Neal drew for me, on a piece of card, a map of the inner city. Streets in indian ink were ruled as straight as when the first planners laid down the British grid-iron on tracks tramped out by convicts. The path I was to take was dotted neatly in red.

'Don't you get lonely home from school?' Mr Clarence asked me one day.

'No,' I said. 'I like it.'

'Useful, being able to take satisfaction in one's own company.'

He was a tall fat man with a hard red skin covered with the strange lumps that were said to have put an end to his theatrical career (though this was disputed). In his high starched collar he sweated stoically. Because the word-blocking emanation, so impassable with some people, seldom came between us, I don't think he ever fully gauged the extent of my problem at school. When I tried to explain it to him he said, 'There is nothing wrong that practice and will power will not cure. Now as those s's and f's are the main problem let's tackle those. Start!'

And I would say, in the deathly dragged monotone he advised, 'Seven – silent – fishes – swim – fleetly – in – the – Severn – and – the – Firth – of – Forth.'

'But,' I would say, 'I wouldn't be game to talk like that to anyone else.'

'Fences when we come to them. Now! Again!'

On some days, when my mother was leaving to visit her mother, she would say, 'I'll stop and pick up a few things on the way home, dear, so I shan't be home till after three.'

And I would think, with excitement and trepidation, 'Now I will have time to go past the cement pipe and find the track...'

But my mother would save me by saying, 'The money for the baker is on the pantry shelf, and I've left a note for Mr Sloper. Don't let him leave Cavendish bananas. I want Lady Fingers.'

How pleasant to hear the gate click behind her, and to feel my treasured privacy softly invading the house. At some time in the day I would remember to take the French cachou tin from its hiding place, and to look steadily, in a magic provoking way, at the two pebbles.

When I offered Pickwick a carrot he twitched his head away, and when I slouched round talking to him and leaning against his warm bulk, I got no nuzzling response. Nor was he perturbed nowadays when an aeroplane flew over and I stood waving my white cloth. I got used to seeing him out of the tail of my eye, standing in his yard like a horse painted on plywood. My father remarked one evening at the table that the old fellow was getting blind and deaf, but we three girls immediately set up a clamour of begging for his life. Old animals, we knew, were put down. 'But he is *Pickwick*,' we said.

'I don't think we should prolong the poor fellow's life,' said my father (son of the poor farm), 'for three sentimental girls.'

'No, by Jove,' said Neal. 'I didn't kick up a fuss when Cobber had to go.'

'Oh, aren't you marvellous,' said Rhoda. 'Aren't you wonderful. I am stunned.'

'Oh dear, oh dear, oh dear,' murmured my mother, while my father said, 'Well, we will have to see.'

Every lunch hour, when I heard the aerial hubbub from the school across the park, I felt a riotous joy that I was not there. All the same, at three o'clock, I ran with the same riot of joy to meet Betty and Clare. Usually it was to Clare's house we went. Her young mother let us rouge our cheeks, look at film magazines, and play euchre on the fruit-bottling table under their house. One day, when I ran to meet them, Clare was walking across the park alone.

'Where's Betty?'

'Gone home. I've got to tell you something.'

'What?'

'I'm not allowed to play with you and her any more.'

'Hey,' I said, 'what have we done?'

She looked at the ground. 'I'm not supposed to tell you.'

'Come on!' I said indignantly.

'I'm going to the convent school next year. Mum and dad say I have to get to know girls from there.'

'Can't you know us both?'

'No, *truly*, I'm not allowed.'

We were both crying. '*Truly*,' said Clare.

I went to Betty's place. She was sitting on the swing in her back yard eating a sagging slice of bread and peanut butter.

'I know,' she said. 'It's because we're Protestants. Isn't it mad? She needn't think I'm going to care.'

'Me either.'

'You've been crying, you mad thing.'

'I have not.'

'Wait till I finish this, and we'll have a doubler.'

As we were swinging, Betty said, 'Mum says it's the mick priests. They always stop them mixing with Protestants.'

I said we were not Protestants, and that except for Sybil, we were free thinkers. I told her my father's father had begun it. 'He threw off the yoke,' I said.

'Is that the one whose horse bolted, and who was thrown out of his buggy and dragged along by one foot till he died?'

'Yes,' I said.

'Well,' said Betty, 'you see?'

'One of his boots got caught in the reins,' I said, 'that's all.'

'We always go at Easter and Christmas,' said Betty.

I went home and told my mother, as she stood at the stove, about Clare. 'Betty's mother says it's the mick priests,' I said.

A look of peace and satisfaction settled on my mother's features. 'Betty's mother has no right to talk like that,' she said. 'Mick indeed. That's prejudice.'

'Anyway,' I said, 'I don't believe it. I bet they won't keep it up. I bet Clare will play with us.'

'I wouldn't count on that,' said my mother serenely, 'if I were you.'

During that second span of time when my mother and I were alone in the house together every weekday, she used to go to her bedroom to sleep or doze for about three hours every afternoon. Her bedroom door always stood open, and when I heard her stirring I would take in a tray of tea and serve it from the camphorwood chest at the foot of her bed. And because she had nothing else to do, and because I was there (hanging around again) she would talk as volubly as Aunt Eliza once had done, often saying the first thing that came into her head, while I, sitting beside the tray on the camphorwood chest, would listen, and occasionally launch into talk myself.

One day, she arrested herself in a tangle of anecdote to remark, with the altered diction of clarity, that all of her adult life she had needed a few hours of each day to herself.

'It was like a medicine. If I didn't get it, I would feel quite out of sorts, and all kinds of things would get on my nerves.'

'What about that year I was kept home from school?' I asked.

'What year? Oh-oh-oh *that* year. You were nine.'

'Didn't I get on your nerves? Depriving you of your time alone? You didn't show it.'

The keen angle of her head seemed to substitute for her baffled eyesight. She said, 'I enjoyed that year.'

'So did I,' I said. 'That school – the relief.'

On her own reflective course she said, 'You were the last one. That was it. I knew that was the end of it.'

I recalled how sometimes I would look up at the house and see her turning away from one of the windows. 'You were very indulgent,' I said.

'Not too indulgent,' she said sharply.

My mother had been netted in the postwar media web of child psychology, which had turned out to make suggestions very different from the ones she had once commended. 'Of course you weren't,' I said. I did not like to hear guilt and defensiveness in her voice; I was nudged by my own parental mistakes. 'But what about the hours you needed to yourself?'

'Well, dear, I'm sure I don't know.'

'Or did you get them?' Now I was teasing her. 'I seem to recall I was often sent with baskets of paw-paws and persimmons to Aunt Annie's, all the way to Clayfield.'

'Twopence each way, and you didn't have to change trams. You used to like it.'

'And then once a week to Mr Clarence,' I calculated, with my teasing. 'To say nothing of the times you sent me down to play draughts with Kenny Fry, when he had meningitis. Saying, "That poor boy does enjoy your company."'

'I'm sure I didn't do anything underhand.'

'Not underhand at all,' I said. 'Diplomatic. Good stuff. I know about those few hours. I need them myself.'

'Kenny Fry limps to this day.'

'Kenny didn't mind being home from school either. They used to call him Sooky Fry or Lamb's Fry.'

'Did they indeed? Well, he was a brave boy. He fought that thing.'

'What else could he do?'

Too late, I saw where this lazy enquiry would lead us. I had almost forgotten the look on my mother's face when it set in those lines of disgust. She said, 'Some give in. Your father gave in.'

'Mum,' I said, fated to say it once again. 'That was a very sick man. That was a man in his sixties. He had survived diphtheria. He had survived typhoid fever. He had chronic bronchitis. He had emphysema. The marvel was that he lived as long as he did.'

'I kept him alive,' said my mother.

'It was wonderful that you did,' I said, 'for so long.'

'It could have been longer. But he gave up the fight.'

'That was his right, mum.'

'It was no such thing.'

I got up from the camphorwood chest and picked up the tray. My mother was still speaking vehemently about my father being the last person she thought would have given in, but when I stood beside her and indicated her empty cup, she stopped, looked bewildered, then said, with vague sweetness, 'What? Oh, no, dear. No more thank you. That was very nice.'

Walking with the tray through the dining room and into the kitchen, I wished I could go back and dispute with her. I wished I could be an adolescent again, challenging everything, so that I could have jumped up from the camphorwood chest and said, 'Don't forget, I was there that day when he came home. I was changing the table cloth.'

My mother told me to put a clean cloth on the table, and as I stand by the sideboard with the cloth still unfolded in my hands, I hear my father crossing the verandah with fast but heavy steps. He reaches the door, ignores my mother at that point in their ritual where they always kissed, and instead of hanging his hat on the rack, casts it spinning on to the bare table.

'I am done for.'

These, the first words I ever heard him speak to my mother untempered by the presence of 'one of the children', were the last words I ever heard him speak.

Kenny Fry was ten. He could not walk yet, but could sit up. We played draughts, ludo, noughts and crosses, and join-the-dots, also called boxes.

'Do you know the way to Budjerra Heights?' I asked him one day.

'Yes,' he said, 'I went there with my uncle when he was a surveyor.'

'What's it like?'

'Just old bush.'

'But there are camps,' I said persuasively, 'where people live.'

'Humpies? I only saw them between the trees. One had a red geranium growing in a half kero tin.'

'Let's go there when you can walk. If you remember the way.'

'Sure,' said Kenny. 'We can ride your horse.'

'He's too old to ride. Let's walk.'

'Sure,' said Kenny. 'We'll walk. I'll take you next year.'

'Promise?'

'God's honour.'

It was as easy for Kenny to promise as for me to rest on his promise. For him, as for me, that year had become a time of postponement, of the latitude of daydreams. Kenny's mother, after an initial interrogation in which she discovered that my father did not spit blood, diligently wooed me. She was a widow, and had little other respite from the grizzling of her sick and lonely boy. She gave me cup cakes lapped with pink icing and let me take home a magazine I had picked up from where she had left it beside Kenny's bed, and had started to read.

'All right, if you want it so much. Better not let your mummy see it, though. Mummy's a bit old-fashioned, eh?'

Heroine had fair curls, cad and villainess were dark and sleek. Hero believed sleek one's lies about heroine until last pages, when heroine's loyal chum cornered hero at last and (stamping her foot) told him the truth. Into the cloudburst of vows and kisses at the end I insinuated Des Kellaway and myself. Peggy was the loyal chum. I took the magazine home hidden in my pants and crackled when I sat down. Rhoda heard and took it out. She laughed as she read it, disdainfully flicking over the pages, but let me hide it under her mattress.

Kenny's mother, in her desperation to entertain him, had taught him to plait her hair, and now suggested that he should plait mine. I sat drowsily while he made numerous thin plaits in my short hair. One day while he was doing this he said, 'I might marry you when I grow up.'

Half-asleep, my forehead resting on a pillow over his better leg, I said, 'I'm going to marry another boy.'

'What's his name?'

Sleepily improvising, I said the boy's rich uncle had made us vow to keep it secret.

'Just tell me his name,' begged Kenny.

'All right. Desmond.'

'What does his father do?'

'I'm not allowed to tell that either. You can marry his s-s-s-sister.'

'What's she like?'

'Tall and s-s-sll-'

'Slim,' said Kenny kindly.

'With pale golden hair and blue eyes.'

'Sounds all right. She can't be too thin, though, because I would have to sit on her.'

Rhoda had told me about the sexual act, she and her friend Gwen having wheedled the information out of the more knowing girls at her high school. To shut her up, I had pretended casually to believe her. Or perhaps I really did believe her, but was utterly resistant. It is difficult to go into the labyrinth and bring out my reason for rejecting her information. I, too, have been subjected to popular child psychology, which supplies the easy answer that I associated the information with the 'showing' of our genitals that had been a rite of admission to the society at the creek, and that I turned it away because it revived my shame and guilt. But Kenny and I didn't make much of showing each other our genitals, which makes me think that the shame and guilt were easily overcome, and that a much weightier reason was that I did not want to face the alteration which a belief in Rhoda's information would force in my perception of my father and mother. I could not face this; it was too different from what I had always supposed. Though my father had become one of those to whom I could not speak without stammering, he remained, if less beloved as a man, a beloved and remote *figure,* while my mother, in spite of the simple conversational tone, and my new comfort in her company, was to be viewed, when in conjunction with my father, as merged with that remote *figure,* as slightly immaterial. While willing to assail their material selves, I did not want that figure brought down; I valued its distance. Under Kenny's flickering fingers I kept my head quite still, hoping he would say no more. But he said, 'My uncle sits on his wife, anyway. I saw them.'

Rhoda had not mentioned sitting. Curiosity broke through my guard and made me ask, 'But what was his wife doing?'

'Just lying there.'

'Were they talking or anything?'

'No, they were too puffed.'

'Had they been running?'

'No, they were just on the bed.'

Rhoda had told me this act took place in bed. I said, 'Hurry up, Kenny. At three o'clock I'm going to Betty's.'

'I've finished. You can look now.'

I got up and went to the mirror. 'Phew-agghh!' I said, as I always did, violently unplaiting my hair while Kenny gave his sweet high laugh.

'When can I meet your boy's sister?' he asked.

'As soon as you start to walk.'

'Next year I'm going to play cricket.'

In that year of postponement, we seldom contributed to each other's fantasies. Our fantasies ran parallel, veering sometimes to touch, but never for long. Each was content if the other did not oppose. Standing with my legs apart, shaking my hair about, I said that next year I was going to a small school built of stone, with a tower, and big shady trees all round it.

'What's Desmond's sister's name?' asked Kenny.

'Marguerite,' I replied.

The day when I was finally shown the way to Budjerra Heights must have been a Saturday. Everybody was at home. Neal and my father had settled to one of their long talks, sitting in canvas chairs on that part of the verandah called 'the porch'. On the other part of the verandah, which was divided from the porch by a lattice screen, Sybil and I were loudly quarrelling. My father raised his torso from his deck chair to call out a rebuke, when at the same time my mother, at her marching step, came through the room I shared with Sybil, emerged on to the verandah, and clapped her hands together.

'Come on, all you girls. We are going for a good tramp in the bush.'

Rhoda drifted out of her room, sullen. It must have been afternoon, all our morning chores done, and for some reason, none of Rhoda's friends, nor any tennis, available. She said, 'I don't want to go for a good tramp in the bush. Thank you.'

But again my mother struck her hands together. 'Come on. There's been nothing but moods and bickering all day. All put on good hats. I won't take no for an answer.'

Fifteen minutes later we had crossed the tram lines at the top of our street and were walking under the awnings of the local shops. This was a long way from Soden's Corner; I did not dream we would go anywhere near Budjerra Heights. My mother said quietly to Rhoda, 'Now, dear, you know what to do when we go round Hough's Corner.'

On Hough's Corner the larrikins of the local push stood slouched in a row. Their hands were in their pockets, cigarettes waggled from their lower lips, and many stood with one foot on the wall behind them, as I had done when I was one of the trouble makers in Miss Rickard's class at the school. Their white shirts were big and ballooning, and they had no creases in the crowns of their hats. I, on my messages to the shops, could walk past them unnoticed, but unaccompanied girls with breasts were subjected to raucous appraisal, yodelling and jeers. Rhoda had told me how her friend Gwen, forced to run past the push so that she would not miss her tram, had burst into tears which she tried to hide, as she clutched the strap in the swaying tram, against the flesh of her upper arm.

The push was silent as, conducted by my mother at her marching pace, and looking neither to right nor left, we passed round Hough's Corner. Evident among the larrikins was the pink of form guides; on Saturday afternoons they would slip over to the pub to lay their bets. My mother was experienced in passing pushes, and when we got round Hough's Corner and were walking on the wide suburban road that would eventually run into bush, Sybil begged her to tell us again about the chaperone who had conducted her and the other young women when, at the end of each working day, they had come from behind the desks and switchboards of the General Post Office, and had emerged into Queen Street.

'Well, naturally,' said my mother, as if reluctantly, 'Mrs Quinane went first.'

'Go on, mum,' said Sybil, *'Please.'*

In that second span of time when I was alone every weekday with my mother, listening from the camphorwood chest, I was to hear this story so often that when I sensed it coming I would try to head it off. But in those days I loved to hear how our mother, with Amy, Lily, Annie, Maud and the others, led by booted stout black-bosomed Mrs Quinane, had run the gamut of the jeering larrikins (abetted by those who had come to shout that women were taking men's jobs), and how the group of girls had followed Mrs Quinane with their heads held high, and had looked neither to right nor left.

'We had passed our examinations. We had earned our positions. We were the first in Queensland. And who else, I would like to know, would have kept the younger children in school after my father died? One afternoon Amy started to cry and said she couldn't face it, but we said, "Come on, Amy, be a soldier. Go out there with dry eyes, or stay back alone."'

From the camphorwood chest I would coax her conversation elsewhere, but when I was nine, I loved these tales of her heroism, and the way she relived them with her head held high and her grey eyes kindling and flashing. Walking up broad Caledonia Road towards the bush, I respectfully took her hand. Sybil said they must have been horrible men, and Rhoda, speaking for the first time since we had set out, asked how long they had kept it up.

'Their ranks soon started to thin. In a month or so we saw that they were tired of it. We weren't surprised. We never doubted we would win.'

'But you still had to have a chaperone,' Sybil said anxiously.

'It was thought best to keep Mrs Quinane.'

'It must have been a bit of a let-down,' said Rhoda, 'when they stopped.'

'Indeed it was not, girl.'

My mother carried a handbag in one hand, and cupped in the other, a clump of maidenhair fern wrapped in damp newspaper. This we took in to Mr and Mrs Tulius, whose new house was near the straggling end of Caledonia Road, and whose garden was hardly started.

'Now put it in straight away, dear,' my mother said to young Mrs Tulius. In case she should be thought overbearing, my mother, when instructing anyone other than her daughters, did not wag a forefinger, but only a little finger, which gave rather a charming and helpless air to her admonishments. 'It died last time because you let it dry out. Look, I've a suggestion. Now don't laugh at me.'

She took from her bag a small hand trowel wrapped in oil cloth and in a naughty and secretive voice explained that she would not believe bush flowers wouldn't grow in her garden, and even though she had failed with them so far, she was simply refusing to give up.

'So since I'm standing here with a trowel, just give me that fern.'

To put in the fern, she straddled the garden bed instead of bending at hip joints and knees, as she always told us to do. Her skirt lifted at the back and disclosed white thighs above her rolled stockings.

'She does that on purpose,' said Rhoda; but Sybil and I said together, 'Oh, she does not,' and Sybil added, 'It's so that she won't get the hem of her good pleated skirt dirty. Come and look at the new baby.'

Rhoda pulled a face. I felt uneasy with Rhoda when she was in one of her depressions. 'Mum will stand there talking all day,' she said morosely, as we wandered over to join Sybil at the baby's pram.

I did not take long when it was my turn to lift the gauze. The baby was too young to interest me. Four thin red appendages waved feebly above white swaddling. Lips, surprisingly big and grey, smacked. As Rhoda and I turned away she said, 'Wouldn't it be easy to kill?'

Now I pulled a face. 'What's the matter with you?' said Rhoda in a light fast voice. 'I'm only stating a fact. I bet a lot of people think that. I used to think it about you, when mum first brought you home.'

Our mother, flanked by the smiling Tuliuses, was still talking as they strolled towards us. 'I wish she would stop being winsome,' said Rhoda. She raised her voice, 'Mum, I think I'll push off home.'

'Oh no, dear. What about our walk?'

'I don't want to tramp in the bloody bush.'

'Goodbye,' cried Mrs Tulius, clutching both my mother's hands in sympathy. 'And *thank you*. You're a *real chum*.'

'You bet!' said her young husband, looking indignantly at Rhoda.

Rhoda sauntered to the gate. 'Well hurry up then, mum, if you want this tramp so much.'

In Caledonia Road, my mother said, in a low voice quivering with affront, 'That word! On the lips of one of my daughters!'

'On the lips,' said Rhoda, laughing.

'I have never been so ashamed in my entire life.'

'Don't exaggerate, mum. You're always telling us not to.'

'Quiet, please,' my mother intensely whispered. 'People

may be in their gardens.'

I picked up a eucalyptus twig and pretended to be interested only in flicking palings. I was miserable in this conflict between my alliance with Rhoda and the blossoms of comfort I had lately taken from my mother. Sybil, who had run ahead to take our mother's hand, turned and said softly to Rhoda, 'You wait. Mum will tell dad.'

'She won't,' said Rhoda calmly to me. 'It would upset him too much.'

'He got told when I played the wag.'

'That was different. That called for family management. But it's no use trying to do that to me. They can't do a thing to me. I'm too big,' said Rhoda, swaggering, 'and they know it.'

My mother's right arm was fluttering against her body in that gesture so characteristic of her, like the abbreviated fluttering of a wing, but in an idling voice she asked Sybil to observe that those people over there who had painted their house pale blue would be sorry; it would not stand up. We passed the last of the spindly-legged houses, each rising behind white pickets derived from an English cottage, and embarked in our divided cavalcade on a ragged bush track. Almost at once we came to the impediment of a fallen tree, and here, out of earshot, my mother halted, and turned on Rhoda.

'Now,' she said. 'Now, my girl, you will apologize.'

'All right,' said Rhoda. 'I apologize.'

'I should think so,' said my mother falteringly, looking at Rhoda with suspicion.

Rhoda dropped to her knees beside the fallen tree and burst into tears.

'Now, now, girlie,' said my mother, patting her shoulder.

'See, everything's all right,' shouted Sybil; and I hopped on to the tree trunk and dramatically teetered.

'Come on, dear, we'll go on. Stand up now, Ro dear. There's nothing like the bush to clear all our troubles away.

Let us all stand for a moment and draw in good deep breaths of this splendid tangy air, better than any scent I know.'

I looked nervously at Rhoda, but she stood up obediently, drew a short breath, and said, 'Yes, it is nice.'

'Now, girls, I want you to keep your eyes open,' said my mother as we went on, 'for that yellow flowering bush I tried before. It's very very small, remember, so we'll have to be sharp.'

Rhoda was languid, but Sybil and I soon cried, 'Here,' and 'Here.' 'Very good,' said our mother each time. 'Mark that place with crossed sticks and we'll collect them on our way back.'

But presently she halted, and did not seem to hear what we said to her, and took a few steps downward off the path.

'Now here's a funny thing.'

We said 'What,' not much interested.

'Here's some cultivation. If I'm not very much mistaken, that's watercress down in that hollow.'

We said 'Oh come on,' but she stood perfectly still, and spoke as if we were not present.

'We had it at the old place. Charlie is so fond of it. I wonder if I put it where the old sump used to be . . .'

'Mum,' said Rhoda. 'Look. Barbed wire. It's a fence.'

'Nonsense,' said our mother, without taking her gaze from the bottom of the hollow. 'This is all crown land. There's no freehold past Caledonia Road. One of you girls just hold my bag.'

Sybil took it. The single strand wire fence had sagged almost to the ground. Our mother, holding her trowel, stepped easily over it. Rhoda, the tallest of us, said suddenly, 'Mum, there's a brick chimney through those trees.'

'Oh dear,' murmured our mother, standing straddled again at the bottom of the hollow, 'it's quite nasty and muddy down here. Here's a nice young clump.'

Heard before seen, the woman who stepped out of the scrub on the opposite bank screeched, 'What d'you think you're doing?'

I see this woman standing in black clothes, her grey and black hair streaming loose from its pins. She wears men's boots. Her arms are tightly folded, her head is thrust forward, her mouth is still screeching. My mother stands straddling the cress, the lifted clump cupped in one hand, and on her face an unforgettable expression of shock, amusement and propitiation. Her mouth soundlessly opens and closes, so that I, standing with my hands covering a gasp, think of the baby's lips, smacking. Sybil has dropped beside me whispering, 'Mum mum mum . . .' Rhoda is crouching behind a bush, shaking with giggles, weakly moaning that she would wet her pants. The woman shrieks and howls on but then stops and says with quiet menace, 'All right. I'm off to get the gun.'

'I will put your cress back,' said my mother (Rhoda rolled over on her side, sobbing with laughter). 'I am so sorry. I had no idea there was any freehold land here.'

Only the first few words of the answering howl – Didn't you now? – were intelligible. The rest of the terrible howl followed my mother as she clambered up the bank.

'Oh dear, I'm rather muddy.'

'Now git, you and your brats, off this *freehold land.* Git, git, git.'

'Come along, girls. Sybil, get up at once. Yes, Rhoda, it's very funny, but don't let her see you laughing.'

Rhoda staggered into the open, holding her stomach.

'Do you think she really has a gun?' whispered Sybil.

'Certainly not. Nor has she any freehold land.'

'Mum,' said Rhoda, 'there was a *whole proper house* in there.'

'I am not often mistaken,' said my mother.

In the shriek that still followed us we heard again the word 'gun'. Sybil broke into a run. 'Come back, you silly girl,' said my mother, laughing. 'We will just walk at a nice normal pace. And remember to keep a lookout for those crossed sticks. No apparition will appear to prevent my taking up a bush plant, I hope.'

But we could not find the crossed sticks, and soon it was apparent that somehow or other, in our retreat from the woman, we had taken the wrong path. Presently Sybil enquired, 'Are we lost?'

'How can we be, girl?'

'Lost in the bush!' Rhoda bent at the knees and staggered to and fro. 'Lost! Lost!' I laughed and copied her. 'Lost!' we cried. 'Water! Water!'

'Do stop that. I can't think for your noise.'

'Water! Water!'

'It's getting dark,' said Sybil.

'It's nothing of the sort.'

'Will they find our bleached skeletons?' asked Rhoda.

'This track is more clearly defined than that one. Come along, girls, stop that tomfoolery and let's go.'

'No, seriously, mum,' said Rhoda, 'we ought to take the downhill track. I'm sure we've worked our way uphill.'

'The downhill one will go back to the cress place,' said Sybil. 'Lost people walk in circles.'

'Is there no landmark?' murmured our mother, looking about her in wonder.

'My legs are tired,' said Sybil.

'Let us sit upon the ground,' said Rhoda, covering a yawn, 'and tell sad stories of the death of kings.'

'They are tired as anything.'

'Girls, it will save time in the long run if we all stand quietly and have a good hard think.'

While our mother stood thinking, and we stood leaving it to her, we heard the tread of feet and the crackling of sticks, and on the downhill track, hat first, a man came into view. Our mother stepped forward and said pleasantly, 'Excuse me.'

The man wore ragged city clothes, boots with big rounded toecaps, and carried a cardboard suitcase furry at the angles. He had a small trimmed beard which, Sybil whispered to me, was like King George's. He halted and looked us over.

'What is it, missus?'

'Could you tell us the way to Caledonia Road?'

'Not from here I can't.'

'We *are* lost,' cried Sybil.

'You can't be, kiddie,' said the man, 'not in this bit of bush.'

'Certainly we can't be,' said our mother. 'Tell us how you came in.'

'From Soden's Corner.'

'Soden's Corner will do us nicely. That means we don't take the uphill path?'

'Uphill one goes to Budjerra Heights. That's for me. Downhill to Soden's Corner. Haven't got the price of a meal on you, have you?'

As my mother opened her bag I stepped forward and said, 'Is there a landmark on the way?'

'Landmark.' He looked at me closely, with a lop-sided smile in his beard which I chose to take as a signal that he understood my secret allegiance to his society. He said, 'You come to a cement pipe, running over a bit of a gully.'

As we set off on the downhill track I was proud to hear Rhoda say, 'He seemed quite a nice sort of man,' and even prouder when my mother agreed.

'He had a beard like King George's,' said Sybil again.

'That's a great distinction,' replied our republican mother.

'The king's isn't the only beard in the world,' I told Sybil.

The track opened out, but became rougher, so that we had to jump and clamber down eroded hollows; and then suddenly the bush ended and there was the road with the glinting stones on its margins and in the middle the soft yellowish dust. I moved over to the side from which I knew the cement pipe could soon be seen, so that I could openly declare it while keeping its real significance to myself. Sybil came over and joined me, repelled by the dust, but found the stones no better, and soon lagged behind. My mother and Rhoda, now the best of friends, walked in the middle of the road in their puffs of dust, talking in an adult sort of way.

'That's true, dear,' I heard my mother say, 'but remember we saw him for only a minute or two. In times like these, when there's a job for any man who wants to work, there's usually only one reason for living like that.'

'He didn't look like a drunkard.'

'A drunkard or an idler, I'll be bound. Who else would be going there?'

'What do you know about it?' I shouted from my stony margin. 'You've never been there.'

'For pity's sake,' said my mother, 'don't you start.' And Rhoda said amiably, 'Yes, Bea, shut up. Is it true, mum, what Gwen's father says – that there have been outbreaks of sickness there?'

'There have indeed. That's why many people think the place should be broken up and the people moved on. Your father's against that, and on balance, so am I. It's traditional, you know, to allow it. It's a relic of the early days, when so many had to take whatever makeshift shelter they could. And yet, and yet, one of the health inspectors went in, and very strongly urged that something be done. Do you know, he said that some of them don't even have the decency to dig themselves a cesspit.'

'Pooh-ooh,' said Rhoda.

'And that when he went into one humpy, all he could smell were fried onions and urine?'

'Oh, mum, stop it.' Rhoda waved a hand in front of her face. 'Pooh, pooh, pooh.'

'It wouldn't be true of all of them, dear. I believe there are women there, and always, everywhere, you find some women who manage to keep themselves and their children clean.'

But the assurance (though it did bring a fleeting image of the rough-dried cloth Peggy and Des drew down over their sun-scaled arms) came too late for me. We were passing the cement pipe, but I hung back with Sybil, and grizzled that I was thirsty, and that my legs were tired.

Almost as if they were in conspiracy, my mother and Rhoda wore the same kind of private smile as we crossed the park to the house. Both hurried, outdistancing Sybil and me, and by the time we laggards got home, Rhoda had begun, for the benefit of my father and Neal, a dramatic account of my mother's criminal activities. My father lay back in his canvas chair, his laughter visible but hardly audible above Neal's. My mother, falsely coy and indignant, marched in and out of the bedroom, to deny or to laugh, while she took down and brushed and repinned her hair. Sybil joined in, running from one to the other saying, 'And she said she had a gun,' and 'Then we met a man with a beard like the king's.' I heard more of this than I saw: I was lying on my side on one of the beds on the verandah, crying, and saying (when at last attention could be spared for me) that my legs were terribly sore. And in fact, when I had to get up to go that evening to the table, I limped, and did not myself believe I was pretending.

I took the two pebbles and threw them over the fence into the park, and when Kenny suggested that I should supply 'some kind of tin with a lid' I gave him the French cachou tin. When Kenny's mother was out, he and I shared one of her cigarettes, and he said the tin would be handy in case we had to butt it out in a hurry.

I never heard what became of the Kellaways, nor am I sure that I ever saw either of them again. I think I once saw Des standing with the larrikins on Hough's Corner, but I could not go near enough to confirm my impression, because by that time I had breasts, and had grown into my face.

THE AVIATOR ·

We spent those school holidays in a rented cottage at Burleigh Heads, sleeping on lumpy beds on a splintery-timbered verandah, our sleep entered by the thundering water and driving salt wind that possessed us by day. When we came back to Brisbane Rhoda resumed high school, Sybil the school across the park. My father and Neal had returned earlier than the rest of us, and were already into the routine of dressing in hot suits and felt hats and going each weekday in the tram to work, adding mackintoshes and rubber boots in the violent storms of late summer. I alone could keep my seaside bare feet as I settled again to the days at home with my mother.

But there were differences. The horse Pickwick was no longer in his yard, and none of us 'three heartless girls' who had pleaded for his life noticed his disappearance for three days. Sybil was the first suddenly to raise her head at the breakfast table and say, 'Where is Pickwick?' I had to run down to verify his absence, for I thought I had seen him, since our return, standing in his yard half-blind half-deaf, a simple brown shape, always in profile. Neal and my father, who had had the doing of the thing, leading him across the park to the yard behind Soden's forge, were not lenient, and none of us three, when confronted with our heartlessness, dared openly to mourn, nor I to say that I continued to glimpse, from the tail of my eye, that brown shape, that imprint of memory, his ghost.

105

Another difference was that my year of freedom was nearly over. My plea for an extension, at first considered by my parents in one of their bedroom colloquies, was dismissed when they learned that my enemy Miss Rickard was transferred to a school nearer her home. It was decided that I no longer stammered enough to claim exemption. The mystery of my paralysis of speech when confronted with a few people, notably my father, was set aside as simply that – a mystery, to be cleared up in due course. Or perhaps they suspected (since my father was the one with whom final decisions were said to rest) that I was using my stammer to escape the school. I was not. I knew I was doomed. And although I was wonderfully gifted in ignoring dreaded events until the hour they were upon me, in the matter of the school this endowment failed me. It was February; my year would end in April. My impending return to the school began to spread like a stain across my life, or like the huge flotilla of seaweed Rhoda and I had watched one dawn rocking closer and closer across the blue and silver and turquoise sea.

Meeting my doom by enhancing it, I told myself as I mooched about that after I went back to school I would 'lose the sea'. When, each lunch hour, the miniature aerial tumult reached me from the school across the park, I would shut my eyes and try to fill my sight with the shining hump of a breaker or the race of foam up the hard sand. When I went to help to relieve the invalid boredom of Kenny Fry, I would pause over the draughts or ludo board to describe how, if you went out beyond the breakers, you could feel for a split second that you were standing upright in the swell. I blushed with awe and fear as I told him.

Kenny had grown while we were away, and could now walk a few steps on crutches. I expected him to respond by saying that soon he would learn to surf, buy a board, be a champion, and at that signal we would each go off into our parallel fantasies. But he said, 'What about the sharks?'

'Pooh, they rang the bell sometimes, but it was always a false alarm.'

'Did you know,' he said, 'that I almost died?' The pupils of his eyes enlarged as he watched me. 'I was a feather away from it.'

His mother intercepted me on my way out. 'Have you no consideration? Skiting about all the things you do?'

Shocked, I clasped my hands in appeal. 'I wasn't.'

'You were. You were and you always do. How do you think Kenny feels? Rousing his envy.'

'I didn't notice.'

'Well, try. I know you're not mean-natured. Just actressy. Look at you now. But I'm not saying to stop coming.'

One sweltering March day, when my mother went under a green-lined parasol to see her mother at Albion Park, and left me alone in the house, I found one of those currents of air that move at floor level and spread myself on the verandah with my hands under my head. The treasures of space and privacy, usually so valued by me whenever I was left alone in the house, seemed already cancelled because they were soon to be lost. When lunch hour at the school became audible, instead of opposing it with visions of the sea, I sullenly let it work on me, recalling the ticking shuffling restless tedium of the classrooms from which those hundreds had just marched out, some to stay in the concrete spaces under the leggy buildings and others to swarm over the pale bare dusty ground – into the sports oval reserved for the boys, or to climb bars, ride on iron-chained swings, or to hop out diagrams drawn with a stick. Beyond the sports oval and the trampled dust, the ground dipped to a small area of rough bush, and here, one day, I had joined in a war game called Medes and Persians. And perhaps because, for once, I was listening for individual sounds in that hubbub, I remembered the intensity and exhilaration with which I had played this game, and how pausing for a moment to renew my breath, I had become aware for the first time in my life of bodily heat as an abnormal condition.

Now, above the aerial hubbub of the school, I heard another noise. The school lay to the west. This noise was coming from the eastern sky and resembled a wooden rattle rotated with absolute regularity at very high speed. I leapt to my feet, raced through the house to the kitchen, seized the old white cloth from the cupboard, and in half a minute was standing in our back yard ready to wave when the aeroplane, which I estimated was somewhere over Caledonia Road, came into sight.

One of my cousins had seen an aeroplane fly so low that he had seen the aviator's goggles, and Betty's mother, pegging clothes on their line, had run into the garage because she did not want to be seen with her hair in metal curlers. I had never heard that rapid regular sound so close before. A ground noise, a chain of barking, ran beneath it.

Sometimes when I waited with the white cloth, instead of coming closer, that noise would veer off and recede, but now the swift rackety sounds were merging into a vibrant roar which I located as only a few houses away up our street, and then the barking and the sounds of the school became nothing as the aeroplane emerged from the tops of the tall trees lining the Coolidges' back fence.

Too shocked to prance and yell, I stood with my arms stretched as high as they would go and violently shook the white cloth in the windless air to keep it aloft. The aeroplane was passing over our back yard. I saw the aviator in profile, his helmet, his goggles. He turned his head, he looked down at me. Up my legs, through my body and arms, a cold electric current ran. The aviator raised a gloved hand. The aeroplane flew over Pickwick's yard, veering towards the park, and disappeared behind the Beathes' mango trees. Down the street a new chain of barking began.

The image of Pickwick I caught as I lowered my gaze from the sky was quite incidental. Had the aviator smiled? I dropped the cloth and ran towards the park, hoping to watch the aeroplane out of sight.

As I ran, vaulting vegetable beds, the hubbub of the school abruptly stopped. Then I heard the hundreds of voices springing in unity into the air, crying oh ah oh ah oh ah oh, rising and expanding until the roar of the aeroplane was matched by an airborne concert of joy and triumph and wonder.

From the top of our back fence I saw the aeroplane fly beyond the school and disappear in the direction of the river. The billows of rejoicing from the school subsided into an excited babble in which individual shrieks and yells were again audible. A few of the dogs were still barking.

The aviator had waved to me. Perhaps he had smiled. I dropped from our fence into the park and began to run along the line of back fences. Aunt Jean stood in her yard, holding the black Orpington hen she always spoke of as the one she loved the best. 'Did you hear that, Bea?' she called to me.

I stood at her gate. 'The aviator waved to me.'

'What a big thrill,' said Aunt Jean, pretending to be excited. She scratched the ruff of the hen and added crooningly, 'He scared the living daylights out of every creature in the street.'

Old Mr Bell stood in pyjamas at the Greenlees' gate, his daughter Mrs Greenlees beside him. 'They have no darned right to fly so low,' he was saying angrily.

'All right, dad. You write a letter to someone about it. But come on in now, out of this heat.'

'The aviator waved to me,' I said.

'Ol? Ol? Hear that? He waved to this kiddie here. That's how low they come.'

'That's right, dad.' Mrs Greenless gave me a wink, either of warning or disbelief. 'But you just come on in now, dad.'

Clare's mother was taking washing from the line. I ran quickly past, fearing to be diverted by the embarrassment she always showed since forbidding Clare's friendship with me. Now I was sure the aviator had smiled. I could see him; he smiled as he waved. I passed under the shadow of the Beathes' mango trees and came to the Frys' house. As soon as I saw Kenny sitting in a cane chair on their back verandah, randomly chanting and banging the verandah rail with a crutch, I knew his mother was out.

'Hey, Kenny!' I shouted.

He struggled out of the chair as I crossed their yard. 'Did you see it?' he shouted back.

'Yes.' I ran up his steps. 'And do you know what?'

'I was inside, worse luck. I only got out in time to see him disappear.'

I stopped short, watching him sideways, plucking my dress in peaks from my sweating skin.

'I heard them over at the school, though,' he said. 'Gee! Didn't they sing out! They still haven't calmed down. Listen.'

Listening, flapping my skirt with both hands, the newly revived memory of intense exhilaration made me cry out, 'I *can't wait* to play Medes and Persians.'

And having already transgressed, I added in a triumphant rush, 'Kenny, the aviator waved to me.'

'Did he?' Kenny did not look at me, but kept his head cocked as if still listening to the noise of the school. I noticed again how tall and white he had grown while we were away, and how the bones were distinct in his hands and wrists. As he turned his eyes to mine I could discern his struggle.

'Why didn't you say so straight away, then?'

My s's had improved more than my f's. 'I wasn't sure. It was all so f-f-f-f-'

'Fast,' said Kenny.

'Quick,' I said.

'It was a Baby Avro,' said Kenny, with languid certainty, 'by the sound of it.'

'I don't know their names.'

Kenny began again, as if absent-mindedly, to bang at the verandah rail with a crutch. I sat on the top step, turned away from him, and looked down at my evenly tanned feet. When I had to wear sandals again, a fan of deeper brown marks would appear on each foot, burned through the three tear-shaped vents in each sandal. Kenny was going inside. I felt the boards of the verandah vibrate under his crutches; but presently, as I got up to go, he came through the door with one of his mother's cigarettes in his mouth, alight.

'Here,' he said, offering it. 'There's no wind today.'

So we leaned on the railing, drew the aromatic smoke into our mouths, and expelled it in rings that writhed a little before they were absorbed into the shimmering air.

SYDNEY STORIES

THE MILK ·

When Marjorie's son Emlyn returned to Sydney from Europe, he demanded to see the little flat she had rented but had not yet moved into. She divined his opinion from the way his feet came together in such an abrupt stop on the threshold. 'See the nice broad window sill,' she said, going briefly to sit on it. 'And I shan't be here for ever, you know.'

He was in the tiny kitchen. 'It's not secure,' he shouted.

'What?' She stood beside him. 'What isn't?'

'That.'

'A servery. Oh, good. I didn't notice that.' She opened it with one finger. It was certainly dirty. 'It's for the milk,' she said.

'They put kids through those.'

'Not in these parts, surely. There can't be much to steal.'

'Everyone has a television.'

'I haven't.' She shut the servery. 'It's only for a while,' she coaxed. 'Only till the divorce.'

Although it was one of Marjorie's rules never to do anything drastic in the January heat, it was in January that she had managed at last to convince her husband that she was serious about leaving him.

'No contentious matters at dinner' was another of her principles, but no principle could stand against the momentum

115

gathered, and it was at the dinner table that she achieved that communication.

Bruce rose abruptly. The look on his face was murderous, as was the one brief and thickened sentence he spoke. Even in the immobility of her astonishment, she did not believe he would actually murder her, but did realise that such venom not only made impossible the amicable kind of divorce she had just proposed, but made it impossible for her even to stay in the same house. She packed two suitcases and went to a private hotel suggested in a hurry by her friend Carla. She went by taxi because, while she was packing, Bruce took her car keys.

The hotel, on the northern shores of the harbour, was a place of somnolent residents and soggy beds. 'Well,' said Carla, in Marjorie's room there, 'you did say somewhere cheap.'

Marjorie noticed that Carla avoided looking at her face. 'Poor old Brucie,' said Carla.

This was in 1976. The divorce laws had been reformed the year before, sweeping away grounds such as adultery, cruelty, and desertion, and putting in their place only breakdown of marriage. Carla said, 'He can't believe you can leave him, and not be legally punished.'

'Nonsense. He reads the newspapers.'

'But he can't take it in. It doesn't seem natural.'

'Oh,' said Marjorie, 'I dream about him.'

'He says it must be your change of life.'

'It probably is.'

'Well, Marj, in that case,' said Carla.

'Why shouldn't it be?' said Marjorie. 'Why shouldn't change of life be like adolescence? The two great changes. So? The two great chances.'

'Chances of what?'

'Exaltation. Remember?'

'Not really.'

'And suddenly seeing the truth. And knowing just how to do things.'

'Oh my,' said Carla. 'Perhaps now you'll be able to draw feet.'

Carla and Marjorie had been at art school together. Carla had become a commercial designer and had continued in it in spite of marriage and children. Marjorie, an illustrator specializing in botany, had dropped that, and all of her training, until the sixties, when, under the influence of a group of local women, she had begun to sculpt in the garage. But, abstract and incisive though her pieces were in conception, all turned out to have a trivial and fiddled-with look. Nor did persistence bring improvement. 'It's the surfaces,' she said. 'Like badly iced cakes.'

But when she returned to small-scale drawing, she found a new enjoyment in her materials, and an excitement in each day's first contact of pen or chalk with paper. She also discovered in herself a reluctance to say anything to anyone about these pleasures. Her stylish and accurate pen drawings soon began to earn her money, but even though the unsparing truth of her instinct told her she would leave Bruce, she did not face that truth to the point of providing for it, and remained lax in commission and shy about naming her price. All her drawings were of plants or objects, although she could usually manage a figure hovering behind the cooking ingredients, or a distant child in the garden. 'With its little feet behind the herbaceous border,' Carla would say. It was often Carla who commissioned these drawings. Now, in the hotel, Carla said, 'It makes it harder to find work for you.'

'I've a book of West Australian wild flowers to do. All from photographs. Easy.'

'Then for God's sake, get it in on time, and see that you get decent money. Have you a lawyer?'

'Of course not. I always thought Bruce and I would talk, you see, discuss—'

'Oh, Marj, get one, get one.'

'Legally, I am sure I am—'

'Within your rights. Yes, but the law's a new one. Not many precedents. Martin, of course, won't – well, he can't can he?'

Carla's husband, Martin, was a lawyer. 'Of course he can't,' said Marjorie. 'Do you think I expected it?'

'Not really.'

'Does he recommend anyone?'

'No.'

'I see.'

'Sorry.'

'So I'm to be put in solitary.'

'Marj, give people time to get used to it.'

'I can't work here. I'll have to get a flat. Look, there isn't even room for a table. Carla, am I imagining it, or are you really trying not to look at my face?'

Carla laughed, abashed, and picked up her bag. 'It's just that I'm so sorry for Brucie.'

But she still did not look at Marjorie's face, kissing her goodbye instead.

All the flats Marjorie saw in the territory familiar to her, the north and east, were too dear. It was Bruce's edict that they should communicate only through lawyers. Marjorie went to see her lawyer, who was named Gwen.

'Look, since I'm not claiming maintenance, or even my full legal share of our property, don't you think Bruce should allow me something to go on with? I've got a thousand or so in my own account, but the rest of it is all muddled up with his. I'm earning, but I must rent a flat, you see, working space. And here is a list of the things I need from the house. Basic, as you see. Bed, table, etcetera. But will you ask about the money?'

Gwen, like Carla, did not look at Marjorie's face, though for a different reason. A big peachy Rubens beauty, she set herself up to be looked at rather than herself do any surveying. She swung aside her waist-length hair and directed at her bookshelves the sweet pensive smile often seen on television, where she spoke on women's affairs. Her voice was very soft.

'I'm afraid he still insists that because you're the one who left, you're not entitled to a cent. Of course under the new act he's wrong, but I'm afraid it does mean that unless you're prepared to put out a good bit of money, you're going to have to wait till the case comes to court.'

'Which will be?'

As she watched Gwen shrug, Marjorie in her imagination cut her hair to shoulder length and removed some of her eye-shadow. She never made these fast and absent-minded rearrangements in the appearance of her friends; they simply seemed to take place of their own accord in suspenseful or awkward moments with people hardly known. 'Will it be,' she asked, 'say, three months?'

'More like six,' said Gwen.

'Then he's just being *mean*,' cried Marjorie, like a child.

'We so often express our injuries through property,' murmured philosophical Gwen.

'What about that list, then? Can Trevor persuade him to let me have those things?'

Trevor was Bruce's lawyer. 'Oh, I expect he can, yes. I'll ring him now.' Gwen put a hand on the phone and gave her delicious smile. 'Leave a hundred with Isolde on the way out, will you?'

Marjorie went south to Newtown, where she found a small flat – one room, kitchenette and bath – with good light, in a big old block set among patched-up terrace houses, small shops, and light industry. Her son Emlyn and his wife Fiona returned from Europe two days before she was to move in. They had heard nothing of the separation. Fiona was agog but amused. 'It gave him a bit of a shock, I bet.' But sweat had broken out under Emlyn's eyes. 'Shut up, Fee. Mum, tell us what we can do to help.'

By now Marjorie was used to people who avoided looking at her face. She understood that Emlyn's modernity was in conflict with his grief and disapproval. All the same, she was pleased to see his censure deflected to Fiona, who only hugged him and said, 'Shut up yourself. Yes, Marj, what can we do?'

'I want to look at this flat you've taken,' said Emlyn, pushing Fiona away. 'Wouldn't you know this would happen when we're overdrawn on our Bankcard?'

'Don't worry. I've two books to do. You can look at the flat tomorrow.' Marjorie smiled at Fiona. 'And on Thursday, if you like, and of course if you can get time off, you two could help me to move. I've got this sore shoulder. Here, at the back.'

'Get it looked at,' said Emlyn with ferocity.

'It was the suitcases. It will go. If you like, you two could go with the carrier to pick up the things Bruce – your father – oh, what shall I call him? – anyway, the things he is letting me have for the flat.'

'You won't fit much in one room,' said Emlyn.

'I adore Newtown,' said Fiona.

'Fee got that dress from Valentino,' said Emlyn.

Marjorie laughed when she saw how Bruce had interpreted her list. A weathered outdoor table with its two slatted chairs, a folding bed, a pale-blue chest of drawers from Emlyn's childhood, a bagful of worn linen and blankets, a box of pots and pans without lids, and her work-table, stool, and the old tea trolley on which she kept her materials. She laughed out of the strained amusement she was finding it more and more easy to summon, and because his meanness relieved her guilt, and because she did not want to further inflame Emlyn, but to co-operate with Fiona in keeping it light and funny.

'Love that window sill,' said Fiona. 'Wow.' She sat on it. 'I want it.'

'Well, mum, if that's really all?'

'Thank you, dears.'

'Come on, Fee. I'm late as hell.'

'See you soon then, Marjie.'

In the doorway Emlyn stopped, as he had done the day before, and morosely surveyed the room. Fiona could be heard running down the stairs. Unzipping the bag she had marked FIRST THINGS, Marjorie hardened herself against her son. She was tired. Her shoulder hurt. There would be cock-roaches. Emlyn had himself divorced his first wife (under the old laws) in order to marry Fiona.

'I wish you would let me nail up that bloody servery.'

'I don't know how long they let you park down there, Emlyn.'

As soon as he had gone, Marjorie abandoned the bag and went to the window. As she had hoped, the sill was wide enough, and broad enough, to contain her sitting figure. She sat resting in the embrasure, her legs along the seat, her back against the wall, her face turned to the window.

No tree broke her view of the street, which on this late afternoon was fairly busy with traffic and pedestrians. After a while she noticed that most of the people were burdened. Shabby young mothers bore heavy, sleeping babies. Women were weighted down on both sides with plastic sacks of pro-visions. Men carried bulging airline bags and packs of beer. Those waiting on the bus seat had bags and cartons on their laps or at their feet. Only the boys and those children not tethered by an adult hand were free. A group of boys, Aboriginal and white, came running. Knocking into each other, yelling, guffawing, inventing dangers, they brought a neat Chinese for a moment to the door of his grocery shop.

When travelling in Europe, Marjorie had looked down from hotel windows on traffic and human activity, but in Sydney she had lived all of her life from infancy in quiet neutral streets, where the neat squat houses were separated by splendid trees, and where almost the only pedestrians were school children. She had nursed a longing for the sea, and after the friendly divorce she had planned from Bruce, she had intended to find a small cottage near the beach where she had spent holidays as a child. She looked down on the street with an alertness that asked for no explanations, as if she were living only with her eyes. The cafe next to the grocery came alight through its netted shopfront. Lights came on in the terrace houses and revealed people cooking in corners of bedrooms. In the flats a television roared and was cut down. A phone rang; water throttled in a pipe. When heavy steps ascended the stairs outside her door, she was amused to be able to match them with the visible gait of a man she had just seen crossing the street. She got up and went to the peephole in the door.

She had never looked through a peephole before. The man had disappeared, but the distorted perspectives were mesmeric, and kept her there. The corridor looked so long, almost noble, but threatening too, the towering doors curving inward at their height. She told herself that one of those doors must open and admit a figure to her view, and under the alertness of this expectation, the scene grew more and more eerie. It was only a game, but when she withdrew her eye, having seen no figure, she was touched with solemnity.

She turned on the small battery radio Emlyn had left her, seized the bag marked FIRST THINGS, and took from it cleaning gear, a spray can of insecticide, and two rolls of Marimekko paper. She quickly washed the kitchen shelves, the drawers, and the servery, then lined them all with the paper. She refused to care that the chastity of the paper, its gloss and small vivid geometric daisies, made so sad the scarred and discoloured paint. In the room she took from among her work things a piece of card and a felt pen.

MILKMAN—When you see the servery door open, it means I want milk. Bottles only please. I don't take milk in cartons.

M.T.

She folded the card and set it like a neat tent on the paper. Beside it she put the clean milk bottle she had remembered to bring, and beside that, the exact money. She pushed open the outer door of the servery, and shut the inner one.

She held her breath as she rapidly sprayed insecticide behind the stove and refrigerator and along the skirting boards. On an explosion of breath she staggered out of the kitchen, kicking the door shut behind her so that the poison could lose its first stench while she ate and slept.

Carla had brought to the hotel that morning a little wicker hamper. As Marjorie examined its contents she compared herself to Carla. She would have remembered the wineglass, but forgotten the bottle opener.

She ate and drank in the window embrasure. The wine eased the pain in her shoulder, but relaxed her strained alertness and returned her burden to her. As bad, precisely as bad, as going back to Bruce, was the burden of her guilt. She longed above everything (everything but that) to be forgiven. She jumped up and stood boldly, with one knee on the sill, and finished the wine. She became drunk enough to be quite pleased with the improvisation of the folding bed, and to be comforted by the semblance of a cubby house given by the dim shapes around her of her unpacked, mismatched things.

In her dream, Bruce is hurrying to meet her, as he had done that time at the airport. He almost runs, shouldering his way through the crowd, his face congested with the familiar sizzle before his laughter would break. But in her dream, she was not appalled by his joy, as she was at the airport, having brought herself on the long journey to her irrevocable decision. In her dream, indeed, she is not at the airport, but is in the folding bed in the Newtown flat, and Bruce is advancing, one hand extended, across the floor. She sees behind his laughing face the floral curtains she has drawn against the street lights. She sees her work-table and trolley. She is amazed to be forgiven; the bliss of his forgiveness makes her gasp. She reaches for his hand and sees not the laughing face, but the malevolent face that had looked down on hers as he rose from the dining table. His extended hand would kill her. It presses on the bone between her breasts. She rolls off the bed to escape, and as she scrambles, sobbing, to her feet, she hears a loud crash, and a door slamming. She fumbles along the wall and finds the light switch. The room is exactly as it was when she went to sleep. The crashing is no longer loud; she recognises it as the joggling of milk bottles in a carrying crate. Her search for the light switch has brought her to the door. She rolls against it and puts her eye to the peephole. Far down the long and stately corridor she sees a dark little gnarled figure running weighted on one side with his milk and disappearing round a corner.

The suffocation in her chest becomes a searing pain. She considers a heart attack, but cannot believe in it. When the pain grips her entrails and forces her to a bowed position, she remembers the wine so quickly drunk. 'Fool!' she sobs. 'Fool!' But she is able to be amused by her ignominious cramped run into the kitchen. Milk will help. Even to envision the calm white bottle on the clean paper is a solace. She opens the servery. Her card stands there, and there, on the Marimekko paper, is her money, and there stands her empty bottle. The milkman has been, and has rejected her request. She drinks water, glass after glass. The pain leaves her belly, but spreads across her chest again, and goes on and on, attended by the old steady pain in the back of her left shoulder.

It seemed to help Doctor Furmann's powers of diagnosis if, as he tapped, as he listened, as he pressed fingers beneath her rib cage, he looked into the distance. But when she was dressed again, and sitting opposite him at his desk, he did look fully and very attentively at her face. He was a ferret-faced young man with notably intelligent eyes.

'I think you have a stomach ulcer.'

'Is that all?' said Marjorie.

'All? Ulcers are no joke.'

'No, but the worst pain last night was across my chest, and the pain I've had for weeks is behind my shoulder, so naturally, you know,' said Marjorie, with her shrugging, 'I thought, heart.'

'Would you prefer that?'

'I don't care one way or the other.'

'You're divorcing, did you say?'

'Yes, I did say that.'

Marjorie guessed by the sympathy in his eyes that he thought her the abandoned one. She would have liked the luxury of allowing him to think so, without the discomfort of deception. She said coldly, 'I left my husband.'

The sympathy remained. His splendid dark eyes reminded her of Emlyn's. His hairline was so uneven that in this pause she began to straighten it by electrolysis. 'It seems to me,' he said at last, 'that at your age, it doesn't matter who leaves who, not so far as my work is concerned. I want you to have an X-ray.'

'What will it cost?'

'Don't you belong to a fund?'

'My husband did all that.'

'You're still legally his wife.'

'Please give me a referral.' Marjorie knew she would pay for it herself. 'I'll go to a hospital.'

'You'll wait longer.'

'Never mind. I can take something, I suppose, in the meantime.'

He gave slow instructions as he wrote the referral and two prescriptions. 'No alcohol. And you don't smoke, so that's okay. No coffee. No aspirin. Not much tea. Eat little and often. If not solids, milk.' He handed her the flimsy sheets. 'If you find milk helps.'

'Milk!' Marjorie laughed, then lifted the top prescription and said sternly, 'Tranquillisers?'

'Don't indulge your opinions at the expense of your health.'

'But I told you, I must work.'

'Then take one when you stop work, and another at night. That pain in your shoulder, by the way, it's my guess that's referred pain.'

Coming home one day with her plastic sacks of provisions, Marjorie encountered the woman who lived in the next door flat. Marjorie would have been diffident about knocking on this neighbour's door, but when she saw her in the mundane and undistorted corridor, she was bold enough to accost her.

'I wonder if you could tell me what I must do to get milk delivered.'

'Easy,' said the woman. 'Leave your money out. No money, no milk.'

'But that's what I do.'

'And I always leave the servery door open.'

'I do that, too.'

'Well, I get milk, no trouble. Except when I forget to leave the money out. Then I get a carton across at Wong's. It's no trouble to slip across to Wong's.'

'That's what I've been doing. But I like bottled milk. Besides, I just don't understand it.'

'Well, it's no good telling you to ask him. He comes at three-thirty. Why don't you ring the company?'

Marjorie rang the company in the smelly public phone booth on the corner. Her name and address were taken, and delivery promised, but the next morning, and the next, when she went to the kitchen and opened the little door, she saw only her note, her money, and her empty bottle. She knew her disappointment was ridiculous, but it was unconquerable; it gave a lagging start to her days. She went again to the booth on the corner, but vandals had been there, and the receiver lay smashed on the floor. She hoped it had not been done by the group of boys she had come to like and watch for. She walked to the post office and found an undamaged phone. The company passed her from person to person, and while waiting for someone named Miss Vinson, she was cut off. After that, she would open the servery door merely to exercise her cynicism, and would smile as she banged it shut.

Emlyn was furious with her for having no phone of her own.

'Mum, even professionally—'

'Emlyn, if you would listen—'

'Even professionally, it's crazy. Fee and I are financial again. We'll shout you a phone.'

'Emlyn, I've been trying to tell you, I've paid for my phone. I asked Harrap for an advance on the cookbook. They didn't mind a bit. It was amazing. Now I'm waiting for Telecom to connect me.'

'God! What a service! How long are you supposed to wait?'

She hoped that Emlyn was expressing his affection through this indignation, since at present he was inhibited in expressing it in any other way. She did notice also that he had begun to look at her face, though as often as not his glance would slip quickly to her collar.

'And what about this milk Fee tells me is so important to you? Cartons are okay. We get cartons.'

'It's just that I wanted to get up in the morning, and open the servery door, and see it there.' She made the shape of it with her hands. 'And reach out, like that, and take it in. But you're right. Cartons are okay.'

Emlyn went to the servery and opened it. He picked up her note. 'What's he like?'

'I've seen him only once. He comes before dawn. I don't wake out of my drugged sleep. In the distance he was little and dark, not young. Don't worry about it.'

'I guess he doesn't read English.'

'That's not it. He wouldn't need to.'

'No. The bottle, the money. That says it.'

'Right. So.' She took the note, tore it up, then padded in her bare feet to throw the scraps into the carton of waste paper beside her worktable. She hoisted herself on to her stool and spread her hands. 'Look at all the work I've been given.'

'Mum, I had a go at talking to dad. Useless.'

'I don't want to know about it.'

'Yes, but look here, mum, this – ' Emlyn slanted his head to indicate the room ' – this just isn't a fair go. You need better legal advice than you're getting from that Mae West character. If ethics mean you're stuck with her, which is bloody nonsense in my opinion, instruct her to engage a barrister. Carla's husband would recommend someone. Or I'll find someone.'

'My dear—'

'Don't talk to me about money. Don't insult me.'

'My dear, I am here in this room, and I wish to stay here, working every day, until the case is heard. I have set myself on a course. Don't divert me. Don't upset my balance. I mustn't fall off my rope.'

He was looking her full in the face, but as if it were the face of a stranger. After a while he said absent-mindedly, 'Right.' Then he said, 'When do you get those X-rays done?'

'They'll let me know.'

'You look well,' he said in the same tone. 'Fee was saying you're looking really good.'

'I feel fine.' Now that Emlyn had dropped his ferocity, she seemed to have picked it up. 'I don't believe there's anything wrong with me at all. And I don't need help. And I don't need to know anything about your father.'

'I get it,' he said. 'And anyway, look here, dad's okay.'

His sympathy had brought her to the point of telling him how intensely she was enjoying her work, but she drew back out of the superstitious fear that to reveal it was to risk losing it. She did not overvalue her work. She knew its first importance was that it earned her money, but she was surprised and grateful that in her present circumstances it could so deeply engross her, could give her such a sense of urgency. Every day in the humid heat of January, February, and early March, she rose and folded up her bed, ate her breakfast and bathed, then put on one of her loose dark batik dresses and went to her worktable. She pinned her hair high on her head to free the nape of her neck; she wore no pants nor bra, no shoes. The dress itself was a concession to her visibility from the street. Curtains or blinds reduced the light, and she had besides become accustomed to making quick little sketches of the people in the street, and dropping them, done or half-done, beside her worktable, where they lay gathering grit and dust. When she had to go out for food, she put on pants and the rubber thongs she had bought at Woolworths. She wore these same clothes to the hospital, where she was given a barium meal and X-rayed. She had to wait four hours, which slackened her sense of urgency and made her feel restless and tense. The urgency was exciting and exhilarating except during enforced waits or when she had to go to the city to collect or deliver work. She hated these occasions because she felt obliged to wear full underclothes, a dress of a more formal sort, panty hose and shoes, even make-up. To dress like this she felt as a serious and even dangerous intrusion, and she would arrive back at her flat in a state of anxiety or even of slight hysteria, and would violently pull the hated clothes off her sweating body. She wished she could afford couriers. If it were Carla who had given her one of these jobs, Marjorie would beg her to bring it herself. Carla riffled among the drawings on the floor, casting some aside and picking out a few at which she cocked her head and lifted one corner of her mouth. 'It's no miracle that you can draw feet,' she said one day. 'It's just this.' She tapped the drawing she held. 'Practice, practice, practice.'

'I can draw feet because I need the money.'

Carla appreciated the humorous hardness of this. Marjorie wondered if Carla believed it to be entirely true. Carla wisely nodded, in any case, as she returned the drawings to the dusty pile.

The glass of milk Marjorie kept on the window sill she covered with an envelope. Dust and grit gathered also in the servery, on the coins, the bottle, and the Marimekko paper. Although Emlyn had been assured by the milk company that there was no possible obstacle to Marjorie getting her milk, the servery continued to present, on each morning's sardonic inspection, the same picture as before. She pretended to Emlyn that his complaint had been effective; she did not want him to go on a crusade about a bottle of milk a day. He had already been on a crusade about her telephone, and whether or not as a result, it was now connected.

Once, in the early afternoon, hearing faintly the clink of coins, she slipped quickly from her stool and ran into the kitchen. The money had gone. Feet in thongs were slapping down the stairs. She heard the laughter of the boys, and yelled down the staircase after them that they were devils, as she had heard Mr Wong and the people in the street do. She did not replace the money, but in bed that night found the omission gave her a superstitious uneasiness, and impatiently she got up and put the three coins in the servery. The rolled newspaper she carried in the other hand was for killing cockroaches; she never went into the kitchen at night without it; another superstition she had developed was that insecticide would kill her as well.

The radiologist reported that Marjorie had a large ulcer crater on the posterior wall of the upper third of her stomach. As Marjorie read this, she heard Doctor Furmann remark, in a pleased and enthusiastic voice, that he had been quite right about that shoulder pain.

'Referred pain. Come here, and I'll show you the crater on your X-rays.'

'I can't stop work to have an operation,' Marjorie warned him swiftly.

'I don't suggest it. Now, that silvery area is your stomach. Now, see that dark intrusion? I'm tracing it, see? That's it.'

'And that is my monumental backbone. And those wavy things, which I must say are quite pretty, are my intestines.'

'If I may have your attention.'

'Perhaps I could wear myself inside out. Well, all right. It's awful. It's huge. It looks like the Gulf of Carpentaria.'

'Yes, it does. It's deep, all right. That one hasn't grown overnight. Well, it's our job to close it up. On each X-ray you will see it get smaller.'

She asked with horror, 'How often must I have these X-rays?'

'Every month.'

'And how many months will it take to cure?'

'That's partly up to you.'

'Give me some idea.'

'No less than three.'

'Which I suppose,' she said bitterly, 'means six.'

'Sit down,' he said, 'sit down. There's a drug recently developed. Cimetidine. Perhaps it's for the lucky future. I don't prescribe it yet. It's still at the trial and error stage.'

'Like the divorce laws.'

'I know it's no use telling you not to worry.'

'I thought not worrying was exactly what I had been doing.'

'I know it's hard.'

'I've been feeling so well,' she said angrily.

'Fine. You've responded to treatment. So now we're sure of our ground, we'll give you something stronger.' Again his voice went on as he wrote. 'These may have the side-effect of raising your blood pressure, but we'll keep a weekly check on that.'

'Weekly!'

'Yes, and give you something for it if the need arises. It's a matter of maintaining a balance.'

'Oh, I see. A balance.'

All the next day Marjorie lay on the bed in her nightgown, stubbornly reading out-of-date magazines. She read about Patty Hearst and Princess Caroline of Monaco and how to stretch your budget. Carla rang. Emlyn rang. 'Mind your own business,' she wanted to say. But their solicitude was her own fault, for having told them anything at all. So she said it was only a small ulcer, nothing really, easily fixed. She ignored a knock on the door, but when she got up in the evening, and saw the agent's card under the door, she remembered it was rent day. There was hardly any food in the kitchen. She got dressed and went over to Wong's.

'And your milk?'

'Yes, please, Mr Wong.'

Just before dawn on the following day, she dreamed again of Bruce. He stood at the dinner table, looking down at her. 'From now on,' he said, 'every mouthful you eat will poison you.' It was near enough to what he had actually said to make her rise and spend the remaining hour till daylight hunched in a shawl on her worktable stool, looking out of the window at the street cleaners, the garbage collectors, and the derelict men and bag women freshly routed from their cubbies. But just as she did not remember what she had read about Patty Hearst or Princess Caroline, so she did not now absorb what she looked at.

She was too tired to work that day. In the evening Emlyn and Fiona came and presented her with water biscuits, creamy cheeses, and a book on herbal medicine. They were still there when Carla came with her husband Martin. Carla bore the food of childhood, a milky rice pudding in a homely earthenware dish. Marjorie had to open the folding bed so that they could all sit down. She noticed that now everyone could look easily at her face, except Martin, and even he was able to address her in a natural tone of voice. The next day, via Carla, he suggested the name of a barrister Marjorie might instruct Gwen to engage. Marjorie refused. Though she had returned doggedly to her work, she could not afford to add this factor to all the others to which she must now adapt her balance. At the end of the week, when Doctor Furmann prescribed tablets for her raised blood pressure, she accepted the instruction passively and in silence, and as passively took the tablets at the ordered times.

She had lost her sense of urgency. She did her work faithfully, but without her former delight. One day, warmly complimented on it, she was startled, and took the piece back and looked at it again, and saw that, yes, it was better than she had done in her exalted state. She sighed with incomprehension.

Perhaps because the cool days had come, she no longer found it hateful to dress to go to the city. She did not dream of

Bruce again, but although she increased her dose of tranquillisers, her sleep was often broken. When she heard the milkman's bottles jangling away down the corridor, she assumed that what had brought her awake was his banging her servery door. In the morning it was always shut, and she would viciously slam the inner door she continued to open for her inspection. Then one night, as she was about to go into the kitchen for water, she heard him stop outside her servery. It was not a full second before he banged the door and jangled away. She threw down her rolled newspaper, seized the money and the bottle, and ran in her bare feet down the corridor after him.

She caught up with him while he was scooping money from a servery. She stood with arms extended, proffering the money in one hand, the bottle in the other.

'What about me? Flat forty-one?'

He put two bottles into the nearby servery and shut the door. 'Good,' he said. He took the money and the bottle, gave her a full bottle, and picked up his crate.

'Wait! Why don't you deliver it?'

He was certainly Italian: small, lumpy though thin, with black mordant eyes and a look of disgust on his simian mouth. She had seen his counterpart among his comely people, and concluding him to be a relict, almost bred out by prosperity, she had been surprised that he had so often crossed her path. He had cheated her in five Italian cities, and in those same cities had directed her lost footsteps with kindness and even gallantry if she were quick to understand, and with testiness and contempt if she were not. In Sydney he had spared some of his time and authority to help her to buy unfamiliar food, and last year, when she had bent to the driver's seat of his taxi and offered a fifty dollar note he could not change, he had all but screamed his anger and abuse. She was in awe of his inheritance, the implant of poverty and unnatural labour. She said (for his English had been no better than her Italian),

'Everyone else,' and pointed to the row of doors, 'but not me,' and pointed to the door at the far end. 'Why not?'

He scowled as he put down his crate and took money from his bag. 'You do this.' He extended his hand, the money on his palm. 'I give milk.'

'That's what I *do*!'

But he had picked up his crate and was moving away, and when she called again for him to wait, he responded with what sounded like a curse, and gave a backward flip of his free hand. In none of his manifestations had he been patient. Herself cursing under her breath, she ran after him, but he had turned the corner, and when she reached it his only visible part was the small head bobbing down a narrow service stairway she had never seen before.

Without gratification she put the bottle of milk in the refrigerator. She knew he did not expect her to run after him in her nightgown every time she wanted milk. He meant her simply to pay him. Her end of the corridor was dimly lit. She put another three coins on the paper, then went out into the corridor and opened the servery door. The money was clearly visible in the light from her kitchen. But usually, the kitchen was dark, the inner servery door shut. She went back, shut the inner servery door, and turned off the light. And this time, she saw that it was difficult (though not impossible) to distinguish the coins from the small geometric daisies on the Marimekko paper.

In the morning she went out and bought sandpaper and a tin of white enamel. She sanded down the old cream paint and put fresh white paint on all planes of the servery except the base. For the base, she folded a sheet of layout paper to the right size. In the evening, after her work was done, she polished three coins and washed and dried a milk bottle. A soft laugh broke from her as she did this, and again as she slowly and ceremoniously set down the three coins. She did not know if he had failed to leave her milk because, in days filled with the same desperate impetus as hers had been, he had not bothered to give the second glance that would have distinguished the coins, or whether it angered him that he found them hard to see, and he was forcing her to show them as clearly as he had done when he had displayed them on his extended palm. She thought the latter more likely, but did not care, such was her certainty that the milk would be there in the morning.

Yet she could not have been so certain, because, in the morning, when she opened the door and saw it standing there in its simplicity, amazement preceded her delight, and amazement was in her smile as she reached out with both hands and brought it in. During the day she had only to think of the sight of it, standing there, for the sensation of smiling to spread through her whole body.

She did not continue to polish the coins, but took care to set aside for that use the cleanest ones in her purse. During her next restless night, when her wakeful period included half past three, and she heard the milkman's fast padded steps, and the jangling of his crate, she listened intently enough to hear him take the coins and set down the milk. He did not slam the servery door. He closed it gently. She told nobody of the incident. Each night, she changed the white paper, and took pleasure in setting down the three coins in their invariable pattern.

She was disappointed when she studied her second X-rays with Doctor Furmann.

'What?' he said. 'Did you expect a miracle?'

'Yes,' she said.

'I thought you would be pleased. It's so much reduced.'

'Oh, it is,' she said, to appease him. 'Now it's like Spencer's Gulf.'

'You mean Spencer Gulf.'

'Your geography is as good as your treatment.'

'Next time it will be like Port Phillip Bay. Roll up that sleeve, please.'

In the winter, the sunless flat was cold all day. She bought a small radiator, but its heat made her lethargic, so after her morning shower she walked into fur-lined boots and swaddled herself in layers of clothes before she started work. She picked up her sketches from the floor, dusted them, and put them into different coloured folders in order of preference. Each time she added new ones, she found that her order of preference had changed. Though her divorce was not yet listed, she began to think of a garden, the smell of basil and geraniums, and the feel of a warm stone path under her feet. But when she studied advertisements for cottages at that northern beach, she felt less certain about wanting to live there.

Carla, when she came to the flat, would often, as she was about to leave, fall into the kind of silence that made Marjorie suspect her of hanging about to find a chance to say something about Bruce. 'I hope you don't think I'm going to put myself into reverse at this stage,' said Marjorie on one of these occasions. 'I mean, about the divorce.'

'No, I don't expect you can,' said Carla.

'It's no help to talk about it.'

'It was you who mentioned it.'

'It was you who so clearly wanted to. Tell me something. I can't get my money from Manzell and Rogers. I've sent my account twice. Do you know anything about them?'

Her divorce was listed the day after she had her third X-rays. These showed the ulcer crater reduced to the proportionate size, if not the shape, of Port Phillip Bay. 'Don't be over-confident,' warned Doctor Furmann. 'Don't relax your care. When is your divorce?'

'In three weeks.'

'Just what part stress plays is not known for certain.'

The day after this, Marjorie put some documents in an envelope, put money in her purse for Isolde, and went to the city to see Gwen. Early for her appointment, she decided to go to Nock and Kirby's to buy paint for the outdoor table and slatted chairs. It was a quarter to two; the counter was crowded, and while she was waiting her turn she saw Bruce standing on the downward escalator. He wore an unfamiliar tie, held his attache case in one hand, a walking stick in the other, and was carefully regarding his own feet. When he reached the floor, he stepped on to it with a slightly fumbled and panicky step, then with one hip swinging wide, limped quickly away towards the George Street entrance.

Marjorie abandoned the paint and hurried distractedly out of the York Street entrance. She took four antacid tablets on her way to see Gwen, who was magnificent that day in magenta and purple. When Marjorie got home she rang Emlyn.

'Emlyn, I saw your father in Nock and Kirby's.'

'Did you?'

'Has he had an accident?'

'No, mum, he hasn't.'

'Then why is he lame?'

'Mum, we all saw your point when you said you didn't want to hear anything about him.'

'Yes, but now I've seen him, it's better if I do hear something.'

'Well, you remember his arthritis?'

'But that was nothing. He called them twinges.'

'It's something now.'

'Twinges. But I do recall,' she said, since Emlyn was silent, 'that most of the twinges were in one hip.'

'Right, that's where he copped it.'

'Will he always be lame?'

'I don't know. There are things they can do. He's going to a specialist. A top man. And anyway, mum, even if he is always lame, he's not the kind of guy who can't handle it.'

'No,' said Marjorie, 'he's not.'

But as she put down the phone she thought of how characteristic it was of them each that she should take the wound in the soft tissue, while he should take it in the bone. She sat with her hands folded, wondering if it was only bad luck that she had not found, at the right time, the right, miraculous seeming, gesture of conciliation; but after a while she jumped up and turned her mind to other things, knowing she could not afford to enter that labyrinth. She had collected her mail on her way upstairs, and was pleased to see that Manzell and Rogers had paid her at last.

THE LATE SUNLIGHT ·

As Gordon crossed the park on the way back to his chilly rented flat, and felt the stored warmth of the day's sun rising from the terra cotta paving, he was tempted into turning aside and sitting next to an old woman on a sheltered bench. He put his folder and notebooks beside him, let the sunlight settle on him, and felt his body sigh. The old woman said, 'You are taking the sun?'

He did not try to define her European accent, knowing only that it was not French or Italian. Nowadays he tried to provide against his tendency to be too friendly too soon; in his youth it had led him into so many long useless conversations, had wasted so much of his time; warring couples whose only aim was to condemn each other had made him their confidant, and evangelists for the more unusual religions had scarcely been able to believe their luck. Without looking at the woman he murmured an assent.

'The sun in winter is like the medicine.'

Gordon gave the slightest of nods.

'You need the medicine of the sun?'

Gordon had had such a disappointing day at the library that he could not help saying that at the moment, he certainly felt he did.

'You have been sick?'

This was how it had always started. He tried to retreat by shutting his eyes, as if his eyelids especially needed the sun.

140

'You look as if you have been sick.'

Such a voice, so loud and acid, gave him a choice. He could get up and go, or he could turn and talk to her. His old tendency was always inclined to revive when he was away from his wife and family.

Her eyes were a faded black, lustreless yet intense, perhaps hostile. But to their stare she added the smile of long painted lips, the vivacity of eyebrows drawn far above her natural browline, and a sociable inclination towards him of her thick body. 'You are too pale,' she said. 'You have none of the pink.'

Neither had she. Her skin was olive with undertones of lead. He saw now that she was dressed in what his two elder children called 'money-money clothes'. Richness glistened in her fur collar, in the velvety pile of her elaborate asymmetrical hat, in her narrow finely-crafted shoes, and in the handbag, made of the skin of some reptile, which lay rigid and sharp-angled in her lap. 'A young man,' she said, 'should have a little of the pink.'

The inclination of her body seemed ingratiating, but her tone was still acid. Forty may really seem young to her; Gordon absolved her of flattery. 'I suppose I'm so thick-skinned,' he said lazily, 'that no pink can get through.'

'Thick-skinned? No.' She shook her head in absolute negation. 'No, no, no, no, no.' She leaned back on the bench. 'You are refined,' she said, and gave a single sharp nod.

Scottish ancestors had given him a lean gingery ascetic look, and he supposed it was this she called refinement. But from her generation to his, it could be a dubious compliment. He made an ironical mouth and said, *'Am I?'*

Below the thin black arcs, the two lumps of her hairless brows drew together in a scowl. 'You think I don't know?' she said. 'You think I can't tell? When I see these others, all around me?'

Her little gloved hand, curved downward, stabbed towards the other occupied benches, towards the sunburst fountain, where people were taking photographs, towards the paths on which they were daring to pass up and down.

'They are so common.'

The last word was delivered on a guttural of hatred and contempt. Gordon's recoil was swift and instinctive. His parents had put an absolute embargo on this epithet, assuring him that his own inferiority, and possibly wickedness, was all its use would prove. Nor had the sympathies of his maturity tempted him far in a contrary direction. Indeed, if blasphemy existed for Gordon, this painted old woman had just committed it. He folded his arms and raised his face again to the sun. There was no point in anything but politeness. 'Excuse me,' he said. 'I'll take a bit more of this curative sun.'

He knew she would speak again. But now the sun was holding him, as was a reluctance to face the depressing flat. When she asked if he was a writer, he prepared to pay for a few more minutes of the sun, and replied that he was a teacher.

'Those papers,' he said patiently, guessing what had prompted her question, 'are notes I've been taking in the library. I've got time off to do some research.'

'You teach in a school?'

'I teach in a university.'

'You are a professor?'

The word was pronounced with respect. 'I am a tutor,' said Gordon. 'I teach history in Canberra.'

'Ah. Can-*bair*-ah.'

The respect this time sounded false. She asked him what history he taught, and when he said Australian, she asked with dangerous playfulness whether there was such a thing. But the sun was her enemy; it was easy not to reply. Behind his closed lids, light motes sweetly floated. Her voice, like the footsteps on the path, changed timbre, became muffled, retreated. And sweet as a light mote, there drifted into his brain the knowledge that his thesis should not be on the colonial institution he had chosen, but on one man, the one whose character had permeated that institution. There that man stood. Details, so carefully gathered by Gordon, worried over, mauled, but stubbornly disparate, flew to assemble round him. The voice at Gordon's side, continuing to speak of Can-*bair*-ah, still sounded distant, but he knew it was not. Begging his man to stay, not to fade, he jumped to his feet and picked up his papers. 'But what does Can-*bair*-ah matter,' cried the woman, giving her little gloved stabs, 'when there are no real cities in Australia anyway?'

Gordon wished he had a hat to raise, something to placate her for his abrupt departure. But he could only apologise for leaving so suddenly, and hurry away. 'You are a gentleman,' she called after him, loud enough for half the park to hear.

In the depressing flat, which he had taken unseen, Gordon sat down immediately to his books and notes. He worked, with a short break for dinner at the Indian restaurant three doors down, until midnight. By that time his excitement was tamped to a sober hopefulness. More information was needed to confirm that vision. But Gordon thought he knew where to find it.

The next day in the library, he crashed. The information in which he had trusted diminished the man's importance. Yet his vision had made it impossible to return to his old institutional subject, which now spread itself out like so many lumber rooms. He dropped again into the dullness and perplexity that had brought him to search in Sydney. The library, because in his boyhood and youth it had often been a refuge from the enthusiasms of his family, had always rested in his mind like a point of peace. But now even the library was uncongenial to him. He left early, crossing Macquarie Street with the hunched gait by which his wife Marion said she could detect his low moods.

In the park the old woman sat in the same seat. Seeing her before she saw him, Gordon recalled the words she had called after him yesterday–'You are a gentleman' – and speculated on their meaning: they were a sarcastic reproach for his abrupt departure; they were flattery to make him come back; they were simply wild and heedless. He intended to pass her by, but she saw him, and gave him her slow red foxy smile, and for some reason – perhaps because disappointment had made him apathetic – he went and sat at her side. 'Today I will tell you of my son,' she instantly announced. But then she turned the red smile downwards, brooded, and said, 'No, I will not.' She eyed his notebooks, became sociable. 'You have been at your library.'

He nodded. He kept the notebooks in his hand, and did not relax into his seat. Today she was dressed with a richness that at four thirty in this scrap of a park amounted to grotesquerie. Her jacket and cap were mink, he was sure. Only diamonds could have the flashing power of the stones in her dangling ear rings, and in that case, the stones surrounding them must be–yes–rubies. That was to say nothing of the rings on her fingers, perhaps six. She wore no gloves today. The handbag was the same one. She opened it, shook a pill from a tiny round silver box, and shut the bag with a satisfied snap of its double clasp. In some recess of his mind he had already decided she was middle European, and now, from those turbulent countries crushed together on the map, Hungary stood out. She rolled the pill in her mouth and eyed him sideways. Both her painted and real brows were at rest, but the smile of her sucking mouth was anticipatory. She was waiting to finish the pill before speaking. Her legs were shapely; she crossed them and kicked out the upper one. Had she been a performer of some sort? An actress? Perhaps she had even ridden a white horse round a circus ring. He could see it. And then had married a rich man, and puffed herself up with jewels and furs, and begun to call people common. He wondered why he rather liked her. She finished her pill.

'You are married?'

'Yes.'

She was at her most ingratiating. 'You have the look of a man nicely married.'

'Well, I am.'

'Your wife's name?'

'Marion. And,' he said, before she could ask, 'we have three children. Peter, Tess, and Joel. Twelve, eleven, and seven.'

'I once knew a Marion.' She deepened her voice and drew a hand downward from her chin. '*Such a chin!* That was when I was first in Australia. Has your Marion – *such a chin?*'

He foresaw an analysis of Marion's appearance; he would not encourage it. 'Have you been long in Australia?' he asked.

She subsided into disgust. 'One hundred years.'

'But actually?'

'But actually, since during the War.' She was watching him keenly. 'No, I am not Jewish, in case you will now want to forgive me everything. Yes, that is what some people do. My husband, who was also not Jewish, acted in a political way, so we had to leave.'

He knew from experience that if he replied to this, the conversation would certainly be long, and if not useless, infinitely knotted. He put down his notes and leaned forward with his elbows on his knees. 'What part of Europe do you come from?'

She spread a hand on her breast. The stubby little ringed fingers sank in fur. 'I am Viennese.'

He made a swift mental appraisal of his inaccurate guess, and another of his passing thought that it had been near enough. But now she said, with sudden prim finality, 'And you, sir? You are Australian?'

He said he was.

'Of Australian parentage also?'

'On both sides.'

'From one of the big country estates perhaps?'

He could not help laughing. He thought of the little bunga-
low, so flimsy that in memory it shook with the thump of
argument and exhortation, and threatened to burst with the
people who had nowhere else to go. Worthy causes had slept
on the verandah or on a mattress in Gordon's room, and a
victim of society had stolen his Cambridge histories. Leaning
back on the bench, he gave a long soft laugh not only at the
contrast of the suggestion with the reality, but in tribute to
his dead parents, so good, tireless, and indignant. But she was
looking at him with her long mouth shut as tight as the clasp
on her handbag. He stopped laughing and said, 'Sorry. In fact
I was born right here in Sydney. My father was a teacher too.
Only he taught little kids, in primary school.'

Her hard angry calculating look did not waver. She said,
'You should not tell anyone. No one would ever know.'

He could have laughed again, but did not want to anger her
further. Nothing she said could matter. He half-shut his eyes
against the sun, and at that moment knew at what point in the
day's research he had taken the wrong direction. He saw his
own hand as it wrote the request for the misleading material.
She was speaking, but he shut his mind to her words, while
quickly he allowed to enter the knowledge of the path he
should have taken. But he could not help hearing that he was
the very model of an Englishman she had once known, who
was a very great aristocrat, and a model of refinement, so
that when he rose quickly to his feet, and picked up his notes,
he gave her a little bow of farewell. He had never bowed in his
life before, but he wanted to please her. Today's insight, like
yesterday's, was without doubt the result of relaxation after
hard mental work, but she had been present on both occasions, and though he knew he was not superstitous, he could
not afford to take risks. Bowing, he explained that he must
hurry back to the library. She gave her consent with a nod,
but did not let him go until he had told her his name, and she,
again with that precise gesture of hand on breast, had given

him hers. It was long, and he was too distracted to listen with his usual care, and all he retained was her Christian name, Vera.

On his way back to the library he bought a pack of chicken and gobbled it up behind one of the advertising fixtures on the railway platform. He was glad Vera could not see him. He did not have much time in the library before it shut, but enough to assure himself that this time he was not mistaken, and to reserve his material for tomorrow. When he got back to the flat he rang Marion. While he waited for an answer he envisioned her walking through their pleasant haphazard rooms, wearing the padded black Indian dress and the boots she had hardly changed out of lately. Her fair hair would be loose on her shoulders, and as she walked she would slip a hand beneath it and massage the back of her head, where the knot had been pinned all day. When she answered she sounded tired.

'Darling,' he said with a rush, 'I'm sorry I didn't ring before. Is everything okay? Kids okay? You?'

'Everything's fine. How's your work?'

'Oh – all right.' He knew she would understand, from his guarded yet airy tone, that at this stage he wanted to keep it to himself. She would recognize it as a good sign. 'What about yours?' he asked.

'Guido is sick, and I'm taking one of his tutorials. But don't worry. Don't hurry home. Peter and Tess cooked dinner tonight, and Joel set the table. How is the grisly flat?'

He had not even noticed it tonight. 'I guess it serves its purpose.'

'I long to see you, Gordon.'

'I long to see you, my love.'

'How much longer?'

'Two more days.'

'That's not bad.'

'At the most. Has Joel got his glasses yet?'

'No. Tomorrow.'

'Home on Friday, then. I'm fairly sure.'

'Try hard. Goodnight, darling.'

'Goodnight, sweet.'

He felt deeply contented as he undressed. He sometimes felt more genuinely a part of his family when away from them than when at home. There, he occasionally had the curious feeling that he had had no part in their making, but that he had come gambolling to their door one day, and they, calmly, smilingly, kindly, had taken him in and given him a good home. Marion was a mathematician, and so, potentially, were all three children. All passionately loved music, though never to dance to, as he had once done, and none read fiction for pleasure. They disregarded their own beauty, and in their cupboards hung few more than the essential garments. Interchangeable hats hanging on pegs in the hall guarded their fair skins. The oddest thing of all about them was that on Sundays all went to the Anglican church, Marion simply insisting when he teased her about it that that was how she had been brought up.

But when Gordon was away, none of these differences caused him the alienation (which sometimes became resentment) that they caused him at home. The contentment with which he went to sleep continued into the next day. In the library he proceeded with absolute certainty to find his material. It was one of those rare days when nearly everything he turned up was useful, and could be accepted without surprise. The congeniality of the room – the peace of its polished timber and high pale panes of glass – was restored to him. Flickering only on the margin of his consciousness were the morbid shadows on Vera's skin, her disquieting eyes and the long red lips sucking at her pill. As he walked to his train in Martin Place, these settled into a conclusion that she was very sick.

The first sight of her seemed to contradict it. She sat in the same place, and when she saw him, she kicked up a leg and patted the seat at her side. She had no pill in her mouth, and again her smile was mocking, deliberate, and foxy. She was dressed entirely in black, on her coat an astrakhan collar, on her head an astrakhan toque incredibly twisted to one side in a kind of cockade. 'So today you carry the brief case,' she said as he sat down.

She took no notice of his explanation that he had had some documents copied. She seemed excited, bursting with talk. 'My son also carries the brief case. He is like a good little doggie, carrying the brief case. I do not mean you are like a doggie. You are so tall. But he is little and neat, and should not carry the brief case.'

'Is your son here in Sydney?' asked Gordon.

'Of course he is here in Sydney. He is Australian. His wife is Australian. His children are Australian. He is a little Australian doggie. And now my neighbour tells me how I must see him, this doggie, how I must ring him and tell him to come.'

It disturbed Gordon that she had only a neighbour to tell her this. 'You have no other children?'

'I have no children at all. I do not count doggies. He will get everything. That is the law. That is enough. I will not see him also.'

Her handbag was again the same one. She shook out a pill from the little silver box. 'Last time I see him was two years ago. He comes to me and he says, "Mutti, you must do this thing for your health, you must do that thing." I say yes, yes, and now go home, good doggie, to your *Sand*-ra.'

She pronounced the name with even more hatred and contempt than she had used for the word common, but because this time it was merely personal, it did not shock Gordon so much. The late sunlight was having its usual benign effect. His thoughts settled contentedly on his work. His colonial man stood before him in promise of full life. He estimated that tomorrow about three hours of work would give him enough to go on with for months.

Vera finished her pill. 'Now I wish to speak of your wife.'

He was good-humoured but wary. 'What about her?'

'You have her photograph?'

'Not here.'

'Please to describe her.'

Gordon laughed. 'She is slim and fair. You want to know if she is beautiful, don't you?'

She gave one of her consciously dignified nods. He had changed his mind about her having been a circus performer, but the suggestion of theatre lingered. He said, 'Yes, she is beautiful.'

'And – excuse me – is she common?'

'I'm amazed that you excuse yourself. I don't quite know how to answer you, but if in your opinion I am not common, then neither is Marion.'

'That is good then. I would like her to have the dark beauty, but the fair is also good. Though not so good for the men to have.'

Her son, she went on to say, was of that fairness they call washed-out. Gordon was not attending. He was thinking of the tick Marion had found the summer before last in her pubic hair. They had been bush walking, and that night she had found it, and had lain on the bed while Gordon anaesthetized it and plucked it out. Now he could never hear darkness and fairness contrasted without seeing again, in the light of the halogen lamp drawn down to the bed, the black tick in the curling shining flaxen hair, its head already embedded in her white skin. Nor could he ever think of it without feelings of tenderness, lust, and romance. The prospect of an early start at the library tomorrow, his certain return home in the afternoon, made him tolerant of Vera's vehement wanderings about Sandra and the doggie, for both of whom he felt a humorous sympathy.

'Before that last time he came to see me, he would come every Friday. Alone, of course, without his *Sand*-ra. He would make the conversation. First he would want to speak of the old days, as he would call them. But I do not speak of the old days to doggies. And then there is the weather. Or the news. He would make the long face. "The news is bad, Mutti." And I would say, "If it is Australian news, do not tell me. Here is no news." My husband used to get the European papers, you understand. And when they would come, he would put away your *Heralds* and *Telegraphs*, and he would say, "Now we will have some real news."'

Gordon wondered how often she must have been asked why, since she hated Australia so bitterly, she didn't go back where she came from. So many times, he guessed, and with such hostility, that she now scornfully invited the question. He said, 'Have you never been back?'

'We went back, but it is here my husband makes the money, so it is here we must stay. Then my husband dies,' she said, with one of her angry looks, 'and it is too late to go back.' With one gloved hand she stabbed the air. 'And of Vienna what is left anyway?'

'I have never been to Vienna.'

She said with calm contempt, 'Of course you have never been to Vienna, my dear. In your lifetime is no real Vienna left.'

He was about to reply that he knew people who said there was no real Sydney left, when a voice above them said, 'Well, Vera, you look happy enough today.'

A tightly stout and smiling woman stood beside the bench. She was perhaps not much younger than Vera. 'All the same, Vera,' she said gently, 'I wish you would come home with me.'

Gordon got to his feet and picked up his briefcase.

'This is my neighbour,' said Vera, beginning to kick up her leg again, to smile and to mock.

'Mildred Reed,' said the woman. 'Vera and I have lived next door in Charton Towers for ten years.'

'Gordon Harbage,' said Gordon.

'Well, Mr Harbage,' said Mildred Reed, 'I suppose it's no good asking if you have any influence with Vera, but I wish someone had. I wish someone could persuade her to see Arthur.'

'Arthur is the name of the little doggie,' said Vera complacently.

'I understand your concern, Mrs Reed,' said Gordon, 'but as for influence, I've none. We've simply met a few times here in the park.'

'He is the very image of that Englishman I was once talking you about.'

'Talking me? Vera, you're tired. And it's getting cold out here.'

'Yes, I will come,' said Vera calmly.

'I think we'll get a taxi.'

'Wait,' said Vera. 'First I will give my new friend this. I will not see him again.' She opened her bag. 'I wish for him to take this little gift to his beautiful wife.'

The little parcel she offered was wrapped in a twist of red paper, tied with a crumpled red ribbon. 'It is one of my pill boxes.'

'Those pill boxes are solid silver,' said Mildred Reed with respect.

'Well, thank you,' said Gordon, taking the little parcel, trying to imagine Marion using a pill box.

He got the two women a taxi. He was surprised that Vera did not look at him after he had helped her into it. It was Mildred Reed who smiled and raised a hand, while Vera sat hunched, her faced turned away, as if offended. He had, he supposed, omitted some ceremony natural to a great gentleman.

At the flat he rang Marion. 'Three hours is all I'll need tomorrow. I'll go straight from the library to the airport.'

'The two o'clock plane?'

'For sure. I'll be home before you. Has Joel got his glasses?'

'Yes. He keeps screwing up his face. He says he can't forget those things are on it.'

'Poor old boy.' Gordon suddenly clapped a hand to his
pocket. 'I've got a present for you.'

'What?'

'No. Wait.'

'All right. A surprise.'

'It certainly surprised me.'

The next morning, when Gordon was getting ready to go to
the library, he saw the little red parcel among his papers, and
impulsively opened it. He knew by the worn embossing that
the box was very old, and he smiled to see that, small as it
was, room had been made for minute cherubs to loll about it
here and there, linked by garlands. Marion would probably
become fond of it, and keep it on the shelf with the sea shells,
pieces of blue glass, and the Chinese figurine with the missing
hand. He opened it and took out a piece of stiff paper which he
thought may be a note, but from which fell into his hand the
diamond and ruby earrings Vera had worn in the park on the
second day.

He felt himself flush hot with anger. Now he must get them
back to her; now he could miss the two o'clock plane. And
now, above all, the precious steadiness of his investigation
would be disrupted. He stamped about dressing, he cursed,
scowled, chucked papers into his case. Then he abruptly
checked himself. Like this, he was compounding the danger.
Instead, he could congratulate himself on remembering the
name of Vera's building. It would not take long to go there
and return them – nothing, nothing, would induce him to
argue or talk – and if he maintained his steadiness, kept his
goal immovably in sight, neither his research nor his return
to his family need suffer.

A taxi took him to Charton Towers in five minutes. The
directory in the foyer showed M. Reed in 99, but both 98 and
100 were shown only as occupied.

Without more than a few seconds of grinding his teeth, he took the lift to the ninth floor. As he walked down the corridor he saw Mildred Reed coming out of a door. She saw him, and stood with the knob in her hand for a moment before shutting it. She waited until he was within close speaking range. 'Vera is dead,' she said then. 'I found her two hours ago.'

He breathed out an automatic 'Good heavens'. The door behind her was marked 98. When she moved towards her door, 99, he followed her, not wanting to, yet not knowing what else to do. 'Will you come in?' she said.

'For a few minutes.' As she opened the door he looked quickly at his watch.

They sat on opposite chairs in her hall. 'It could have happened any old time,' she said. 'It was just good luck it didn't happen in that park.'

'Her heart?'

'Yes. Hopeless. Hopeless. But when it came to the last, she wouldn't take advice. The moment they told her she would have to go to hospital, she went straight to the bank and got all her jewellery out, and every day after that she had to get dressed up and go wandering about talking to people in shops, and sitting in that park.' Mildred Reed grimaced, close to tears. 'I'm going to miss her. I'll tell you that.'

Though still uncertain what to do, Gordon had drawn his case on to his knees. He took out the pill box. 'There's this,' he said.

'It's valuable, do you mean? That's right. But Vera wanted your wife to have it. I heard her myself. But if it puts your mind at ease, ask Arthur.'

'Her son's here?'

'Of course. I got in touch with him at once.'

'Good. Splendid. Because there are these, too.'

He tipped the earrings into the palm of his hand. She plucked one of them out, held it dangling, and smiled while she shook her head.

'They're not genuine?' he asked.

'Oh, they're genuine. I was just thinking of the time Sandra had the cheek to try them on. Which, I might mention, was the absolute end.' She smiled again, dropped the earring back into his hand, closed the fingers of both her hands around his, and put her face near his like a plotting schoolgirl. 'That's what Vera was doing. Making damn sure Sandra wouldn't get them. If I were you, I wouldn't ask Arthur anything. He never stood up to her, that was his trouble. If I were you, I would do just as she wanted.'

Gordon disengaged his hand. 'No chance.'

'It was her last wish.'

But now Gordon was standing, looking openly at his watch. 'I want to see Arthur, Mrs Reed.'

'Well, all right.' She sighed and laughed as she hoisted herself out of her chair. 'But I only wish you could see Sandra too.'

Vera's furnishings were as rich and weighty and tortuous as her clothes had been. They dominated the man who stood among them. Gordon found in him no resemblance to the little doggie projected by his mother. He was of medium height, slender, with grey among his fair hair, and a finely moulded and thoughtful face. In other circumstances, Gordon would have liked him on sight, but at present he knew what he had to hold on to; he knew what was threatened; he would not divert himself by taking one of his sudden likings. He noticed that the man had been crying; the flesh about his eyes was puffed, the eyeballs were inflamed. He did not offer his hand, but stood straight, his arms hanging.

'Of course you must keep them.' He spoke coldly, or perhaps only distractedly; Gordon could not tell. Gordon's explanation had been too much interrupted, too much vouched for, by Mildred Reed, and to his great irritation, he saw that she was now about to burst out again.

'Mrs Reed,' he said, 'please let me speak for myself.' He turned to the grieved man. 'The point is, I simply don't want these. I'll give the pill box to my wife. That's okay. I consented to that. But I won't keep these.'

'I understand,' said Vera's son. But he did not extend his hand to take the earrings, and Gordon was forced to lay them on the nearest surface, which was a small inlaid table. He did this gently and with great relief. 'I wouldn't have chosen to come now,' he said, 'only I leave Sydney early this afternoon. I'm sorry about your mother's sudden death.'

Tears filled the eyes of Vera's son, and he turned away. 'I am sorry about her whole life,' he said. He opened the door of an inner room. 'Goodbye. And thank you.'

In the corridor again with Mildred Reed, Gordon saw by his watch that he had lost less than half an hour. He had remained steady; the day was fine, and taxis would be easy to get. He said, 'I liked her son.'

'Arthur's all right.' She lowered her voice. 'She did have a cruel streak.'

'Still, I can quite see how you will miss her. She had such a strong presence. Was she an actress of some sort?'

Mildred Reed drew in a breath of half-pretended shock. 'Lucky you didn't ask her that. She was a countess. That's why she used to go about saying everyone was so terribly common.'

'I thought they didn't,' said Gordon.

'What, countesses? Titled people? Well, she's the only one I've ever known, and she did, no doubt about that. And no doubt about the title either. It was in her own right. I saw the documentation. I suppose there are lots of them in those countries. Her father was Hungarian. But still.'

'Well,' said Gordon. 'I see I've been badly educated.'

He was alone in the sealed lift on the way down. At the rim of his steadiness he knew there was some disturbance, some little clamour. He said aloud, 'May God rest her soul.' The words dying away left him surprised. She had made him bow, she had made him pray, and each time for the same purpose.

In the two o'clock plane, with the morning's solid work behind him, Gordon allowed himself to wonder what would have happened if he had agreed to keep the earrings. He imagined Marion, in front of the mirror, laughing as she held them up to her ears. He imagined one of the children – it would be Joel – saying with anxiety, 'But they're worth a lot of money.' He imagined Marion saying, 'Then we can sell them, and buy Tess her violin.' Beyond that, he would not allow himself to imagine. He knew he would never regret having refused them.

OUTDOOR FRIENDS ·

Owen Thorbury and Freda Thewen met when Owen's elder daughter, Blanche, and Freda's only son, Justin, decided to marry.

Justin and Blanche had already been living together for more than a year in a decrepit house in Leichhardt, where they had gone in order to put themselves, ideologically, as far from their parents as possible. During their year in Leichhardt, Blanche had introduced Justin to her parents, and Justin had introduced Blanche to his, but these meetings had taken place unceremoniously, in fact incidentally; and when Linda Thorbury suggested to Blanche that she and Owen would like to meet Justin's parents, Blanche had laughed in pretended amazement and asked, 'But why?'

Blanche however was so obsessed with Justin that when she visited her parents she could not stop talking about him, and it was inevitable that now and again she should mention his parents as well. In this way, Owen and Linda Thorbury learned that Justin's father, Rex, was eighteen years older than his mother, Freda, and that he went on terrible drunken binges, but that in between, he was just great; and Freda – Blanche went on in what her father called her jargon – was absolutely terrific, and terribly supportive. They also learned that Rex had done all sorts of things. He had had a motor agency, a trucking business, fast food shops. And now, said Blanche, he had a sheep property with his brother, and he and Freda were sometimes there and sometimes in Sydney.

'That sounds as if they have money,' said Linda, and though Blanche pointedly did not reply, Linda added swiftly, 'Or debts. They can't be unaffected by the drought.' Blanche then said that what she liked best about them was the way they were always so nice to each other, 'so really caring'. As Owen and Linda had not been at all nice to each other for some time, and in fact were shortly to separate, this brought the conversation to an end, leaving Owen to reflect on the marital legend Blanche had just presented, and to wonder what the Thewens were really like.

By the time Justin and Blanche decided to marry, Linda and Owen Thorbury were on the point of separation. Linda could no longer pretend to ignore the intention of a man who had engaged a lawyer, advised her to do the same, and begun to pack his books and maps. The mood of the house was tense and dangerous. When Blanche said she supposed the two pairs of parents should meet, Owen suggested a restaurant, but Linda insisted that the meeting should take place in 'Blanche's own home', and Owen, glad to concede her anything but the one thing she wanted most, agreed.

Even when their younger daughter Hester declined to come home for the occasion (their son Timothy was in New Guinea), Linda persisted; but the indignant sound of her high heels, as she walked about making preparations for the meal, warned Owen that it would not be a success. She was a light woman with a heavy tread. Owen forced himself to accost her in the kitchen.

'Linda, I think we should be frank with the Thewens about our plans.'

'What plans? I'm busy.'

'That we are separating.'

'That you are leaving me.'

When for so many years she had refused to let him say it, she now always insisted on his spelling it out. 'All right,' he said. 'That I am leaving you.'

'Please let me get to the fridge.'

'Do you agree?'

'Certainly not. Let Blanche and Justin have this one family evening to remember.'

Yet Owen was not surprised when, at the end of the dinner, she brought a cheese and a dish of walnuts to the table, sat down, and said, 'You might as well know that my husband is deserting me.'

The Thewens had done nothing to disturb their legend. They had been affable and united. Rex Thewen was drinking only mineral water. He picked up his glass and said, as if it were nothing much, 'Separating, are you?'

'He is deserting me.'

'Oh, mum,' sighed Blanche. 'Deserting. Really!'

Freda Thewen's eyes, calm and interested, were moving from Linda's face to Owen's and back again. Her arms were folded on the table, her hands resting on her long sleeves. She did not, as the others did, take food or drink to cover the awkward moment. Owen cut cheese and said, 'True, I am the one leaving the house. Linda wants very much to stay here, and as I am the instigator, it's fair that I should be the one to move.'

Linda cracked a walnut and said with force, *'To desert!'*

Blanche shielded her eyes with a hand. 'It's enough to make people have second thoughts.'

'That's for sure,' said Justin.

'Oh, don't do that, you two,' said Freda lightly, kindly.

'No,' said Rex. 'It's a gamble. But if you're not game for that, you're not game for anything.'

'A gamble,' said Linda. 'How strange.' She put one hand on her breast and widened her eyes. 'When I, in my innocence, took it for a solemn vow.'

'Come off it,' said Owen (protected by company, bold with wine), 'you said we had better marry because if we didn't your mother would hit the roof, and you giggled all the way through the ceremony.'

'I wonder if it was quite like that.'

She said this so gently that even Owen was surprised when in the next moment she threw the nutcracker in among the walnuts and rose wailing from the table. He did not turn to watch her run from the room, but heard her stop in the doorway to cry, in a voice rising to a shriek, 'I know all you good people will excuse me.'

Nobody moved for a few seconds. Then Blanche rose, threw down her napkin, and with heavy desperate steps, followed her mother. Owen picked up the wine bottle. 'It's been agreed for ten years,' he said, 'that when all the children left home—'

But suddenly he could not be bothered explaining, could not even be bothered saying, 'But now, it seems, Linda was only humouring me.' Let Blanche tell the story to the Thewens, if they asked. Let her present another marital legend. In a firmer voice he said, 'Look, if there was anything else I could do, I would do it. But there isn't.'

He was holding the bottle above Freda Thewen's glass. She shook her head. He poured half into Justin's glass and half into his own. He raised his glass to Justin, and at once saw that the gesture, meant to be consoling, would be interpreted as shockingly jolly and crass. Justin, sitting opposite his mother, folded his arms, like hers, along the table. He looked nowhere but into his glass, but in his raised brows and the line of his mouth, Owen saw the insulting forbearance of his generation.

He put down his glass. 'When are you and Blanche to be married?'

Justin did not reply. Rex said genially, 'Next week. It's to be a registry office job, according to Justin.'

Justin said nothing, but his mother, though she frowned, slowly nodded.

'Simplify the matter,' said Rex. 'No guests. Best thing.'

After they left, Owen cleared the table and threw his and Justin's untouched wine into the sink. While he was stacking the dishwasher, Linda came in, childish in her neat and pretty nightgown, and as always without her high heels, surprisingly short. With her back to him she poured a glass of water, and stood drinking it so slowly, and with such deliberation, that he knew she would presently turn to stare at him. She would stand quite still and silently direct her stare wherever he went, so that though his body would continue to move, his consciousness would be impaled on her otherwise impotent malevolence. If he had foreseen, when he had first spoken of divorce, that his intention would bring them both to this state, he would have lacked the courage to continue in it. But now he could not find a way back. He felt that her insistence on victimization had created a sticky web in which it would be indecent to allow himself to be trapped.

Yet it was a temptation to fly straight into that web and never to struggle again. It hurt that Linda should see him only as callous and brutal, and that others should, and especially that he should sometimes be influenced by the opinion of those others into appearing like that to himself.

Linda's stare, and her soft slippered feet, followed him from the kitchen to the door of his room, causing a crepitation of the skin beneath the back of his shirt. In bed he lay sleepless under the onslaught of images left by the night's events. He heard again Linda's shrieked excuse, saw Blanche's face as she threw down her napkin, saw the set of Justin's mouth, had a glimpse of Rex turning a thick shoulder, and his glance, genial, knowing, and indifferent. But he did find at last a shade of clemency. He heard his own voice saying, 'Look, if there was anything else I could do, I would do it. But there isn't.' And Freda Thewen's headshake he now saw not only in refusal of the wine, but in assent to his words. He saw her hands resting calmly on her purple sleeves, her commiserating eyes, and her mouth shaping a silent 'no'.

This image occasionally returned to comfort him in the two remaining weeks of his life with Linda. It was a hideous fortnight. Linda's complaints became loud, public, and amazingly untruthful. Owen had never been slandered before, and was dumbfounded by the credence she was given. The slanders were unanswerable except by flat denial, and when he tried to counter her more reasonable complaints, to put his side of the case to the friends they had in common, those who were not openly hostile diplomatically withdrew their attention and let his cavilling aggrieved voice go on alone. Blanche, now married, assumed a posture of modern impartiality, but could not help eruptions of soreness and hostility. Timothy, in a letter addressed to them both, stiffly acknowledged 'the inevitability of the divorce' in the only unnatural note in five pages of dashing enthusiasm for his work. He was an archaeologist, and this was his first site. Owen's younger daughter Hester, when he rang her and suggested that this would be a good time to see a bit more of her mother, replied blithely that unless she could actually save a life, she was staying away until after Gloomsday, thank you. This amused him. He envied her confidence that she was quite entitled to protect herself, thank you. But it did not offer him clemency. And nor did he get it from his energetic and sociable mother, at a remove from all this in the Blue Mountains. She listened to him without interruption, and replied in tones of sympathy, but once or twice looked amused, and more than once or twice took a little peek at a gardening catalogue. She left it until they were at her gate to murmur that Linda had been at her day and night on the telephone, and she really thought she had better stay out of it. And as she bent to pull a weed as she spoke, she was able to conclude the conversation by saying loudly, 'Of course, the drought is not obliging enough to kill these.'

Owen determined on silence. He would be calm, he would let it pass, he would be silent. He tried to steel himself against the need for clemency, yet almost avariciously longed for it. The image of Freda's face recurred more and more often because there he thought he found it, though Freda herself, weeks later, told him he had read too much into the incident. Standing before him on the path in the park, the first time they met there, she shook her head. 'No, I'm fairly sure that's wrong,' she said. 'I'm sure I was only saying no to the wine.'

The flat into which Owen moved belonged to a country family who had let it because they were financially affected by the prolonged drought. They had used it as a family pad, and although it was not big, it had five beds in it. The letting agent promised that all but two would be removed. 'All but one,' Owen grimly replied (one of Linda's stories being that he was leaving her for a young woman who used to work for him), but a week passed, then another, and nobody came to take the beds, and in the meantime Owen spread clothes and maps and papers on them, and began rather to like them, partly because of how much Linda would have hated them, and partly because they added to his sense of being temporarily alighted, freed. Sooner or later he would get a more suitable flat, but he was short of money because he had bought Linda out of Thorbury Maps, the small cartography firm he had inherited from his grandfather, and in the meantime, this would do.

His fifth storey windows, southern and almost sunless, looked out across a narrow street at the stained side of a building with small windows and big downpipes. He would park his car in the dim echoing space beneath the building, go up in the service lift, then, if he had not brought work home, he would shower and change and have a self-congratulatory drink while he cooked himself a meal. His children had drawn him into the anti-nuclear movement, and if he were going to a meeting, he would eat at one of the nearby restaurants, but if there were a letter from Timothy, he would cook himself something quick and begin to answer it as soon as he had eaten. Timothy's letters were now sober and passionately enquiring. Owen felt reverential before this expansion of his son's intellect, and to try to do justice to it, he went deeply back into his own books on the subject, so that a reply to Timothy often took him many nights. He knew that Timothy would not have got quite the same attention before the separation, but did not let this concern him. He was compelled to keep busy, to keep his mind either occupied or entertained, leaving no space into which his anger and grievance could rush, for Linda was still broadcasting her wild tales, and Owen had nobody with whom he could decently break his silence except, occasionally, his lawyer.

His lawyer said, 'She can no longer make you change your mind, so she's making you suffer. But she'll get tired of it in the end.'

'Will she? You've no idea of her tenacity.'

'You could take out an injunction.'

'No question of it.'

'I agree. It's best avoided. You'll just have to hang on.'

'I'll do that,' said Owen.

'At least there's no wrangle about money. Though I still think you've been over-generous.'

'Anything,' said Owen. 'Anything.'

'Considering she's a rich woman. Was she always a rich woman?'

'No. She inherited her money ten years ago. I must say *she* was very generous with it too.'

'Ah, well, then,' said the lawyer. And he added, 'Even worse than the money wrangles are the custody wrangles. They're the ones that make you question the whole box and dice. But all your children are grown.'

'Yes,' said Owen.

'You're standing up to it very well. I get some ravers in here.'

Owen smiled. 'I'm raving inside.'

The lawyer was an old man. 'Best place for it,' he said, 'whatever they say.'

Owen was pleased to hear his manner commended. Drama and anger had so unsteadied him that in company he could only counter it by assuming this stately and slightly weary composure. In private, catching sight of his face in a mirror, he saw that he looked affronted.

Though rid at last of the burden of gardening and household maintenance, an almost immediate physical slackness warned him that he must find a substitute. When the warm weather began, he meant to recover his skill in body surfing, but on these winter days, he got into the habit of coming home, throwing his case and papers on one of the beds, and walking briskly out in the direction of the harbour, down stone steps and descending streets until a last flight of steps, narrow and darkened by high stone walls, always damp, brought him to the curve of sunny parkland embracing the bay. During the day he had usually collected a few fresh insults to be walked off, and he would walk fast but steadily to the end of the green arc and back, while looking out beyond the clustered masts and breathing, Freda Thewen said, as if he had just discovered how to do it.

He did not see her; she had to stand in his path to make him stop. She laughed at his puzzlement. She pointed. 'We live just over there, you know.' 'Of course,' said Owen. But he had forgotten. He was thinking that here, in his path, was the one person who would listen to him, because the confidential tone had been established that night at the dinner table. He asked her if she often walked in the park, and when she replied that she might come often for a week or two, then for weeks not at all, he wondered if her appearances there were governed by her husband's addiction. He saw that addiction as setting her apart, as he, at present, and for the first time in his life, was set apart.

'I'll show you something,' she said. They were standing at the low stone wall containing the bay. She drew him along a few paces and pointed to a park bench in the water. Vandals, she said, tore them from their concrete footings at night and threw them into the harbour. This one was upright. The incoming tide was rippling over the painted green bars of its seat. They said it was a shame, an outrage, and agreed that someone ought to come and winch it up, but both began to smile as they looked at it.

'It looks so intentional,' she said.

'It's waiting for a mermaid.'

It was a cold August day. Seagulls were gliding slowly, as they did (startling him at first) across the windows of Owen's flat. As they turned and walked on together, she thrust her hands into the pockets of her jacket, and Owen tucked his into the high pockets of his windcheater. He told her where he was living, and about the beds.

'Do you sleep in a different one each night?'

It was what his draughtsman Charlie Hill had asked him. 'No,' he said, as he had done to Charlie, 'one is for maps and papers, one for shirts and coats, one for trousers and socks, I sleep in the fourth, and the fifth is for anything left over.'

Here she differed from Charlie by saying thoughtfully, as if the subject were worth seriousness, 'I would like that.'

'So do I,' he said.

It was almost dusk when they got to the end of the green arc. She spoke on a yawn, covering her mouth with the back of a hand. 'Well, goodbye.'

'Do you drive down?'

'No. There would be no point, when it's a walk I need.'

'So you have to climb that hill?'

'You have to climb one, too, on your side.'

The park was as low-lying as possible, slung between two points, both thickly built upon, mostly with apartment blocks. Crossing it on the way back, Owen walked slowly and deliberately, letting his memory linger on her soft olive skin, her dark attentive eyes, and longing to submit his story to her sympathy, or even to her judgement. The tennis courts and the football oval were deserted and locked. As he ascended the narrow stone steps in the half-dark, he saw at the top four jet black legs appear, and a few seconds later he passed a pair of those ragged and emaciated youths whom he always regarded as occupying the depths of that society of which his daughter Hester, and her dandified fantastic friends, occupied the heights. At least, he hoped they did. He supposed the park was about to begin its notorious night life.

The second time he met Freda it was high tide. The bench was inundated, its bars appearing to twist under the ruffled water. 'If we watch,' said Freda, 'we might see her come.'

'No, she comes only at night.'

'Yes. In the depths of the night.'

'With twenty-eight grams of heroin,' said Owen, sobered by a fear for Hester.

It was earlier than last time. The dry unpleasant wind struck rigging against the masts and filled the air with single-noted bells. In the open field behind them footballers moved in the pattern of their game, dogs barked, children shouted, and lovers and readers lay in sheltered places. Absolutely without forethought, he turned from the wall and spoke of the night when he had offered her the wine. He spoke warmly and fast. He told her how he had interpreted her refusal, her silent 'no', and how the memory of her face at the moment had persisted in his mind. He did not speak of the comfort it had given him, but in refraining was aware of an inner voice saying, Not yet. A runner dashed by them panting. She began to frown, and before he had finished speaking she was shaking her head.

'I'm fairly sure that's wrong. I'm sure I was only saying no to the wine.'

But he still believed he was right. She doesn't know, he thought, what her own face shows. He was so certain of this that he did not insist, but went on kindly to talk of other things. They walked on at Freda's strolling pace, hands in pockets, passed by other walkers, by women with babies and people with dogs, and talked of Justin and Blanche. Justin and Blanche had moved to a narrow terrace house, which they were buying on a deposit given to them by Linda and Rex. Owen was interested that she should specify that it was Rex, and not 'we', who had given them this money. Owen, who was definitely out of favour with Blanche and Justin, had not yet been allowed to see the house. He was careful to sound amused when he admitted this to Freda.

'Oh, but they've been too busy to blink,' said Freda. 'They're doing most of the restoration themselves. I don't know why they didn't buy a good sound modern flat, since they don't want children. Rex won't think much of it. He hasn't seen it yet either. He's in the country with his brother.'

'It seems to be very bad up there.'

'You've no idea. It's ruinous. They're starting to shoot their sheep.'

'Do you often go up?'

'I can't. The dust gives me hay fever. Or I'm a coward, and am sparing myself. No, I'll tell you what it is – Rex was born in the country, but I wasn't. I'm a city woman. Anyway, Rex is all right. There's no one better than Clive for keeping Rex all right.' She emphasized her strolling pace, and with her hidden hands, raised the pockets of her jacket. 'Well, I feel so free.'

The following Sunday seemed so warm that Owen was deluded into driving to Coogee and letting himself be battered by a cold surf. On the way home it occurred to him that he was near Justin's and Blanche's new house, and he impulsively turned the car and sought out their address.

The number of the house was nineteen. The bright new brass numerals were conspicuous beside a tall gate in a palisade of freshly painted olive green. He knew that sanding and painting were still going on inside, and intended to ignore all the rules and protocol they had set up around themselves, and bluffly to offer his help. But as he fumbled with the unfamiliar latch of the gate he saw through its bars Justin and Blanche lying naked and entwined on a rug on the tiny square of grass. Both held books at an awkward angle and were reading with a concentration evidently unaffected by the conjunction of their limbs. He was close enough to read the big print on the spines of their books – CHEMISTRY on Justin's, NOURISHMENT on Blanche's – and almost laughed aloud when he realised that they were studying. A ladder was propped against the wall of the house and sanding blocks stood on the sill of an open window. He guessed that the unusual heat of the day had tempted them into this enclosed space to sunbake and read, and that as they read they had instinctively drawn themselves into this cocoon of sensual contentment. Blanche, whose book was held sideways and aloft, pursed her lips and blew open a page as Owen watched. They did not see him. He retreated to his car. He was filled with love for his daughter, and respect and envy for them both. The beauty of their youthful flesh gave him a sharpened vision of his own hands on the wheel, and regret for his and Linda's twenty-three years of good intentions and feeble deeds felt leaden and immovable in his body. Yet out of that marriage had come his beloved children – Timothy, Blanche, and Hester. He repeated what had become a familiar warning to himself: because he saw those three as his and Linda's only justification, he must not burden them by investing in them too much hope for himself.

For about a week, Owen did not see Freda in the park. Either he was too late and missed her, or she did not come. Then in the next week he saw her every afternoon but one, and after that week, their meetings became accepted instead of accidental, and a strain developed between them. She lacked, or refused to respond to, the flirtatiousness that can make a pleasure of sexual tension. There were periods of silence, or dogged small talk. Or she would behave as if she had forgotten he was there. She would stop and kick a stone from the path, taking her time, with a neat and accurate aim. Or she would stop and bend to one of the dogs running about. 'You're a good dog, aren't you?' Owen would watch her puffing out the words through fond lips. 'Yes, you're a good dog. But where is your leash? You know what the notice says.' The dog's owner would usually come up with the leash, and he or she and Freda would have a smiling animated conversation. When Freda rejoined Owen, she would bring some of these smiles and this animation with her, and for a while they would be more relaxed.

The park bench in the water provided the same kind of respite. '*Still here!*' they would say each day, and would point out the changes, the sand beginning to cover its footings, and the paint lifting from its seat, abraded at night by its scaly occupant. At these times it always seemed possible to talk to her of his troubles with the same ease and energy as on that first occasion, but something always deterred him. Once she suddenly spoke of 'poor Rex and Clive, up there,' then turned to the park and said reproachfully, 'And see how green it still is here.' But more often, the warning rose in his own mind, saying, Not yet, and he knew that he was waiting until they were lying side by side, in an intimacy that could now be established only by the shared surrender of sex. At their first meeting friendship had flowed between them, whereas now there was care and even hostility; only then could they be friends again. But in his pursuit of this amorous friendship, and this sympathetic audience, Owen was checked by Freda's involvement with his family, and especially by thoughts of Linda.

Just after his marriage to Linda, Owen had fallen in love, with a fervour that defined his feeling for Linda as mild, with a girl named Annie Ford. He and Annie's first approaches had also been made out of doors, under cover of casual friendship, as they walked across a park like this one, on their way home from work to their respective flats and spouses. But he and Annie, both scarcely twenty-one, had been driven and bold. They had found shelter in leafy culverts, in a sandstone cave, and once, in a cupboard under the stairs in a rooming house strange to them both. As soon as they tried to regularize their arrangements, down had come the disastrous detection.

Detection this time could not drench him with such tears, nor besiege him with such agonies and rages. But he found it hard to bear the prospect of Linda's triumph, and the tale that would go out everywhere; she would make it sound like incest. And what of Blanche? He did not believe that Blanche's love for him was damaged beyond repair, but asked if it would survive an assault on Justin's loyalties such as she herself was suffering. This advanced the shade of Rex Thewen. But Rex's was an intermittent shade; he was far away, and though Owen occasionally recalled, with a sensation of disturbance, his manner, all he could remember of his appearance were his thick shoulders, unhealthy eyes, and red-veined skin. Freda's comments on him, frequent but dull, part of a boring social patter she sometimes adopted, added nothing to the marital legend provided by Blanche when she and Justin had been living in Leichhardt; Owen still did not know what the Thewens were really like.

Nor did he manage to learn much, factually, about Freda herself. He would realize this after parting from her, while making his way quickly back across the dusky park, passing the first of the night occupants on the path or the stone steps. She sometimes drove down to the park now, and as he walked back he would see again, from his viewpoint above her car, her sallow hand on the ignition key. He wondered what she did when she got home. What, he wondered, were her interests? Owen had heard it said of some women, with disparagement, that they had no interests, but he knew no such women himself. All the women he knew worked, except, in some cases, when their children were young. If they didn't work for money they worked voluntarily, giving themselves efficiently to causes or the arts. Linda had been a librarian with Shell Oil before Timothy's birth, and fifteen years later she had retrained as a welfare worker. Lately she had spoken to Blanche (who had passed it on to Owen) about getting a job. Blanche had added that her mother would find it hard to get a job in times like these, but that of course she would do *something*; she would not sit at home and do nothing. Owen had murmured agreement as a matter of course; it was taken for granted that everyone did *something*. He knew no one else like Freda Thewen, who, when not looking after one man, was evidently quite content to do nothing, who could stroll along and raise the pockets of her jacket, and say, 'I feel so free,' who could stop and hold conversations with dogs and their owners, who could spare concentration so neatly to kick stones from her path. When, to ease one of their strained times, he turned the conversation to women's work, it seemed to him that she was impatient, perhaps even evasive. One day he spoke to her of the anti-nuclear movement, and asked if she had considered working in it. It was the first time he had seen her annoyed.

'It's too late. Work ought to have been constant from the start, straight after Hiroshima, instead of everyone getting side-tracked by Vietnam.'

'That was important.'

'Not *as* important.' He had never heard her dogmatic before, either; he didn't like it. 'It's too late,' she said again. 'Now all we can do is to have faith that it won't happen.'

'You can still try to ensure that it won't.'

173

'Not by creating a mood of doom. I hate it when I hear young people saying they won't reach middle age. Justin and Blanche – I think they're timid beyond words in deciding to have no children. How can they! Is it a pose?'

Owen wondered how much she really liked his daughter, who had married her only son. He drew away from her, and left the park early; but the next day, when he saw her car under the fig trees, he felt joy, as if there had been a breach.

When Blanche had spoken to him about her mother's intention to find a job, she had also asked him to come to see the new house.

'Come to lunch on Sunday, dad. I'll make my scaloppine.'

'I'll look forward to that very much, Blanchie.'

The invitation made him so happy that he only incidentally thought of it as a chance to learn something about Freda. Of his three children, Owen most admired his son, but an element of sensuality in his love for Blanche had made her secretly his favourite. She was his first daughter, his beautiful child; he loved her more than he had ever loved her mother, and since leaving Linda he had been almost entirely deprived of her. He had seen more of Hester. Hester lived and worked not far from his flat, and he sometimes visited her workroom, bringing the preserved ginger she loved, and which never made her fat. (She said that she would rather die than be fat; also that she could not live without pierced ears.) His visits were not satisfactory. There was so little room that he could talk to her only while executing the shuffling dance dictated by her need to climb up and get that box, to answer that phone, to try bronze appliqué on that dress instead of silver, to lean over her impassive machinist, with her chin on his shoulder, and whisper in his ear, to run and throw open the door to a group of those figures he thought of as the modish equivalent of those on the damp steps in the evening park – but whom he now began to see as not so distinct. Looking, then looking again, he saw that one of these could have been one of those, with the same deterioration, beyond chic, with the same sheeny eyes and clusters of spots on cheek and jawline. When they came in the door, little Hester leapt at her father and hugged him round the neck, and he departed, leaving her guests utterly, even uncannily, absorbed in consuming his ginger. He was perturbed by her association with them, and tried to trust in his unobtrusive checks on her eyes and skin, and her assurance that a bit of marijuana was as far as she went.

Only for Hester, he would have been attracted by those figures. It teased him that they, like him, had one life, but whereas his had to be planned, worried over, adjusted and readjusted, they were prepared to sport with theirs for a while, to risk it, even to throw it away. In a wild impatience that suddenly rose in him now, it seemed that his very planning, worrying over, adjusting, were a means of throwing his away, but it was a slow dull bleeding, whereas theirs was fast, and conscious, a gesture. But when his impatience had been subdued by the details, sometimes interesting and charming, of his daily round, he admitted that his way, the usual way, was what he wanted for his children. Between those figures and his appreciation of them stood his concern for his children. He wanted his children to be safe; love for his children had ensured his respectability; he was a respectable man.

He took daffodils to Blanche, and though there was already a basket of daffodils (from Linda's garden?) in the hall, Blanche joyfully exclaimed, looked amazed, and hugged him with one arm while holding the daffodils out of harm's way with the other. She was wearing her fair hair as she had done when a child, flat to her head and hanging straight to her shoulders. She looked tired, voluptuous, and excited.

'Justin. Look. Daffodils. It's spring. Imagine. Spring. Darling, you show dad the house while I put these in water and get on with the scaloppine.'

Between Justin and Owen stood that bad start, and they approached each other with courtesy and care. In each room Justin stood off and explained what they had done, his eagerness and slight nervousness demanding a response that gave Owen no chance to introduce the subject of Freda. Except in his light bones and olive skin, he could find no trace of her in her son.

Justin and Blanche had been energetic and clever. 'We thought we might as well do it properly, get it right up to the mark from the start,' said Justin, 'so that we could keep it that way.' And Owen nodded, for that is what Linda and he had wanted, and this is how hard they had worked, and how hard he had continued to work for so many years that he had come to hate the consuming task of keeping everything right up to the mark. Regret weighted him again as he followed Justin from room to room. Feeling stupid and passive, he heard his voice go on in lively and well-informed commendation.

The weight lifted as they drank white wine before lunch. He read aloud his last letter from Timothy, and Justin read aloud part of Blanche's last one while Blanche cooked.

'Tim's a great guy,' said Justin.

'He is,' said Owen.

'Timothy is a *saint*,' cried Blanche, anxious over her cooking.

As they sat down to the scaloppine, Owen said to Justin, 'I've met your mother a few times, in the afternoons, walking in the park.'

Justin turned to Blanche. 'Mum must have given up tennis.'

'She has, darling,' said Blanche. 'I thought I told you.'

Owen was startled to hear his daughter in such a thoroughly married aside. It was as if he had just realized she was really married, and not only playing at it. He said to Justin, 'Did your mother play tennis often?'

'Can't you call her Freda?' asked Blanche, with one of her sudden irritations.

'Freda, then.'

'Very nice,' said Justin of the scaloppine. 'Yes, regularly,' he said to Owen.

'Her work left her time?'

'It isn't as good as the last time,' said Blanche.

'Well, it's a lot of trouble for just a stew,' said Justin. 'Mum was a very good player, Owen, as a matter of fact.'

'A veal stew,' said Blanche. She lifted her glass and drank, while her eyes above its rim cast a melancholy glance at Justin.

'It's fine,' said Owen. 'The sauce is perfect.'

Blanche nodded. She put an elbow on the table and chewed sadly and languidly.

'Does Freda play any sport now?' asked Owen.

'He didn't cut the veal thin enough,' said Blanche.

'Look, Blanchie,' said Justin, 'don't do it to us. It's good. We're enjoying it. Have another drink.'

'Thank you.' Blanche drank half her wine and said, 'It may not be perfect, but it is scaloppine, and not just a veal stew.'

'Jesus Christ!' said Justin. 'It has to be some bloody thing. So now you pick on the food.'

'*You* picked on the food.'

'Owen,' said Justin resignedly. 'Your glass.'

'No more, thanks. I'm above .05 now.' Across the table, Owen took his daughter's hand. He found it resistant, but continued to smile. 'I'm afraid you were always a perfectionist, Blanchie.'

'What's wrong with that?' said Justin, while Blanche said meditatively, 'Afraid.'

As they finished the scaloppine, almost in silence, Owen could feel the current swirling and turning against him.

He got to his feet, picked up their three plates, and remarking that they must be tired after all their work, he took the plates to the kitchen. To get out of earshot of their low but intense voices, he went into the courtyard, where he lingered, sighing and bored, and reminding himself of the allowances that must be made for a couple scarcely out of their teens.

When he returned to the dining room he saw that Justin had pulled his chair up to Blanche's and was holding her in his arms while she wept. Owen hated women's tears, but by these tears of Blanche's he was immediately softened and moved. He took them for tears of reconciliation, which, he trusted, included him. All the same, he thought it better not to linger, and was about to assure them that he must leave straight after lunch, when Blanche jerked her head upright and blurted out that perfectionism had nothing to do with it, and neither had tiredness. It was something else. She had meant to keep quiet, and not to say a word.

'Darling,' said Justin, 'don't say it.'

'No,' said Owen, lightly and coldly, – 'whatever it is, don't.'

'Oh, no wonder you don't want me to. Neither would I, if I were a man, and had given my wife gonorrhoea three months before my daughter was born. And I don't mean Hester. I mean me.'

Whenever Owen was deeply shocked or indignant, he spoke in a weak tenor. He said, 'Now, now, now – I can't believe your mother would say—'

'I feel so unclean,' shouted Blanche, falling back into Justin's arms.

'No, really,' said Owen, in the same high voice, though half-laughing now, 'I can't have this, you know. There was a slight infection—' he remembered it only as he spoke '—but it couldn't be diagnosed. Nobody knew how she got it.' And now he did laugh. 'My dear girl! Unclean!'

But through her louder sobs Blanche told him to get out, and Justin tightened his embrace and angrily mouthed above her golden head that Owen had better go. So Owen, who had heard those two, in the Leichhardt days, refer to gonorrhoea as the old gon, summoned all his stately calm, and marched off in the direction to which Justin was now violently pointing.

His fury and offendedness far outlasted his amusement, but he managed to draw on the same stately calm when Justin rang the next day. Justin said they were both very sorry and ashamed, and that Blanche didn't really believe that story about the gonorrhoea.

'We talked it over last night. It's really interesting, what she's done. She's made it into a metaphor, and is using it to express her real worries.'

'Oh,' said Owen. His only concern was to let none of his anger out. His face bore its dignified or affronted look as he listened to Justin.

'Her real worry, of course, is that Linda keeps saying you really left her for another woman, and when Blanchie denies it, Linda tells her just to wait and see.'

'But why exactly should Blanche care so much?'

'Why? Why? Because she really believed in that hopeless incompatibility, that's why. And if it turns out to have been just a cover-up—'

'It's a pity incompatibility is invisible. If only it would take some physical form. I see it myself as geometrically shaped. It could have a name tag.'

Justin was silent for a while. Then he said quietly, 'I wonder if you quite understand just how hard this has been on Blanchie.'

'I've tried to. That's why I've considered an injunction against her mother.'

'So you think,' said Justin, 'that would help Blanchie?'

'No, I don't,' said Owen, at his calmest. 'That's why I'm not doing it.'

'The whole thing's been terribly traumatic for Blanchie.'

Owen was still rampaging with secret fury when he went to the park that afternoon. His silence had again become hardly bearable. He had been tempted to confide in his draughtsman, Charlie Hill (making an amusing story of it). He had been tempted to ring his mother. But it was Freda, only Freda he wanted to tell. He wanted her murmurs, her attentive eyes, the physical sympathy he knew was behind the barrier of their reserve.

He was not able to leave work till late, and instead of going home first he drove straight to the park and left his car under the native figs, where Freda left hers when she drove down. Her car was not there, and he thought at first that this was to be one of the days when she did not come, or when their presence did not coincide. He considered this to be just as well, and that she was a most dangerous person to draw into his life, while all the time he continued anxiously to look for her. The park was divided by a tidal channel. She was nowhere in the nearer part, but in the distance of the farther part, over against the tennis courts, he could see a figure, not her, perhaps, but with a stance resembling hers.

As he crossed the timber bridge over the channel his footsteps sounded purposeful to his ears. He had not recognized her from a distance because she was dressed in a dark silky suit, and shoes with rather high heels, and carried a small red shoulder bag, not over her shoulder, but by the long strap held in both hands behind her back. As she watched the tennis she rocked slightly from foot to foot, so that the small weighted bag swung like a pendulum. She always made some gesture, he thought as he approached, to establish her idleness. He felt increasingly anxious as he walked to her across the grass, and though he had never deliberately touched her before, it seemed quite natural when he reached her to lay a hand on her shoulder.

She turned only her face to him, but the rocking stopped. He nodded curtly at the Japanese four on the court. 'Do you want to watch this?'

'Not especially.' Her own nod was directed at the hand on her shoulder. 'Don't do that.'

He dropped his hand at once. 'I'll tell you why,' she said. 'I've just been to lunch—' she nodded again '—over there, on your side of the park, with a friend, Susan Guiser, who's down from the country, and staying there. Such a view from her window, the whole of the park.'

He said sourly, 'A long lunch.'

'A long talk. I was just walking home.'

She set off again as she spoke. He walked at her side. 'I left my car over there,' he explained.

'Did you have a nice weekend?'

'I went to lunch with Blanche and Justin.'

'Then you've seen the house. Could you bear that spiral staircase? Well, not spiral, but you know what I mean—'

He let her voice go on uninterrupted. He was resentful of being trapped in such talk. She went on with the social animation with which she spoke to the dog owners. He wished he had not come. He wished he were home alone, having a drink, and did not have to listen to such rubbish. He thought it must be her clothes that gave her this unusual animation today, and as their four feet rapped the boards of the bridge he was sure that this time it was only her sharp heels that gave them their sound of purpose. There was no wind; the tide was low, and a warm stench reached him from the harbour bed. Once he turned a hand sideways across her path to warn her to side-step the excrement of a dog, an habitual gesture, understood at once. She did not stop talking.

It was also habitual to stop when they came to the park bench. They had never seen it quite beached before; it stood on a mound of sand among plastic containers, sodden bread, fruit peel, and drink cans. 'So she drinks Fanta,' said Freda.

But Owen struck the top of the wall with a fist, 'Barbarians. Barbarians. Barbarians.' He tried to conquer the weakness of his voice. He was glad that the rough stone was hurting his hand. 'Despoilers—'

But he could not find words strong enough, nor a strong enough voice. He unclenched his fist and banged his hand down hard on the wall. She quickly took his free hand, and in the shelter between their two bodies pressed it in hers. He was not surprised, and still felt hostile, towards her as well as towards all barbarians and despoilers. He noticed that her other (public) hand casually fingered the strap of the bag over her shoulder.

'I'll show you something,' she said, as she had done at that first meeting, when she had shown him the bench.

Smiling, in a secretive playful way, she directed him out of the park, along the road, and on to the deck of the marina. He had never been here before, supposing it to be reserved for the owners of boats. The agency for boat sales was shut, and so was the shop selling marine gear. Here she brought them to a stop. Between them and the park, and the windows in apartment blocks, were not only the big motor cruisers, but a screen of masts moving like hesitant antennae. Smiling and murmuring, she took his hand and examined the scratches made by the stone. She held it to her cheek, kissed it, then slipped both her arms beneath his jacket and held his body close, pressing the side of her head to his chest. He put his arms round her and rested a cheek on her black hair. It was strong wiry hair, incongruous to the soft thin body he was embracing. He felt soothed, almost drowsy, but not sexually moved. His surprise at this became a worry, an obligation to take the active masculine part, and he was about to burrow down and force her head back to kiss her when they heard the reverberations of footsteps on the timber deck. They released each other and stood side by side facing their faint reflections in a rack of dark slickers, while in the same reflection they watched a man cross the deck and walk down the long jetty. Freda gave a sigh. 'It would be nice,' she said, 'if we didn't have to say anything at all.'

'Is Rex still in the country?'

'Of course. Or I wouldn't be doing this.'

'Then I may come home with you?'

'No,' she said, on another sigh.

'Then will you come to my place?'

'Yes, please.'

'I might have said please myself.'

As they walked back to the street she resumed her generalized social voice. 'What a good thing you brought the car. You can wait a long time here for a taxi. And we could hardly have walked back.'

'Because of your Susan?'

'It's no use being half-hearted about deception.'

'Is she staying for long?'

'Going back on Thursday.

'Then we're not to be denied the park?'

'Not if we're careful to behave as we did before.'

They had reached his car. After he had let her in he glanced across the hood to the nearest part of the park. On the field of green, intensified by the dusk and fringed by dark trees, only the footballers were left, small in the distance, and bright as plastic toys. He got into the car and said, 'Well, I'm glad. I think of it as our ground.'

'Yes, yes, so do I,' she said, laughing. 'Our ground.'

Feeling her proximity in the car as exquisite yet painful, he inclined towards her. She drew away.

'I have to say this. Sexually, Rex and I are finished. You will understand that, because you two were, too, weren't you? But we are finished *only* sexually.'

'These things are hard to say,' he said with sympathy.

'So that's why I've tried to become skilled at deceit.'

'And have you?'

'Yes. As you must have done, Owen.'

He could have told her that he had been discreet but not deceitful in his infidelities. It was Linda who had kept them secret, who had pretended (in this too) to know nothing. But he did not want to mention Linda. Not yet.

While Freda was drying herself, Owen, already dry, sat on the edge of the bath. When she came close enough he pulled her to him and thrust his head against her belly. 'Freda,' he said, 'we must both have been fasting.'

She touched his cheek. 'Yes.'

'Have you had many fasts?'

'Very long fasts.'

'So have I.'

'People want you, but you don't want them. Or vice versa.'

'What a good colour you are. Like those brown eggs we cooked.'

Laughter shook the small mass he was holding. 'Food again. Well, I am brown.' She spoke neither in her awkward nor her sociable voice, but in another, simple and lazy. 'When Justin was three, we got separated in the showgrounds. They asked him what his mother was like, and he said a thin brown lady, so they didn't look for someone in a red coat.'

Owen was glad he had not poured over her his grievances and acrimony. When the time came, his revulsion against it had been complete. To begin would be to go on; to say one thing would arouse the need to say everything, and to try to say everything would be inevitably to falsify. He was sickened in advance by all the quibbling details that would pour from his mouth. 'The Thorburys' must also have their legend. Let it stand. Let both legends stand. 'Did Justin take long to find you?' he asked, to keep her there.

'Not after they broadcast. Dear Owen, let me go. It's so late.'

When he rose and they stood face to face he was startled by the lines across her forehead and round her mouth. As he had sat with his cheek embedded in the flesh of her belly he had had the illusion that they were both young. And he saw by her eyes, fixed for a moment on his face, and so tense and inquisitive, that she had shared the illusion. They both laughed, but Owen thought it was sorrow they mocked, and to console or assure her he would have embraced her again, but she turned out of his arms, shaking her head, and wrapped the towel under her armpits.

'I'll get dressed and go.'

'No need. Stay the night.'

'Ah no.'

'Why not?'

She was laughing again. 'No no no.'

They dressed in a bedroom, with beds around them – as she had said – like rafts. While putting on her clothes her pleasant laxity left her, and when he asked if she intended never to stay the night, she replied, 'Definitely not,' and when he asked why not, she said briskly, 'Too domesticated. Let's remember this can't go on for long.'

'All the more reason.'

'No. It makes it harder to break off.'

He wanted to drive her home; she said she would get a taxi. Sitting on the edge of one of the low divan beds, he watched her, on the edge of the opposite bed, draw on and fasten her stockings. 'I'll ring you tomorrow,' he said.

'Please, Owen, never ring me.'

'But that's absurd.'

'I'm not always alone. Rex tells people they can come to stay. And they do, without notice.'

'What of it? A man may ring a woman. Unless, of course, you enjoy all these precautions.'

'It's not that.' With one shoe on, and the other in her hand, she hesitated. 'I wish,—' she said. She put the shoe on. 'I wish we didn't even know each other's names.'

She got up as Owen did. She wriggled her feet, settling them into her shoes. 'That's what I wish. Darling Owen, I'm lucky to have found you, I know that. But there's Blanche and Justin, married. And there's Rex. It'll come, you know, all the clutter. But in the meantime – let's just have this.'

She was pleading. Owen divined in her plea a consistency with his own instinct to let their marital legends stand. But he said, 'You told me about Justin losing you in the showgrounds. That's not clutter?'

'Oh, that's so far in the past. Finished.'

'With no sequel.'

'Exactly. A story.'

'Are you one of those women who has fantasies about strangers?'

'Of course,' she said, rounding her eyes and walking to him, putting her body against his so that he instantly embraced her. 'I am one of those women who envy Leda. Swans have no phone numbers. Or one of those women on the old trains. With consequences only to myself.'

'Today, those women would pick up strangers.'

'I've thought of it. I nearly did it once. But it's too dangerous. I would be afraid.'

Well, I should hope so.' He pressed her head to his chest, as he had done on the marina. When he heard her begin to laugh, he laughed too. 'So you are content,' he said, 'to come to this ridiculous flat—'

'The flat's perfect. It's like a motel along the roadside. And we still have the park.'

'I can see now why you like the park.'

'So do you.'

'That's true.'

'So long as we're careful.'

In the rest of September, and in October and November, Owen and Freda still sometimes met in the park before going to Owen's flat. By November the drought that held Rex Thewen and his brother in the country was beginning to affect even the pampered city. The park looked green only when saturated with evening light, and the banks darkening the narrow steps dried out and dropped loosened stones. In the suburbs water for gardens was rationed. Blanche told Owen that Linda had lost her golden elm. She had wept for hours, said Blanche, because she remembered the day she and Owen had planted it – their very first tree.

In fact, Linda and he had never planted a tree together, but he was not tempted to disclose this because Blanche told the story with sly humour, and Justin brought the palms of his hands together and laughed. Lately Linda's stories had lost invention, had become almost a mechanical prattle, so silly that all of the family (except untouched Timothy) were now able to share the amusement formerly shown only by Owen's mother.

'Has your mother got a job?' Owen asked Blanche, and when Blanche said no, he wondered what else could have happened to unloose the tenacity he knew so well.

Blanche and Justin were drinking coffee in his flat. 'But why can't you get them to move some of the beds?' asked Blanche. 'It's ridiculous.'

'I'll get round to it,' said Owen. He tried to subdue suffusions of elation, but they showed. 'Well anyway,' said Justin, 'you're looking great.'

Owen's mother had also heard about the golden elm. 'Good for her if she's lost only one tree,' she said. She was standing with a rake below the ladder on which Owen stood to clear her gutters of leaves. In the mountains unusual precautions had begun against bushfires. 'We all know everything could go up this year,' she said, with the slightly contemptuous pride shown by those in danger to those who are not. 'The whole place is a tinder box,' she shouted proudly up at Owen.

Later she told Owen that Linda had rung her only once lately. 'And that was to ask me how I put down those fruits and nuts in rum. She must have found another feller.'

'Do you really think so?'

'Why not? She's rich, pretty, pathetic, and only forty-three.'

Hester shared her grandmother's opinion. A widower, she said, had moved into the house two doors down, where the Levinsons used to be, with three big school-boy sons. 'He doesn't own only a crummy little cartography joint either. He's the managing director of something big and heavy and greasy, with a lot of initials. I was with Barry, and he was so understanding about us he made me sick. Hester spread her hands over an imaginary paunch and waddled along a few paces, saying glottally, 'Aw, well, wot family mightn't it happen to, in these modden times.'

'This was up at the house?'

'Yes.'

'Then Gloomsday's over.'

'Looks like it, dad.'

'Good. Good. I'm very glad.'

'I won't tell mum that, or she'll bring it back. I wanted some money. She gave me some. I hope if she marries that clunk she doesn't cut us out of her will.'

'She won't. She loves you all.'

'Those footballers will win her. Well, let them. Who cares. I'm actually about to make some money anyway. I really hit it with these Winnerack jackets. And I don't even like them. They were an aberration. Denise loves them.'

Denise, the new machinist, raised her head and said the jackets were real nice. Owen had never seen Hester's work room so quiet before. Outside the door, when Owen was leaving, Hester said Denise was real nice, too, and a wonderful machinist. 'But so boring. She's *shy*. I hate shy people. And she's *thirty*.'

'What happened to what's-his-name?'

'You must mean Barry. You've forgotten the name of my love. How like you, dad.'

Owen recalled the very tall chinless man, with pink and black hair, who had sat at the machine with his mouth open, and never said a word. 'He was your love?'

'Barry. Yes. He's gone to Turkey with Martin. He wasn't as good a machinist as Denise, and some days he usen't to show. But he wasn't boring. And he wasn't *shy*.'

'I hope Denise likes ginger.'

'She will say it's real nice, and wipe her fingers on a little hankie.'

'You're down, Hester.'

'You noticed.'

'You always come up again.'

'Yeah.'

'Have you been to see Blanche and Justin?'

'Jesus. Is that supposed to get me up?'

'Blanche and you were close.'

'Close.' Hester leaned against the wall, picking at her nails. 'Must have been before she got corrupted by all that sociology.'

'Have the others *all* gone away?'

'One way or another. I don't want to talk about it, dad. Or Winnerack jackets, either. What I need is to bust into something new.'

'You will, Hes dear.'

She turned to go, waving both hands at her side and saying, 'And I hate innocent people, too.'

Owen was not weighted with all of his former fear for Hester when passing the black-legged youths, or when he was reminded, as he stood with Freda in contemplation of the park bench, of the little packets said to be smuggled ashore at night. Nor need he ache now for Blanche's anger, nor feel the full hateful weight of guilt for his broken marriage. Guilt began to lodge in milder forms elsewhere. His letters to Timothy suffered; it was time he asked Charlie Hill to come for a drink after work; he had twice postponed conferring with Carl Alpino on the anti-nuclear leaflets to be printed in the new year. At first Freda came only occasionally, but late in the second week, when he defied her injunction about ringing her, she did not even remind him of it, but said promptly, 'All right, I will, I'll come.' And fifteen minutes later they were rocking, moaning, laughing, or speaking in an almost incoherent babble which Owen (when he was alone and able to be ironical) compared with the onset of the gift of tongues encouraged by certain American religions.

Nor were they as discreet in the park as they had intended. When they saw a brown lace brassiere hooked to a bar of the park bench, they leaned together in their laughter. Again and again he took her arm and held it until she murmured a warning. The sexual tension that had once made proximity so painful now made it luxurious and gave to their association a weak merriment. When the park bench disappeared, winched up or borne away, they facetiously mourned it. When she would have stopped to talk to dogs, he carelessly pulled her onward. As the days grew longer, they loitered. They walked on the jetty and he discovered her to be knowledgeable about boats, able to classify the yachts, compare the engines of the cruisers, estimate prices.

'How do you know all this?'

'We once had an agency for boats.'

It was one of their trespasses into clutter. These were inevitable but rare. Her embargo on them usually stood because to break it would be to distract them from their mood. They indulged each other. He had to repress chagrin when she said 'we', and very soon she avoided saying it. Talk of the drought, the declining hope of rain coming in time, the continued shooting of sheep, was reference enough to Rex Thewen. Talk of Timothy in New Guinea, or Hester's success with the Winnerack jackets, was sufficient allusion to Linda. Blanche and Justin, the nearest, the link, were tacitly put in the same category as Rex and Linda, and if they made their way out, were shrouded by generalization. Freda, lying beside him on one of those hot weekend afternoons when they could indulge their laziness, began to talk of children, and of only children, then of only sons.

'Their mothers get so much instruction. From their earliest days they hear how one day they must stand aside and let them go, and how at all times they must be ready for this. Otherwise they'll be homosexual, which is supposed to be bad or sad or something, or else they'll be men who only want mumsy wives. It's imprinting them. That's what has to be avoided. Imprinting. So they do that, the mothers. They avoid that, and they stand aside, and so on. And what happens? The son becomes perfectly indifferent to his mother. And some time later – this is the strange part – so does his mother to him.'

'That's very dogmatic.'

'Yes,' she said, laughing, 'and probably not even true.'

Owen, who was considering Linda's excessive care of Timothy, and her objections to his departure, said stoutly, 'My mother certainly manages splendidly without *her* only son.'

Their absence of a shared future made their talk idle and suave, contention not being worthwhile. They talked of incidents and events so long past that they had become only stories, not always without sequence, but with sequences able to be omitted. For the first time in more than twenty years, Owen spoke of Annie Ford. Annie Ford was dead. Her memory had never left him, but its brilliance and urgency had compacted into a dense and somehow coloured shadow. It was this shadow he now disturbed for Freda. Walking with round-shouldered Annie across that other park, he thrust a hand suddenly into her hair, and found himself confronted by her first serious prolonged stare. Annie, lying beneath him, made her goggle eyes of amazement. Annie whispered in the dim light of the cupboard under the stairs that she couldn't find her bag of groceries; they smothered laughter at this farce, but when they got into the light he saw tears in her eyes. Annie took him by the lapels, pulled him against her behind a tree, and said into his face a line, or two lines, of a poem. He had known it was poetry by its rhythm, but was too shocked by her face to remember it; and as it was the last time he saw her, he had never learned its significance, either for himself or her. Freda tried to coax it from his memory. 'If you could remember even one word.' He could. It was 'pleasure'.

They repeated it together, smiling. It could not have been intended like that, as a gift, a word so welcome to them both.

Linda's presence was implicit in these stories, but Owen was never tempted to admit her. It was always later, when he was alone, that he pondered on her part. Deeply affected by the tears and rages and fisticuffs following that first detection, Annie and he had retreated into their marriages, repudiating their right to inflict such pain. Freda, saying so promptly on the phone, 'All right, I will, I'll come,' reminded him of how he had gone out one night to the chemist, and on an impulse had rung Annie from a callbox. She had come at once, out of breath, and they had spent the following hours walking round the streets, desperately talking. Chilled by a westerly wind, they had seen their faces, bleached, coarse, and exhausted, under fluorescent lights. At midnight each went home to deliver their decision. Linda had responded with the revelation of her pregnancy; and Annie, when Owen reversed his decision the next day, gave a cry, pulled him to her against that tree, and said those words he had forgotten.

Linda had had three children in three years – nailing him, he had thought in the bad times, with the birth of each dear child. Yet look how the loving photographs disproved it, and celebrated the good times. He shook them out of their folders and took them to the light. Here he stood beside Linda, who cooed at Hester in her arms, while Blanche and Timothy sat on the shaved grass at their feet. How contentedly he smiled. How right Linda had been to accuse him of sneakiness and hypocrisy. His hostility had cannily retreated, had become a resolve hidden so deep that its occasional exposure could be mistaken for a flash of intuition, saying, This won't last. Only Linda's inheritance of money, making his resolve practically possible, had brought it into the open.

He could even wonder, now, if her recent accusation – that he had left her for another woman – was a blind thrust in the right direction, though he had been as blind as she.

One day he saw her coming out of a restaurant in Paddington, with a man, she happily stumping in her heels, while the man, in spite of the paunch indicated by Hester, glided. Hester's waddle was a slander; this fat man was graceful and strong. He opened the door of a silver Volvo, and Linda got in, settled herself with the preening and fidgeting so familiar to Owen, while the man glided swiftly round to the driver's side, grinning to himself. He sat down, gave a couple of bumps in his seat, and they drove off.

Owen, his philosophical impartiality shattered, watched them with a dour amusement. It suited him that she should be happy, yet he felt defrauded. In flight from her noisy heartbreak, he had thrown money into her path, he had thrown suffering into her path; he could have spared himself a little of both.

The incident also revealed to him how easily intimacy is detected in the most conventional of gestures. The next time he was walking beside Freda, and caught an inquisitive look from the eyes of a familiar passer-by, a park habitué, he saw himself and Freda through that woman's eyes: the uxorious couple, secretive yet bold, with foolish smiles and wavering steps. He took Freda's arm, above the elbow, and caressed it beneath the sleeve. 'You are doing it again,' she said with a lilt.

'Because it's the last time,' he said. 'We have been silly. Or we want to advertise it. Why else are we always saying we must meet here less often, and be more careful when we do, then not doing it? Now we must.'

She nodded vehemently. He released her arm. They stopped at the harbour wall. She pointed. 'See that. You don't often see those. That was designed and made in Holland.' And in the same informative tone she went on. 'You asked me once if I enjoyed the precautions. You will know me better by now. I know some people like all that, the precautions and complications, but I've always hated them. That's why I tried to make myself good at the planning, and the strategy. But lately I seem to have lost my ability. I need to get it back, because it protects me from what I'm bad at – standing up and telling direct lies.'

'It's your face, you know,' he said. 'It shows everything.' It seemed unnatural to be talking to her like this, while standing apart and pretending to be interested in a boat. 'You don't know yourself what your face shows,' he said.

By early December the drought had advanced even on the park, parching the grass and turning inward the big leaves of the native fig trees, so that those trees looked bronze above their iron-grey trunks. Another park bench was thrown in the water, but upside-down, its jagged concrete feet sticking up, it lacked pictorial charm. Owen and Freda seldom went to the park, and when they did, they left for his flat by different routes, making remarks about strategy. An interview with Hester appeared in the *Sydney Morning Herald*. In a big photograph, she smiled broadly, with one arm around Denise, who still looked shy. Owen cut it out to send to Timothy. Timothy would remember how Hester used to display that tight wide smile when she was very angry. He included a short letter to say that he had got most of the information Timothy had asked for, and would have time over the Christmas break to assemble it. He did not quite take it for granted that Rex would be home for Christmas, but was waiting for Freda to mention it.

One evening he answered his doorbell and saw her there. She had never appeared unexpectedly before, but she did not respond to the interrogation in his eyes as he silently drew her in and shut the door. She let the bag slip from her shoulder and complained of the heat. Her forehead shone with sweat and the armpits of an old brown dress were wet. She had walked over. Brown leather sandals, of the kind children wear, exposed dusty toes. He was moved by her dishevelment and heat, by the suggestion given that she had come hurrying over in her strong need; but she resisted his embrace, turning her head petulantly aside and saying that she must have a shower. He said, 'Of course,' but he felt that an ideal moment had passed. He washed up his dinner things while she showered, and when they went to bed, lying in the hot air with the light off and the window open, he could not recover the impulse. She said, 'Can't we just lie here? 'Of course,' he said again. He got up and fetched a fresh sheet which he spread over them both, and for the first time since they had become lovers, he felt bored by her presence.

'Do I snore?' he asked her suddenly, for they often went briefly to sleep. She said she didn't know, herself sounding bored. He separated his body from hers, explaining it was for coolness, and must have gone immediately to sleep. He was awakened by her hands moving very tenderly over his body, and then her mouth, in small sucking movements. He did not feel quite awake. It was so voluptuous, yet so simple and natural, that it seemed partly a dream. Believing or pretending that it was a dream, he did not move until the last moments, when in absolute silence and certainty he raised himself on to her body. They may have slept again. He remembered saying quietly, 'Don't go home, my love,' and her reply from the darkness. 'I really can't.' But when he woke very early in the morning she had gone. She must have dressed in the bathroom, where the light would not disturb him, washing her pubic cleft and the insides of her thighs, undulating as she drew on her briefs, waving her raised hands into the sleeves of her dress, sitting on the toilet lid to fasten her sandals. The only evidence left was the towel flung down, the washcloth wrung out. He remembered occasions when he had left sleeping women, and wondered if he had seemed to them, as they stood in some doorway, to have been a visitant.

He met her in the park on the following afternoon. She had a dog with her, a white bull terrier on a leash. He was jubilant and aggressive. 'Whose is it?' he asked her. 'That creature?'

'Not ours,' she said, laughing.

To hide his chagrin at her 'ours', Owen bent to pat the dog. The dog looked at him with small, pink-rimmed, humble eyes, and did not move his tail. 'I don't like the breed,' said Owen.

'He's just fully grown,' said Freda. 'Aren't you?' she asked the dog, in her fond voice.

'I might have known you would sneak off,' said Owen. 'What are you doing walking the brute, if he's not yours?'

'A man from the country came and left him with me. He's collecting him before Christmas.'

'You'll be stuck with him. It will be like my beds.'

'It won't be. He's very valuable. Aren't you, Gus? Aren't you very valuable and well-bred?'

'Gus. What a name. It suits him.'

'His kennel name is Kirraweena Spartacus. But he gets called Gus.'

'Gus. And today you're lumbered with Gus, so you can't come home with me.'

'I'm menstruating, in any case.'

'Women who put themselves down like that! As if they had only one function. Go and lock the dog up, and while you're doing that, I'll buy food, and we'll have a long unhurried dinner.'

'With the blinds drawn.'

'That's for your sake, Freda, as much as mine. More. Yes, definitely more.'

'That's true,' she said, looking away.

'Look, you don't want to come, just say so.'

'Well, Owen, I don't.'

'Good.' He put the affable mask of the fair go over his offendedness. 'I'll walk with you a little way.'

They walked over the bridge, the dog, on a shortened lead, obedient on her other side. 'Only ten days till the Christmas break,' said Owen. 'What are you doing?'

'I don't know.' Her voice became cool and formal, as always when Rex Thewen presented his shadow. Owen thought it could even be called dutiful. 'I haven't heard what's happening yet,' she said.

She was entitled to her moods; he did not want to become importunate. For three days he did not go to the park. He spent the late afternoons in crowded shops, buying Christmas presents. A week before Christmas Day, Blanche rang him.

'Dad, we've been thinking. Christmas Day is a problem.'

'No problem so far as I'm concerned, my dear. You'll be going to your mother's. I'll be truthful – I've always been a secret curmudgeon about Christmas Day. I can tell you now. I've sat there, in that house, with tinsel in my hair, playing Mastermind, and wishing I were somewhere else. And that's where I'll be this Christmas Day.'

'Not in that flat, daddy.'

'What's wrong with it? But no, I'm likely to be right here in this office, writing the letter I've been promising Tim. Is your mother asking Fatty and his litter to Christmas dinner?'

Blanche laughed briefly and spoke curtly. 'Yes, dad, she is. Justin and I are trying to get on with them. Don't make it harder. Hester, of course – speaking of curmudgeons – says no thanks, she would rather work.'

Owen was consoled – and simultaneously surprised that he needed consolation – for his exclusion. 'It isn't that we don't appreciate the urgency of her work,' Blanche was saying, 'but with Tim away, we do think she might have spared that much of her time. Justin and I have just about had Hes. Mum asked Rex and Freda too, but they can't come, so Justin and I are going to them on Boxing Day.'

'Now what made me think,' said Owen, 'that Rex Thewen was in the country.'

'He was. He is. But he'll be back by then.'

Owen, tangled in his web, could not ask when she had learned this. He would go to the park that afternoon.

'What I'm saying, daddy,' said Blanche, 'is that that ties us up for both days. And on the twenty-seventh we're going to Seal Rocks until the New Year. So, dad, unless you would like to come to the Thewens on Boxing Day – Justin has asked them to ask you, you live quite close – unless you do that, we won't see you until the New Year.'

'I can't think of a better time,' said Owen. 'Boxing Day's out. I'm going to the mountains to see mum. Mention that to Justin, would you? And we'll make it the New Year. Let me take you both to dinner.'

'All right.' Then Blanche said flatly, 'I'm sorry, dad.'

'Blanche. There's no need to apologize.'

'I'm not apologizing. I'm saying I'm sorry. Which is quite different. I'm sorry you had to leave mum. I know you did have to, or you couldn't have done it, but I'm still sorry. I didn't know Christmas would make me feel like this, feel so bleak. Don't you feel a bit bleak, really, at us being up there, and you down here alone?'

'I did feel a bit excluded when you first mentioned it, Blanche. But bleak, no.'

'Well, I do. And I feel inadequate, as if I've failed mum and you in some way. It's better to say this than to let it boil inside. No wonder they're going to destroy the whole world when so many of the people in it can't even keep faith with *one person*, can't even keep *one promise*.'

Owen tried to say that in fact he kept most of his promises, but Blanche would not let him finish.

'Can't keep the promises that are really *hard* to keep. Justin and I are never going to get divorced. We have sworn it. Rex and Freda have both been married before, and when they married each other, they swore, they made a vow, that whatever happened, this one was going to stick. So that's just what Justin and I have sworn. *Whatever happens*.'

Owen was silently addressing Freda. Well, my sweet love, here comes the clutter. He said to Blanche, 'That's very idealistic, dear, but not impossible. And I hope you and Justin make it come true, as Justin's mother evidently has. Did she tell Justin all this when he was about to marry?'

'No, years ago, when he was only a boy, and angry with his father. And he said he thought it was irrational, and she said yes, that's why there has to be a vow.'

'I see her reasoning, though it's not mine. And I'm glad you said what you felt you had to say. I agree, it's better than letting it boil. But I'm at work, my dear.'

'Dad, I'm on your direct line.'

'Yes, but I'm very busy.'

She gave a sharp sigh, almost a gasp. 'Okay, dad. Justin is dropping in your present during the week. Happy Christmas. See you in the New Year.'

Again Owen and Freda halted when they met, and again the dog stood between them. 'I thought his owner was calling for him,' said Owen.

'Now it's to be after Christmas.'

Owen could not help searching her face, as if expecting her to look different now that he knew more about her, but she looked just the same, smiling at him, then down at the dog. 'Is there a key or something,' he asked, 'to wind him up?'

'There is, almost. I could show you. Why are you looking at me like that?'

'I'm trying to find something extraordinary about you.'

She drew back her head, laughing. 'Why?'

'To justify my feeling for you. And because Christmas is coming. And I'm afraid you'll stop seeing me. When is Rex coming home?'

Her shutter of duty descended. 'That's what I came down to tell you. Do you have time to walk a little way?'

The presence of the dog gave her a disciplined air; she walked with shorter quicker steps. 'Rex will be home tonight,' she said, 'or even this afternoon.'

'I know it's not sudden,' said Owen, 'but it feels like it.'

'Not to me, of course.'

'I must have hoped something would happen to stop it.'

'Clive is coming with him. They've sold the place.'

'That seems sudden, too.'

'They've been negotiating for a while. At the end, it was sudden.'

'So they – he – Rex – will be here indefinitely?'

'Clive will be going back for a while.'

'So it's over?'

'Why ask?'

'You're quite sure?'

'Yes, Owen, and so are you.'

'Freda, I'm not. I'll wait and see what happens.'

'Don't.'

Her certainty was impressive. He glanced at her, but she looked straight ahead. The dog walked fast and neatly at her side. Owen protruded his head and looked at the animal across her body. 'He's an extraordinarily dull looking brute,' he said in a mock-grumbling tone, to make her smile.

She did smile. 'Not always. Wait a minute, and I'll show you something.'

'Like you once showed me that bench in the water. Freda, that promise we made, that agreement we tacitly made, to stop when Rex came back, it seems such a long time ago.'

'It wasn't a promise, or an agreement. It was a condition.'

'Oh, I beg your pardon, madam.'

'Oh, stop it, Owen.'

'Yes, madam.'

She said stiffly, 'I am looking forward to seeing Rex.'

'That is perfectly natural, madam.'

'Oh, hell,' she said, half-laughing. They had reached a part of the park, not much used, bound by the road, the harbour wall, and the high blank brick wall of the yacht club. Freda bent a knee to release Gus from the leash. The dog moved off a few paces, then stood docilely. 'Are you sure he's not a very small cow?' murmured Owen. 'Watch,' said Freda. She took a yellow tennis ball from her bag and held it aloft. 'Gus,' she whispered.

The dog was instantly charged with tension and power. Perfectly still and intent, he watched only the yellow ball. Freda threw it; he sped with it.

'He's certainly fast,' said Owen.

'I told you.'

'You would come if you really wanted to.'

'I'll put it like this. I will really want to, but I won't come.'

'I'll just have to accept it then.'

The dog had twisted to catch the ball before it reached the ground, and was now racing back. She bent to receive the ball, and rose again to throw it. 'I suppose this is what he was bred for,' she said, 'this and fighting. I hate commercial dog breeding.'

He was nettled by this casual way of closing the subject. 'Is that another of the things you've done, you and Rex?'

'No, it isn't,' she said, in cold warning.

The dog returned the ball; she threw it again. He said, 'You mean we can't even meet like this, here? That's absurd. That's childish.'

'It isn't. It's too early to be friends again. Justin suggested that we ask you to lunch on Boxing Day—'

'Blanche told me—'

'—and I just panicked. It's too soon. I would show something. I would give it away.'

The dog, having dropped the ball, gave a brief high whimper of impatience, almost of anguish. 'I'll just have to accept it, then,' said Owen again. He picked up the ball, threw it hard, and watched with his hands on his hips as the dog retrieved it. Now he did not believe in Freda's resolve. If she could not help but show her feelings, how could she help but come? She would stop, he thought, for a while; then she would wander down here to the park, and they would meet as they had before, neither quite by accident nor quite by design. That was the way things went. 'Good *dog*,' he said with enthusiasm, when Gus dropped the ball at his feet.

So sure that it was not over, Owen was happy, sometimes exuberantly happy, without her. Now he could cherish an essential Freda unperplexed by her presence; now he had time to catch up on his neglected obligations. Though the anti-nuclear movement at large was suspended for the holidays, activity continued, and now Owen had time to confer with his printer Carl Alpino about the leaflets needed for next February and March. He had time to assemble the information he had gathered for Timothy, and get it ready for his letter on

Christmas Day. And he had time to go to the pub after work to drink with his draughtsman Charlie Hill. Charlie Hill had been truculent with him since his separation, and in the pub he said, still with a trace of this surliness, 'You're looking well on it, Owen. These days you're even verging on the good-looking.'

'I feel well, Charlie.'

Patting himself for the cigarettes he had given up, Charlie appraised Owen with care. He was over sixty, and had worked for Owen's grandfather. Slowly the surliness gave way to his ingenuous look. 'Tell you what, dad,' he said. 'Wouldn't mind a divorce myself.'

'You're having me on,' said Owen obediently.

'Honest to God, son, I'm not.' Charlie tossed back his head to take a long draught of beer from which he emerged with incredulous eyes. 'It's so easy. No adultery, cruelty, desertion, all that. Nobody's fault now. Breakdown of marriage pure and simple. Just sit out the twelve months. Lovely. If it had been like that twenty years ago, when I was into all that other nooky, would have been into it like a shot.'

'Are you glad you didn't, Charlie?'

'What, glad? Yeah, yeah, sure, son, sure I'm glad. Nothing the matter with Carol. Got married to someone else, sure to have, caught by the old short hairs, would have turned out the same in the long run. And money. Carol being a non-earner, and nothing to speak of in the inheritance line, putting the knife down the middle would have made us both poor. Whereas now we're comfortable. Very comfortable. Fond of each other, anyway. Once you're stuck, know you're stuck, no alternative, you look for the good points. So do they, so do they. All this to say nothing of the progeny. Different for you and Linda, Owen. I see that now, seeing you both looking so well on it. Carol tells me after the divorce Linda's thinking of saddling up for another run. How about you?'

'A dilemma, Charlie. I can't imagine wanting to marry again, and I can't imagine life without a woman.'

'You got a few dollars, plenty of it about. Quality stuff, too.'

'I don't mean that kind.' Owen smiled in accustomed tribute to all Charlie's energetic and deadpan tales of his whoring, his truth disguised in billows of grotesquerie. 'I mean without one particular woman.'

'Linda's right, then. You've found her already.'

'Linda's not right.'

'Keep it on, son. You did say particular.'

'I guess I meant one apart. I meant important.'

'That's what you want, you'll have to marry her. They still want it, you know, still want to be married. Look at your Blanche, our Michele. To hell with marriage, all that ancient stuff, look at them now. Of course you could get one that's married already, gives you a bit on the side.'

'I don't think I want that either. I may hate her husband.'

'Wife of an international pilot or a polar scientist. Of course you wouldn't, you'd love him. Or maybe an old chap who's past it.'

Owen shook his head, trying to laugh.

'Or who's had his cock cut off or something. No? Then tell you what, son, you've got problems.'

'Not yet.'

'Will have.'

'I'll deal with them when they come up.'

'That's the shot, dad. Day at a time. Nothing's ever all roses. Happy Christmas, Owen.'

On Christmas Day, in his office, Owen wrote his long letter to Timothy. He had set himself up with food, wine, and taped music that sounded extravagantly fine in the empty building. In the late afternoon, as the last vibration of an unaccompanied cello died away, he thought he heard a thin cry from the street. Incredulously he hurried to the window. But it was Hester. He saw her pale upturned face, and her foreshortened body making a stumpy L with her dark simple shadow.

He ran down the stairs to admit her. 'Why on earth didn't you ring?'

'Oh,' she said vaguely, 'I came to say thanks for the cassette.'

'Come on up. I thought you might like it. Satie.'

'I haven't played it yet.'

He smelled the marijuana. 'You've been smoking.'

'One or two. It sort of doesn't do much for me any more.'

'Well, come on up.'

On the stairs he put an arm round her, feeling the articulation of the shoulder joint beneath his hand. He thought of patting the head of the dog Gus, and how the cranium was definable under the slithering skin. He thought of his fingers seeking the curve of Freda's arm, under her sleeve. He shook Hester's shoulder. 'You're too thin,' he said, 'even by your own standards, surely? I've food here. Come and eat.'

'How you and Tim,' she said in his office, riffling through his thick letter, 'can keep on getting thrills from all that stuff. The way you pounce on every detail, like grabbing diamonds.'

'Have one of these. It's a piroski, or Russki pie.'

'I don't want anything.' She started to wander about the room, her heels making indecisive taps.

'I thought you were working today.'

'I couldn't be bothered.'

'Then shouldn't you have gone up to the house?'

'They'll all be playing football.'

She looked a little livelier when he laughed; but she said, 'I can't seem to care about work any more. I don't really care about anything.'

'If you don't care about anything, and you still remember your layout, you might as well come sometime and give Carl and me a hand.'

'On that anti-nuke stuff? No thanks.'

'Ungrateful girl. We're doing it for you.'

'Don't bother.'

'It's funny how you and Blanche and Tim got me into it, then all marched off and left me there.'

'Too bad.'

'Indifference is the deadliest sin.'

'Yah.'

She tapped weakly about, looking into the other rooms, then came back to where Owen sat at his desk, stolidly chewing. 'I used to love it here when granddad was alive. The smell, the bare boards, everything about it.'

'It hasn't changed much.'

'I have.'

'Not so much, dear. Even then you used to have low angry moods.'

'This is different. That was because nobody loved me *best.*'

'Have some of this wine. It's good.'

'I don't want any.'

'Just as well, since you've been smoking.'

She picked up his glass and sniffed it. 'All right. I will have some.'

'Not much,' he said, pouring it. 'I'm glad you came to see me, Hes. Come to Gran's with me tomorrow.'

'You mean she isn't burnt to a cinder yet? She said she was going to get burnt to a cinder.'

'Bushfires aren't funny when they happen, Hes.'

'Am I laughing?'

'I admit you're not.' Now that she sat opposite him, he was trying, without making it too obvious, to check on the pupils of her eyes. She suddenly leaned across the desk and propped her eyelids open with thumbs and forefingers. 'Okay,' he said with relief. 'Will you come to Gran's?'

'No thanks. I hate being around geriatrics. There are too many of them. The men aren't too bad, but I can't stand the women.'

'You'll be like them one day.'

'Do you really think so?'

'What *are* you doing tomorrow?'

'Mind your own business, dad. I'm not Blanchie-wanchie. I don't need your tender loving concern. She rang me about Boxing Day. She said would I go with Justin and her to Justin's parents' place. I said no thanks. I was polite though. Polite for Christmas. I didn't say I've never liked Justin, even when they were in Leichhardt pretending not to be straight, or that I don't like his drunk old father either, or his skinny little pasty mother.'

'Pasty?'

'Yes, and she has a *perm.*'

'You're making this up.'

'No, and she wears *navy blue.* I would rather be dead than wear navy blue.'

'You see an option. You're reviving.'

'I do feel better. I always do when I've been right down, isn't it funny. I bet I have a good day tomorrow. Barry and I were in a bus once and we heard a woman say, "I think I'll wear the navy," and we were just getting over that when we heard the other one say, "I always like you in the navy."'

'Have you heard from Barry?'

'Indirectly. He's in jail.'

'In jail in Turkey?'

'No, in Naples, as it happens.'

'That's not quite so bad. Is it?' asked Owen in alarm. 'Is that quite so bad?'

'His father's gone to get him out. Barry used to say his father had Mafia connections. I hope he wasn't only boasting. I love Barry.'

'What was that word?'

'Don't try to be funny, dad. You heard me. I love Barry.'

'He's homosexual, isn't he?'

'That's totally irrelevant. I love Barry. I've unpicked it. I've cut it to pieces. I've trampled on it. I've chucked it out of the window and stuffed it into the bushes. And it always comes out the same, fresh as ever. I love Barry.'

One of his confessional moods came over Owen, making him want to say, 'And I love that pasty woman you recently mentioned.' He wished he had the right to say it, and that it wasn't Freda's secret as well as his own, or that he had no such scruples. He got up and shut the window. 'Then I hope his father gets him out. Is there anything I can do?'

'Apart from driving me home, no. You're too respectable to have the connections. And you don't even have much money.'

'True. But I'll find money if you need it. And I'll drive you wherever you want to go. I'm glad you came to see me, Hes.'

'I'm moderately glad, dad.'

Owen's mother's guests strolled into her garden carrying covered plates and icy bottles and speaking loudly or in exhausted gratitude of 'Hazel's oasis'. They flopped into the striped chairs under the camphor laurels and as Owen served them drinks he heard them tell each other that the smoke seen earlier over the Kurrajong was only an isolated fire. They had rung up. It was well under control.

'Everything under control. Oh, thank you. Cheers.'

'We're in luck again.'

'Don't say it aloud.'

'Cheers. Oh, that's lovely.'

All lived in the neighbourhood. There were fourteen apart from Hazel Thorbury and Owen. Two were middle-aged, two were young, two were children, and eight were old. Owen wished he could forget Hester's remarks, which fed his own surreptitious feeling that there really were too many of them. But as the long lunch went on he carried his plate and glass into their company rather than linger with the young and middle-aged, whom Hester would not have liked either, for they were conventional and stiff, perhaps even shy, whereas the old people had abandoned such precautions and presented themselves boldly. Their references to the Staggerers' Club, which all claimed they belonged to (though some only as associate members, and Hazel Thorbury only as a guest) embarrassed their juniors, and seeing this, they covertly warned each other to stop.

The wise children had taken their food and Christmas games and made a private picnic in the shade beside the old stables.

The oldest of the old was a man Owen had not met before. 'You're Hazel's son,' he said. He spoke as if on a burble of inner laughter. 'Bill. My name's Bill. I'm ninety. Ninety. My wife died in July.'

Owen said he was sorry, though Bill did not seem to be. 'Were you married for long?'

'Not long. She married me out of pity,' said Bill with his amusement, 'when the blacks took away my tea plantation in Ceylon.'

He was a very handsome old man, with fine bony features beneath his limp rag hat, and a great wiry yellowish moustache bursting from his upper lip.

'Sri Lanka they call it now. They owe me two hundred thousand dollars. I'll never get it.'

'A magnificent island,' remarked Owen.

'Was. They've made a mess of it.'

'You've been back?'

'I wouldn't go back if they paid me.'

'Not even two hundred thousand dollars?'

A bit of the laughter escaped. 'I might go back for that. Might. What would I spend it on? I've got everything I want, got the pension. The Ceylonese won't work, you know. They lie down under a tree. We had to bring in the Tamils.' He looked intently at Owen, distending inflamed eyelids, his grey eyes clear and childish. 'Had to bring in the Tamils.'

'Was it a good life?' asked Owen.

'A good life? Suppose it was, in some ways. No society. No society. That's why the chaps got hold of those black women.'

He had caught the attention of the adjacent group, which included Owen's mother, and these he now included in his innocent-eyed scanning. 'A bachelor. Used to go down to Colombo sometimes, when the P & O ships came in, looking for a bride.'

'You can't have looked far, Bill,' said Hazel Thorbury.

'I was in one of those ships,' said another woman.

'Weren't we all,' said a man.

'I was in one of those ships,' said a woman in big dark glasses, who had drunk too much, 'in nineteen thirty-eight.'

'I saw you, Bill,' said Owen's mother. 'I remember it now.'

Bill started a vibration of laughter as he looked at her.

'Yes!' said Hazel Thorbury. 'You were that handsome planter, disgustingly drunk, two tables away at The Golden Face.'

Under a chorus of 'The Golden Face!' Owen heard Bill's laughter come out and burble through his words. 'The Golden Face. Might well have been. Well have been. Yes, that's where the chaps ended up. The Golden Face.'

After the young and middle-aged had left, taking the children, the old began trailing away, kissing, making provisional arrangements, saying that they were tipsy, or drunk, or soberer than some judges they could name, coming back in a drama of ashamedness for things left behind, declaring that this time they were really going. Bill, quivering with his laugh after kissing Owen's mother, put a greyish, sere hand in Owen's for a moment before shuffling off with bent knees between the last couple to leave.

'Crypto-fascist?' said Hazel Thorbury. 'He wouldn't know what you were talking about. I hardly know myself. Crypto means secret. A secret fascist. What nonsense, Owen. And in any case, what does it matter, at his age?'

'I didn't say he was dangerous.'

'I should hope not. He's a dear old feller.'

Owen had helped his mother to clean up before retreating with her into the coolest part of the house, this sitting room shaded by the roof of the verandah. She sat by the window, her big strong legs crossed and her head bent to her crochet work. Owen sat by the fireplace, which was full of potted ferns. The long hot relaxed day had brought on his confessional mood. He was with the one person he could trust with his and Freda's story, and having seen her so free with her friends, he was tempted away from his knowledge that in spite of some concessions, she was as prudish as she was scrupulous. To reduce his blood alcohol level to below .05, he was drinking glasses of ice and water from a jug on the hearth. Awaiting the right time to speak, he rotated his glass for the cool idle tinkling of the ice.

'Bill asked me to marry him,' said Hazel.

'He wants to get hold of of a white woman,' said Owen, moving his glass and laughing.

She raised her crochet work to the window. 'I am making this for Blanche.'

'You've seen Blanche?'

'No. But she rings. She said she would love a lace table cloth. I always knew she would come out of that Bohemian phase. Perhaps one day she would even like my things.'

The things, mahogany and walnut and cedar, gleamed all through the shady house, and cast gentle shadows into the polished floor.

'Her Justin seems a nice boy, and organic chemistry must be a coming thing, since I don't even know what it is. They sent me a gardening book for Christmas. There it is beside you. More colour than use. Hester didn't even ring. Some people never do come out of that Bohemian phase. I got a lovely long letter from Tim, the dear boy. What a good thing he got away before you left. Poor little Linda would have suffocated him, whereas when she had nobody to cling to, look at the way she struck out for herself.'

'Got hold of a fat feller,' said Owen, laughing again.

'Mothers ought to be prepared to stand off from their sons, and let them go.'

'As it happens,' said Owen, alert for the first time, 'I know a woman who would agree with you. And she says when you do that, they become perfectly indifferent to you. And some time after that, according to her, you become indifferent to them.'

'Really? I dislike people who talk like that. And so far as I am concerned, that's simply not true. Are you perfectly indifferent to me, dear?'

'You know I'm not, mum,' said Owen, rejecting her touch of the sardonic. It was so slight.

'Well, there you are,' said Hazel. She drew in her chin so that she could focus on him through the top portion of her bifocals, then set to work again and said absently, 'What are those Thewens *like?*'

Owen reached down for the jug of water. His confessional mood was broken. When he was a boy, the only child of his widowed mother, he had become used to her ability to lightly (and, he was sure, unconsciously) reach out and touch his thoughts. Sometimes she would merely touch, but at other times he knew he was opposed. While cooking, or taking clothes from the line, or washing up while he dried (especially then), she would remark that little Lynette What's-her-name had a pretty figure but was very common, or that Owen's history master was a good steady man, or that those modern American novelists were coarse beyond belief. He poured water and said, 'I don't really know what the Thewens are like. You've met them yourself.'

'I was given my inspection, yes. He seemed very dull, and she struck me as captious.'

'Captious.'

'Only an impression.'

'I wonder if anyone's ever said that about me,' mused Owen.

'They seem to have no background.'

'There's been a lot of social mobility in the last few decades, mum. Backgrounds have got smudged. Justin's the only Thewen who need concern you and me. And we both like Justin. Is Justin captious?'

She rested her work and again retracted her chin to hold him in focus, looking so stern that he nervously awaited something like, 'That woman is your mistress.' He said, 'I'm probably about .02 by now,' while his mother said, 'Stop mocking, dear. And I hope you won't mock when I tell you I have not refused Bill.'

Owen sat back in his chair. He said truthfully, 'I am too amazed to mock.'

She still looked stern. 'He is a gentleman.'

'He is ninety.'

'And so sweet-smelling.'

Owen was moved, his own unreasonable partiality letting him see how the shaky desiccated old man could appeal to this pink robust woman. He said, 'Mum, you are twenty years younger. You would destroy the rest of your pleasant life.'

She took up her lace again, and bent over it, working slowly. 'Well, I haven't done it yet.'

'No, and you won't, will you? He's alert enough, but he's very feeble. He can hardly walk.'

'I told him he could be president of the Staggerers' Club. He liked that.'

'You amuse each other. I know the way it is. But you could keep that up without marrying.'

'There need be no disturbance of my estate.'

'Mum—'

213

'I'm sorry, dear. You were never mercenary. Even as a small boy you were not. That's where Tim gets it. Oh, I don't know, it's my own fault, for isolating myself up here. It was the garden, the bulbs and elms and ashes that don't grow down there. And it was lovely when the children were young and came to stay. I've never been busier in my life. But then they grew up, and my city friends got older, and didn't like the long drive, and couldn't get used to the train. So I had to make the best of the geographically possible.'

'As you are doing with this man.'

'True. But isn't that true of most people who take up with someone?'

'It may begin like that,' admitted Owen.

'And who am I keeping these floors polished for, I would like to know. And my things. I might as well share them now with someone who feels like I do about them. Bill said, straight away, 'Now those are what I call *good* things,' and I felt I wouldn't at all mind him shuffling around the house all day. But you're right. When you take up seriously with some-one, there are always repercussions of some kind. It's the stone in the pond, isn't it? Yes, better to keep it to the amuse-ment. Besides, there's that silly sort of modesty that takes over in old age. Not that there would have been any physical intimacy, of course. But one would have had to remember to put one's dressing gown on before going to the bathroom at night. Boring little things like that.'

Owen was free until Thorbury Maps opened early in the New Year. The tasks that had worried him were done, but the leisure he had looked forward to was hollowed by the kind of boredom he had not experienced since adolescence, when unexpressed expectation had made it seem useless to settle to anything. The intense heat brought humidity but no rain. He intended each day to surf, but his disabling boredom kept him in his flat, torpid and irresolute, deciding to drive to Bondi or Coogee, then leaving it until too late in the day to start.

Each evening with sudden energy he went to the park, walking fast and deliberately, as he had done at first, but Freda did not appear. Perhaps the Thewens, like Blanche and Justin, like Carl Alpino and his family, had gone south or north to the beaches. The second park bench was taken away. In the long hot evenings the marina was very busy, the shops open, the cars coming and going, the shining boats rocking and tinkling. The white daytime moon hung above the masts in the pale sky; seagulls flew low or minced in groups on the parched grass; on the playing fields cricket was played on a brown pitch. Tomorrow, he thought, she would come.

He had bursts of bad temper. Some of the friends Linda and he had had in common, and who had regarded him as a renegade, or had so diplomatically withheld their sympathy, now rang with invitations and with stories of Linda's 'great' or 'splendid' recovery. 'She had to let it all hang out like that,' one woman said, 'or she wouldn't have got over it at all. You ought to have done the same thing, Owen darling. We all understand that now.'

'Thank you,' said Owen, 'but there was quite enough hullabaloo without that. But I'll let something hang out now, Gretel. I haven't forgiven you. Or Tom or Janis or Will either. You were a bloody kangaroo court.'

Will rang him. 'It was the women, Owen,' he said quietly. 'What a cop-out,' said Owen, hanging up.

Under the shower, he spluttered about Bill. 'The old goat!' He rang his mother, spoke to her cheerfully and sensibly, and told her how busy he was. He rang Hester and asked about Barry. His father had got him out of jail, Hester told him, but Barry had chosen to stay in Naples. Barry had taken a fancy to Naples. Hester had made Denise give up her holidays so that they could start on Hester's new ideas. Holidays were stupid anyway, said Hester.

Unable to sleep at night, he thought less of Freda than of Linda. It seemed incredible that her implacable opposition, which for ten years had towered over him like a cliff face, had crumbled and become nothing at the touch of another man. He devised a way of getting back the record albums she had refused to let him have. He would learn when she was visiting Blanche, then go up to the house – her house – open the laundry window, where he knew the catch was weak, climb in . . . He refined it each time; he perfected it; he almost convinced himself that he would do it.

He turned his anger against himself, and on the last morning of the holidays, disgusted, he sullenly collected his surfing gear, banged the door of his flat, and drove to Bondi. The thundering water and splintering light he had once found so exhilarating now brought chaos to his head, but as he drove away he felt cleansed and light. He drove past Carl Alpino's house, but that big and welcoming household had not yet brought itself back.

He plotted to ring the Thewens, and whoever answered, to name himself and ask if they knew when Blanche and Justin were coming back from Seal Rocks. He mocked himself out of this juvenile ploy, then chose another, equally juvenile, and drove past the building they lived in. He had not imagined it as a shabby pink duplex standing in a quiet wide street. When he turned his eyes back to the road, and the red Mitsubishi coming from the other direction, he saw Freda at the wheel. Rex Thewen sat beside her, smaller and more slumped and square than Owen remembered, his head inclined backwards to listen to a man who leaned forward from the back seat. When Freda saw Owen her eyes blazed for a moment with the longing and panic he felt in his own unmoving face.

He knew she would come to the park the next afternoon. He had returned to work; Blanche and Justin were back from Seal Rocks. He ran down the steep steps, full of energy and optimism, and saw her coming from the other side. She was leading the dog Gus, and as Owen and she approached each other she gave her attention to the dog rather than meet Owen's eyes. He noticed with amusement that the background of her printed dress was indeed navy blue, and that it was fairly accurate to call her pasty. He would not agree that she was unreasonably captious. Just short of meeting him she turned instead and walked distractedly to the harbour wall. He followed. 'So you've still got him,' he said gently.

She shrugged and laughed, looking down at the dog.

'I told you it would be like my beds.'

'Now we think that man just wanted to unload him, and that Kirraweena Spartacus may not be his name at all.'

She spoke in her light informative voice, the voice of her small talk. He wanted to burst out in protest against it, but he saw that her shoulders were depressed, and that she was giving him a look of tiredness or helplessness. So he spoke as gently as before. 'I don't know a thing about canine pedigrees.'

'Neither do I,' she said, relieved that he was playing her game. 'But Clive does. And Clive says a bull terrier's head should be egg-shaped, but that Gus has a forehead, which is quite wrong. And so are the pink splodges on his nose. And his claws are the wrong colour. And he's too docile.'

'He failed his birth examination,' said Owen patiently.

'Poor thing. I walk him every day.'

'Not here, you don't.'

'No, in the other park. And I let him retrieve whenever I can. You can see he's overweight. Rex and Clive keep giving him food, and laughing when he gobbles it all up.'

Owen was alert to this suggestion of cruelty; it had not appeared in the Thewen legend before. 'Are you going to keep him?'

'I want to.'

'What shall we do then? Run away together with the dog?'

She shrugged and laughed again, turning away from the wall, avoiding his eyes. 'I've been living a day at a time. I must walk him.'

They started back towards her side of the park. 'So have I been living a day at a time,' he said. 'But our short-term plans haven't coincided. I've been here every day.'

'Not to see me?'

'Of course to see you.'

'We agreed it was over.'

'We agreed it was too soon to meet as friends.'

'It's still too soon. This is the last time I'll come here. I came today to tell you that.'

'Then come again, and tell me again.'

'So that you can disbelieve me again.'

He did not need her anger to tell him he had sounded teasing and complacent, but he was growing angry himself, and when she said, 'Do I have to swear that I won't come any more?' he replied in a raised voice, 'No, don't swear. You may feel obliged to keep your vow, especially as it's so ridiculous. I've got into this jargonish habit of calling people crypto so-and-so's. I think you're a crypto-Christian.'

'And what are you?'

'Oh,' he said, trying now to make her smile, 'it's jargon I only use about other people.'

She did not smile. They had reached the area near the high blank wall of the yacht club. She took a tennis ball from her bag but held it concealed from Gus. Owen laughed when the dog gave a groan and slumped at her feet. She had bent a knee to release him, but instead she rose swiftly to her height.

'Owen, we'll meet one day, when our families make it necessary, and when that happens, it mustn't be like this. You imagine we are standing here talking like casual friends. You say I can't hide anything, but do you think you're any better? Yesterday. Your face.'

Her eyes filled with tears. 'Your face!' she said again. 'Freda,' he said, feeling tears behind his own eyes as he remembered her face behind the wheel, her panic and longing. But she drew away from his hand. 'Your face! And you drove past deliberately.'

'All right. Yes, I did.'

'Do you want me to break everything up for you?'

'No,' he said, sobered, 'I don't want that.'

'Good. So now our plans do coincide.'

'Freda, let's keep on living a day at a time. You don't know what you'll do, and neither do I.' Taking shape in his mind were the long years of Linda's opposition, then the brief period of its amazing dissolution. 'Things change,' he said, and laughed, as if to demonstrate how lightly, how easily, things could change. 'They change so suddenly.'

'Some things don't.'

'They may. Nobody can tell. Here—' He extended his hand, dropped his voice to persuasion'—let me throw that for Gus.'

Shaking her head, refusing to look at him, she released Gus from the leash, and as the dog pranced backward, and took his expectant stance, she said with casual brutality, 'If it hadn't been you, it would have been someone else.'

'Fine!' shouted Owen. 'Great! Go to hell then.'

As he walked quickly away he heard her cry, 'Gus!' The ball sped past him, and the dog after it. Gus caught it in the air, and as he rushed back with it, Owen, without turning around, stepped out of the way with dainty ostentation to let him pass.

Owen felt depressed, exasperated and glad to be rid of her. When he began to visualise how impulsively she must have turned to throw the ball after him, and to remember the anguish in her voice crying, 'Gus!' he argued that he was self-deluded, as when he had once read commiseration into her silent refusal of the wine. But then he would change course, and become convinced that he had been mistaken neither time, and soon he began to dwell on the last night she had been with him, and to hear her voice coming from the darkness, saying that she really couldn't go home.

He supposed it was simply a lucky physical conjunction that made their sexual encounters so simple yet so satisfying, and in such contrast with their other selves, which he now began to think of as their 'waking' or 'verbal' selves. In their waking or verbal state, they had come close to achieving a social equivalent of that ease at the very first, before the clutter had come, but since then, they had felt innocent and at peace only when they were technically most guilty; and while they were technically most innocent, merely walking in the park, guilt – her guilt – had always intruded, had shaped their movements and dictated the evasive trivia of their speech.

He insisted that the guilt was felt only by her. Fear was all he had felt – fear of Linda's triumph, Blanche's anger and Timothy's disapproval. Hester would not have cared.

Her guilt was personified in Rex Thewen. At first Rex Thewen had been for Owen the man who had sat at his and Linda's dinner table – substantial, genial, and sick – but now the smaller slumped man in the red Mitsubishi beside Freda obliterated the first. 'Do you want me to break everything up for you?' Freda had asked; and Owen now rehearsed replying, 'Yes. Yes, I do.'

In great relief, he said it again and again, aloud. 'Yes, I do. Of course I do.'

She became once more a source of hope and exaltation. His confessional mood came over him again. His mother rang to say she was coming to Sydney for a few days. He asked her to lunch, and considered telling her of his love. He would call it simply that: love. He would name Freda, would explain the unnatural circumstances of her marriage, and reveal that he wanted her to end it, and to marry him. In reply to his mother's instant objections, he would say that Blanche and Justin were adults, and that their susceptibilities could not be forever protected, and that he and Freda also had needs – had rights—

But his mother marched into the restaurant, set her Queen Elizabeth handbag on the table, then leaned across to Owen and told him with a shocked voice but with mirthful eyes that as soon as she had refused Bill, he had gone and asked Monica to marry him. Monica was the one in the big dark glasses. But Monica had refused him too. And Monica didn't even have good things. She had a wicker corner cupboard in her sitting room. So much for Bill's appreciation of good things.

'Old goat.'

'No, no. Poor old feller. Now I suppose he'll shuffle around asking everyone. What a fool I was to consider it for a moment, and to lose even the amusement. I admit I'm feeling slightly humiliated. What a good thing I told no one but you. I had an urge, now and then, to tell one or the other of them. Thank heaven I repressed it.'

'One must talk to someone,' Owen said restlessly.

'It's very kind of you to say so, dear, but really, I think repression is a very good thing. Heavens, there's Viv Bolton. She gets more like Bob Menzies every day. Oh, look, she's coming over.'

Owen didn't look. 'She's not bringing her plate, is she?'

'No, she hasn't ordered yet. You don't mind, do you, dear? I'm sure that nice waiter will bring another chair.'

Owen dared to ring Freda's number, putting a wild trust in his own ingenuity if anyone else should answer. It rang unanswered. He took Blanche and Justin to the promised dinner at a harbourside restaurant. Both were sun-tanned, and so beautiful in their pale cotton garments that he was filled again with that hopeless tenderness and regret. He looked often and intently at Justin, trying to discern in his face more than a shadow of Freda's; and soon Blanche began to look at her husband, too, and to move her bare arm so that it touched his, and to say, 'He *is* rather nice, isn't he?'

'Who are you like, Justin?'

'Mum's father, mum says.'

'How *are* your parents?'

'Okay. Well, dad isn't, but mum is. Mum's going to do a computer course.'

Owen could not have said why this annoyed him. 'Like everyone else,' he said curtly.

'Why shouldn't she, dad?' asked Blanche with surprise.

'Sick of hearing about bloody computers,' grumbled Owen.

They both laughed. 'Sooner or later you'll get them at Thorbury Maps,' said Blanche.

It occurred to Owen that it would make marriage to Freda easier if she could earn a living, but he said, in the grumbling tone expected of him, 'Not while I'm there.'

'It must be great,' said Justin, picking up Blanche's hand and looking at it, 'to own a firm your grandfather started.'

'I've never complained,' said Owen.

'Dad's really sentimental about Thorbury Maps,' said Blanche.

'Would your father have run the place?' asked Justin.

'Not while my grandfather was alive. But anyway, the war got my father first.'

Justin put down Blanche's hand. 'It's a wonder your mother didn't marry again. She must have been how old?'

'Under thirty,' said Owen. He had only one memory of his father. He had opened a door and seen him and his mother walking about naked, and had been so startled that he had always remembered them both as huge – a giant and giantess – and did not afterwards associate that giantess with his mother unless it were with intellectual effort. He could not think of a delicate way of leading the conversation back to Freda. 'Why exactly is your mother doing a computer course?' he asked.

'I guess accountants have to, sooner or later.'

'She's an accountant?'

'That was her initial training.'

'I didn't know that.'

Justin shrugged as if to say, Why should you? Or, It's not important. 'She helps dad in his so-called enterprises,' he said.

Blanche turned down her lips and rolled her eyes. The time when she had considered Rex just great was evidently past. Justin said, 'They've gone down the south coast, to look for something there.'

'A great place, the south coast,' said Owen, pleased by this explanation of the unanswered phone. 'Will they be gone long?'

'Depends on whether dad finds anything.'

'Finds a video shop,' said Blanche, rolling her eyes again.

'You don't approve of that?'

'Not for mum,' said Justin, while Blanche said, 'We think Rex and Clive should do it, if they must, and let Freda do something better.'

'Clive is your father's brother?' asked Owen slyly.

Justin nodded. 'They joined the air force together, and Clive got a hole in the head, and dad didn't, and ever since then, Clive has seen dad through his bad spells, and dad has seen Clive through his.'

'Where does your mother come into it?' asked Owen.

'She's the one who's sensible all the time,' said Justin; and Blanche said admiringly, 'Freda is just so tremendously caring and supportive.'

'Before Christmas,' said Owen, 'I used to see her walking a dog in the park, a dull-looking white brute.'

'You can't mean darling Gus?' cried Blanche. She and Justin leaned together again, laughing. 'How about another bottle of Chardonnay?' said Justin.

'I was thinking of asking them over for a drink,' said Owen, to keep to the subject. 'You too. Maybe not Clive. The five of us.'

'Since dad sold that property,' said Justin, 'it's a brave man who asks him for a drink.'

'What a pity,' said Blanche. 'We could each have sat on the edge of a bed.'

Justin called a waiter and ordered another bottle of Chardonnay. 'If dad doesn't mind?' Blanche warned him. 'This one's on me,' said Justin 'Okay, Owen?'

The restaurant was pleasantly crowded, its noise melodious and convivial. Pity for Freda increased Owen's longing for her, confirmed the depth of his love. He became abstracted, and failed to reply to questions. 'Daddy?' said Blanche. He drew in his gaze from the water and saw her looking at him across the table, her eyes anxious and attentive, and Justin as attentive beside her; and in a moment of mental giddiness, when his senses were caught in the cloud of chattering and clinking and borne up into the warm air, he found himself about to make his confession to *them*. It was for the merest moment. It startled him into sobriety. 'Daddy?' said Blanche anxiously again. He said he didn't feel well. They were solicitous, and Justin went and rang for a taxi, though by the time it came they had become coquettish and giggly again.

'Owen is *not*,' Linda used often to say, 'noted for his tact.' But he had never been tempted into such a blunder before. The confession must be made deliberately, soberly, and with Freda's compliance. First, he must make sure of that compliance. He believed he would get it. In the words, 'Do you want me to break everything up for you?' he now found a buried plea.

For a while the incident in the harbourside restaurant shocked him out of his wish to confide at all; then one night he made a partial confession to Caroline Quinlan, Carl Alpino's sister.

He had driven her home from Carl's house. It was midnight, and they were both tired. They sat in his car, stationary at her door, and he found himself saying how strange it was, how mysterious, that one woman could become the focus of a man's thoughts and emotions. He admitted that he spoke of himself.

'Why that particular woman? Oh, it's clear enough in youth, when Nature is using us for her purposes. But now – well, I keep wondering about the component of the imagination, or the memory. Or even the cultural memory, do you think?'

They spoke seriously of this for a while, and were musing on the theory of the desire and pursuit of the whole, and the urge to substitute for lost religions, when Caroline said abruptly, 'But wait, why can't Nature be using you for her purposes again? How old is the woman?'

Owen quickly recalled that he must not give a clue to Freda's identity. 'In her early thirties.'

'Well then? Oh, no doubt it's been taken care of, but Nature's not to know that. And of course, Owen, I notice it's the same old story. You all go for a woman ten years younger, if not more.'

'What have you got against women in their early thirties, Caroline? You're in your early thirties yourself.'

'I care on behalf of my sisters.'

'I didn't know Carl had any other sisters.'

'On behalf of all my sisters, dummy.'

'Oh.'

'I'm interested in the way you say that.'

'Well, I've taken it all in. I've tried to do all the right things. But I get a bit sick of it sometimes. Don't you?'

'I had better go in.' She hauled up a bulging string bag from the floor between her feet. 'Don't,' she said, as he opened the door on his side. 'I can tell what your wife was like by the way you run round the car and open the door like a commissionaire.'

He reached across her and opened the door on her side. 'Only because your hands are full,' he said.

When he shut the door she presented her broad smiling handsome face at the window. The Alpino family was from the Abruzzi, but Caroline, the youngest, had been born here. She said, 'Middle thirties, in fact.'

'Yes?'

'In fact, late thirties.'

'I can tell what a woman's husband was like by the way she hedges about her age.'

'I try not to blame Quinlan for everything. Is your divorce listed yet?'

He nodded. 'October.'

'I wish mine were.'

Blanche was made impatient by his frequent phone calls ('Look, daddy, I'm sorry, but I'm in an awful hurry'), so that sometimes he managed to find out that the Thewens were still away, and that she didn't know when they would be back, and sometimes she did not give him a chance to ask. Now and again he rang the Thewens' number. He no longer thought of it as Freda's number. He intended to say, if Freda answered, 'I must see you. I've something important to say. If you can talk now, give me a time and a place. If you can't, ring me back when you can.'

If Rex or Clive Thewen answered, he supposed he would hang up.

But soon he began to hear the lonely ringing as itself his answer. He stopped ringing, and stopped asking Blanche, and simply set himself to wait, though the silence seeped his confidence.

Timothy wrote to thank him for the information he had sent at Christmas, but remarked with puzzlement on several discrepancies, and on evidence of lines left out. At night, Owen sifted through the rough assemblage of the material, wrote amendments, and supplied the missing lines. At Thorbury Maps he told his apprentice cartographer to go out to Emu Plains to check on a new housing estate. 'I went two weeks ago,' the young man replied. 'The plans are with Charlie now.'

'No worries, dad,' said Charlie benignly. 'We all make mistakes.'

Then Blanche told him that the Thewens had come báck from the south coast, having found nothing.

'Or nothing that Rex didn't dither about until he lost it. Selling that property has really undermined Rex. It's a crucial time for them both.'

Owen's confidence revived. He rang the Thewens' number. Freda answered. He calmly said his rehearsed piece. There was a short pause before she said, with a sing-song cadence, 'You must have the wrong number, sorry,' and rang off. She had been overheard. She wanted time to think about it. It did not diminish his confidence Her sing-song had sounded happy. On waking in the morning he would be certain that today would be the day for her to ring. Or he would open the door and see her standing there. This re-enactment of the only time she had come unannounced was most vivid – his drawing her in and shutting the door, the damp patches under the arms of her dress, her dusty feet, the bag slipping from her shoulder. The continued heat and drought supported his fancy, making it seem like a premonition. He went to the park, walking slowly across the dusty grass, but did not expect to see her there. The parched ground made the lustrous water and bright rocking boats look theatrical.

On a February evening he again drove Caroline Quinlan home. This time she let him take her bags and cartons and put them in the boot. She packed her provisions carelessly, cramming them in. Rice trickled from a broken bag on to the floor of the boot.

On the way she said, 'I suppose your lady is married.'

'Yes indeed.'

'And won't divorce?'

'I hope she will. I'm waiting for an opportunity to put it to her, most seriously.'

227

'You're very brave. I would be afraid to trust my judgement, so soon. Tearing yourself away, prising apart those roots, makes you eccentric for a while, whether it's you who does the tearing, like you and I did, or the other one.'

'My wife went quite, quite mad,' said Owen primly.

'I didn't go mad. But I said and did uncharacteristic things. And so did Quinlan. Didn't you?'

'I did decide to break into my wife's house and steal some records she wouldn't let me have, but I didn't actually do it. And I did almost blurt out some fairly shattering words, but I caught myself in time. Lately, I admit, I've been making more mistakes than usual, but I put that down to, you know—' Owen hesitated before saying it, yet was pleased to be able to say it—'waiting for my lady.'

'Not like my mistakes then. Mine were definitely caused by post-separation dementia.'

'Do they actually call it that?'

'I don't know, but they ought to. I'm not over it yet, either. I still don't trust myself. I don't believe I'll ever marry again, I'll never trust myself enough. I'm on my guard now against the irrational, against someone coming along and imprinting me.'

Freda, lying beside him, had moved one raised knee back and forth while she had spoken in that lazy dissatisfied voice of only sons. 'So that's what happens,' he said.

'If you're unlucky.'

'Or lucky.'

'But Owen, that's the trap,' she said, frowning and laughing. 'It always seems like good luck at first.'

He wished Caroline and he could imprint each other. She was suitable, she was congenial, she was even geographically convenient. She was an anthropologist, and could ask intelligent questions about Timothy, whom she used to meet, with Blanche and Hester, before those three had drifted out of the anti-nuclear movement. She had twin boys of twelve, who spent weekends with their father, and who accounted for most of her impedimenta of string bags and plastic sacks. At meetings at Carl's house, when she leaned across to hand papers to Owen, he looked with appreciation at the bare soft solid arm reaching out to him. He wished he could stop comparing her with Freda, stop saying to himself, But Freda is so graceful, Freda goes like that with her hands, holds her head like that, smiles to herself, carries almost nothing, is not always dropping oranges from a bag, and dropping more when she bends to pick them up. As Freda came towards him from her part of the park, he would not mistake her walk among a thousand.

When he drew up outside Caroline's house, she did not move, but sighed. He realised that at this point she always settled slightly in her seat and gave this sigh.

'Have you heard from Tim lately?' she asked.

'I had a letter today. Remember the American girl? At first she got one mention, then two or three, now suddenly she insinuates herself into this whole letter.'

She laughed as she opened the door. 'Everyone I know imagines they're in love. It's disgusting.'

Owen's premonition of Freda's arrival at his door, though as strong as ever each morning, usually lost conviction during the day, and by evening his expectation would have yielded to depression or ill-temper. But if the day had been distinguished by some incident that had left him stirred or excited, or even if an evening breeze broke the monotony of the heat, he would continue to expect a signal from her. On one occasion his doorbell woke him at three in the morning. He leapt out of bed, the unusual hour turning hope into joyful certainty, and opened the door to see a drunken neighbour lumbering away down the corridor.

On another occasion, early on a Saturday morning, he flung open the door to see Blanche, alone. She had come to ask

Owen to lend them his car. Justin's car had broken down, and because Blanche and Justin had to travel many miles to their jobs, and Owen had only to go to the city, he agreed he could more easily use public transport.

'Sure it's okay, daddy? It's only for a few days.'

'I said it was okay. Though I'm surprised Fatty hasn't a few spare cars.'

Owen could seldom help but mention Fatty; Fatty was a minor itch. But Blanche only murmured reproachfully that his name was Mervyn, and that he was losing weight. Then she said with vigour, 'Dad, why don't you do something about all these beds?'

'I will.' Owen was speculating on how he would feel if Freda should arrive now. He would be pleased; he felt no trepidation at all; it would prepare Blanche for what was to come.

'You always say you will,' Blanche was saying, 'but you never do. It can't be good for you mentally, daddy, all this disorder.'

'I think you're right.'

'And another thing, dad, have you spoken to Gran lately?'

'She was out last time I rang.'

'Or Hester?'

'Yes, but she's monosyllabic on the phone.'

'Then you don't know she has borrowed money from Gran? Gran says we mustn't let her be undercapitalized, just when she's working so hard.'

'She probably is working hard.'

'Who isn't? That place simply siphons off money. First mum, now Gran. Justin and I are really sick of Hes.'

Blanche had never looked more beautiful or lustrously blonde, but Owen wondered if her domestic contentment was not having the unexpected effect of making her complacent, even slightly callous. He remembered Linda, in the days before Annie Ford, and again, when they moved into their first house, and though she was so physically different from Blanche, he was somehow reminded of the way she had preened, tossed her head, stamped about, pointed at things, delivered judgements. He said, 'It's Gran's money, Blanche.'

'Gran's old.'

'Your grandmother is not stupid.'

'She's old and she's too isolated. She's not in a good decision-making situation.'

'Women know so much about the right time to make decisions.'

'Please remember my profession, dad.'

'Of course, dear. But if you wait for the right time to make a decision you may let pass a chance you will never get again.'

'You needn't worry about Gran not getting the chance to give Hes money again. I think you ought to talk to Hes, dad.'

'It's time I saw Hester in any case. Come down and we'll get the car out.'

They were in the hall when the bell rang. Owen dropped his bunch of keys and swore wildly as he bent to pick them up, for now that the formerly desirable moment had come, Blanche, who had whirled at once to lay her hand on the doorknob, seemed a formidable figure with which to confront the face that could hide nothing, which so helplessly let free its truth, love, and dismay. He was almost stunned with relief when he saw that it was not Freda who stood there, but Caroline Quinlan.

'Hello. You're Blanche.' Caroline reached past Blanche to give a bundle of papers to Owen. 'Carl asked me to drop these in, Owen.'

'That's it,' said Blanche. 'You're Carl's sister Caroline. We feel so ashamed of not coming to help any more. Justin too. Tell Carl.'

Owen broke into laughter. 'Tell Carl, tell Carl,' he said in the tenor of his distress. 'Why don't you tell Carl yourself?'

'Daddy,' said Blanche. She turned back to Caroline. 'But of course, we always march.'

'But of course!' echoed Owen, his scorn strong enough to mask his relief and self-disgust. 'We always march!'

Blanche looked amazed and resentful as he bundled her out of the door and shut it behind them. 'Caroline,' he said, angry with her too, 'Blanche is about to borrow my car. Can she drive you home?'

'No thanks, I still have to shop.'

'Shopping for food for your boys?' He hurried them along the corridor, laughing and flicking his keys in noisy desperation. 'I am amused by feminists who wait hand and foot on their sons.'

Caroline pulled her shoulders back. 'Remember I am Italian,' she said tartly, 'and can't help it.'

'You were born here,' he accused her, 'and still can't help it.'

They had reached the passenger lift. 'The boys have their school work,' she said.

He made a scornful face as he pressed the descent button for her. 'Thank you,' she said. 'How useful.'

Blanche and he went on to the goods lift, Blanche giving him side-long glances. 'I didn't know you knew her so well.'

'I don't know her well.'

'Well enough to be rude to her. You were rude to me too. What's wrong with you?'

He was roughly detaching the car key from the ring. 'Nothing I could ever explain to you, Blanche.'

'Dad, I would think it perfectly natural if you became interested in Caroline.'

'Here, take this and get the car out yourself.'

'All right. I didn't ask you to come down.'

He held the key upright. 'Three days, mind. No more.'

'Keep your car. We'll get on without it.'

He dropped the key into the pocket of her dress, then turned and walked back down the corridor, knowing her need of the car would prevent her from following. In his humiliation he laid some of the blame on Freda. She would not stand beside him and lay claim to what they both wanted, yet she always contrived to leave him with a measure of hope. To her declaration that it was over, to her brutal dismissal, she had appended the modification of the speeding ball, the anguished cry. Her timidity and her adherence to her ridiculous vow had abased them both.

Owen rang the letting agent and demanded that someone be sent to remove the beds. He harangued the man, would not let him speak, beat him down with the repetition of, '*Eight months*. It's been *eight months*.' And when the man promised to see to it, Owen could only shout, 'But when? When?'

At Thorbury Maps he squarely faced the mistakes he had been making. He had confirmation of these, and more, from Charlie Hill. 'We didn't want to keep on at you about them, son. We know you've been under stress.'

'I think,' said Owen, 'for a while, I had better not make important decisions without consultation.'

'Good idea, Owen. Just till you steady down.'

He took time off to go across the city in a taxi to see Hester. He found her workroom full of its former, or similar, occupants, all of whom, except Hester and Denise, gathered around his jar of ginger. Those two continued to work. He pulled up a chair beside Hester, and saw her starved beaky stubborn little profile against Denise's, which was plump, white, almost matronly. He had not come to speak of his mother's money. When he quietly asked Hester about Barry, Denise protruded her head and sent him a warning look across Hester's unmoving face. His persistence could get nothing from Hester except a spasmodic pout of her lower lip, a twitch of her nearer shoulder. Her resistance to him reminded him of Freda's: both assumed in him an ignorance so deep that it was useless to try to correct it. He could not allow himself to be goaded into reaching out and slapping her, as he had sometimes done when she was a child. He said goodbye and got up. Hester trailed after him out to the corridor. She leaned against the wall with her ankles crossed.

'Barry's dead. He died a week ago, in Glasgow. His father's gone over.'

'*Glasgow!*'

'Is that all you can say?'

'Oh Hes—'

But she raised a forearm against his apologetic hand. 'I don't want to talk about it, right? And Denise can mind her own business too.'

He kissed her. She allowed it, standing as before, a hard small refractory figure, her ankles crossed.

'Denise is very protective,' he said.

'She's in love with me. She likes doing things to me.'

He could only say, 'And what about you, Hes?'

'I let her. I quite like it.' And she had to add, 'She could get twice the money elsewhere.'

He went back to Thorbury Maps saying to himself with bewilderment, '*Glasgow!*' For Barry's father he substituted a fat man in tight clothes he had once seen moving jerkily and restlessly up and down the aisle in a plane. He could find nothing to substitute for Denise. When his children were growing up he used to tell them, with admirable impartiality, that of course he had nothing against homosexuality, but that life was quite hard enough without the fatigue of belonging to a minority which was still, in spite of reforms, embattled. Thus he had dodged the admission that he could accept those fatigues for other people's children, but not for his own, whom he wanted to be, above all, safe.

The agent's card was in the hall, and all but one bed had been taken away. The removalist had piled his clothes and maps and papers and newspapers in the middle of the sitting room carpet. Even before pouring a drink, Owen pulled the pieces of furniture away from the perimeter of the rooms, where they had been put to make room for the beds, and shoved them into conventional arrangements. He went out to eat, then came back, set a bottle of red wine on the dining table, and began the long task of stowing away. He worked with a fated ironic daintiness, buttoning and neatly folding his clothes, choosing appropriate hangers, beginning at midnight to mark his files.

Justin came into Owen's office, walking slowly and purposefully and as if the ground were hot. He carried a road guide with three markers inserted. 'You said three days,' he said. He sat opposite Owen, opened the guide at the marked places, and with as few words as possible, showed Owen the routes he and Blanche must take each day to their jobs. He traced with a finger the complications and detours of the journey; he spoke of the total absence out there of reliable public transport; he spoke of the time factor; twice he raised his head to send Owen his big-eyed forbearing glance. Well done, said Owen to himself. 'All right,' he said to Justin, 'how much longer?'

'They say another week. It's the transmission as well.'

'If it's a bit more,' said Owen, 'I won't sweat on it.'

In March the drought broke. The rain so beneficent in the country advanced also on Sydney. Driven by contesting coastal winds, it swung and battered down on the city for three days and nights, culminating on the third night in a storm that crashed trees and power poles, blew off roofs, and filled low-lying places with flash floods. Among rumours of calamity, people went cursing and bright-eyed and willing to talk to strangers. Owen, still without a car, competed for taxis or sprang into buses noisy with chatter and dimmed by streaming windows. Standing wedged by bodies, he felt imprisoned, held low by din and chaos, yet was exhilarated too. The sense of enclosure and drama, and the warm wet air, awakened fully his craving for Freda. He was tempted to ring Caroline, to try to fit her into that aching space. He refrained because he liked her too well, and instead beat down his longings with common sense and loud jokes at Thorbury Maps, with sarcasm and fastidiousness, with work and alcohol. At night, drinking while he contined to stow away his possessions, he saw water oozing over the window sills, and went unsteadily round, singing, and stuffed the gaps with towels.

Thorbury Maps, in an old building with thick walls and recessed windows, was a refuge. On the third night, the Friday night of the storm, he worked late with Charlie Hill. Charlie was in high spirits, stimulated by the collapse of a retaining wall in his garden. 'Nothing to be done about it till this stops,' he said with relish. 'And you know how busy they'll all be then. Be bloody months.' At midnight they battled their way to Charlie's car, and sat with wet shoes and trouser cuffs while Charlie, crying, 'No worries, son!' drove Owen very slowly home before setting off north, through the unrelenting descent of water, on the long journey to his own house.

Very early on Saturday Owen woke to a quiet city. He heard a single car pass in the street below and got up to see that the sky had expanded to its usual size and was slowly filling with sunlight.

He took the towels from the window sills and threw them into the bath. He needed to get out; he needed space and unimpeded movement. If he had had his car he would have driven to a beach or to another park, but his and Freda's park was the only nearby open space, and although it did occur to him that after the imprisonment of the last three days Gus would demand walking, and that even as early as this, she may be there, he refused, with strong righteous truculence, to let that possibility warn him off.

He enjoyed the fast downhill walk past awnings blown askew and branches torn from plane trees, but when he came to the steep stone steps, and saw that they were awash with water from the sodden banks, he used the handrail and descended slowly and with care, watching only his feet. When he reached the floor of the park he looked up and saw Freda, about twenty feet away, with the trotting dog at her side, moving towards him with little light slithering running steps, and in her eyes a joyful welcome.

He was so surprised, not by her presence, but by her being on the very rim of his side of the park, and by her haste and joy, that he stopped dead. She caught hold of his wrist when she reached him, as if to make sure that he did not escape while she commanded the dog.

'Sit. Gus. *Sit!*'

The dog sat. 'He's restless,' she said. Owen said, 'You weren't coming to see me?'

She was confidential, still joyful. 'Well, I hoped I would.'

'Has Rex gone away?'

The joy left her face. She released his wrist. 'No.'

'Well, then?'

Dismay was as clear on her face as hostility must have been on his. She pointed at him. 'You don't know. That's it. You don't know.'

'Know what?'

The dog rose and dragged on the lead, making her rock absent-mindedly sideways. 'About the baby.'

Baby. His mind stupidly echoed the word out of his memory of Caroline's remark about Nature's purposes. But at the same time Freda was saying, 'Oh, I'm sorry. I just assumed Blanche had told you.'

237

'Blanche is having a baby?'

'Justin rang and told us last night. Is it your phone? A lot of phones are out of order. Gus!'

Owen pulled the dog back. 'It may be. I've had no calls.'

'You're not pleased?'

'I don't know. They're too young. They weren't going to have children.'

She scoffed. 'Who believed that?'

'What about their studies? No. No. I can't say I'm pleased. You are. That's obvious.'

'I can't help it.'

'All smiles.'

'Gus.' She pulled the dog back again. 'I had better walk him. Will you come?'

They set off towards her part of the park. Except for themselves and a few runners, it was unoccupied. The grass, already quite long, and a soft succulent green, was littered with the debris of the storm. The fig trees had opened their leaves to the gentle air. Seagulls were rising, gliding, banking, everywhere. Following these flights, Owen said, 'It's impossible not to believe they're celebrating.' He saw her smile. 'Oh, for God's sake, not the baby. They must have been cooped up somewhere too.'

'Like poor Gus.' She suddenly threw down Gus's leash. 'Let him go free.'

Trailing the leash, the dog pointed his white wooden-looking muzzle in one direction, then in another, and another. They walked slowly, making themselves a point of return for his angular explorations. Freda put her hands in her pockets and walked with that idle swagger, as she used to do. 'Blanche is three months pregnant,' she said. 'They didn't want to tell anyone till the three months were up.'

'I took them to dinner one night. They were remarkably pleased with themselves. That was why. And why they had to hang on to my car, I suppose. Well, one more child in the world. Who cares? I don't. I've done time as a parent, and I don't propose to do another stretch as a grandparent. I don't give a damn about the baby.'

'You will.'

'Oh, I'll do the usual things. I'll remember its birthday and so on. But tribal joy – I don't have it.'

'Do you have tribal sadness? This isn't Rex's first grandchild. He hates becoming a grandfather, and he hates having a tooth out.'

He looked at her sideways. He said, 'Such clutter?'

'Why not, now?'

'Tell me more.'

'All right. Rex and Clive are furious. They sold too soon.'

'Have we also reached the stage where we can meet?'

'Now and again, if you want to.'

'I don't think I do, Freda. Tell me, if we hadn't met, would you have come to the flat?'

'Well, you see,' she said slowly, 'Rex has been drinking, but last night he stopped, so this morning I told him about the baby. But of course, he was feeling sick. So I just grabbed Gus and came down here. And when I saw all this' – the sweep of her arm included sky, grass, water, seagulls – 'it made me feel so happy that I did want to see you. I wanted to see if you were happy too. I didn't think of coming to the flat. I guessed I would meet you. I knew you would be here, like I sometimes used to know, before.'

'And all this freedom is made allowable by the baby?'

'Yes. You must see that.'

Gus had moved too far away. Owen went after him and brought him back. 'You mean,' he said, handing the leash to Freda, 'it was the end before, but now it's the absolute end.'

She laughed, and threw the leash down again, roughly patting the dog's head before she let him move off. 'But don't go too far,' she told him.

'The absolute end,' said Owen again.

'Owen, it's such a relief. We got through without discovery.'

They crossed the little bridge, preceded by Gus. 'Linda will be pleased about the baby,' said Freda. 'She's marrying that man, Cleeson-Brown, or whatever his name is, isn't she?'

Owen halted. 'Freda, I don't want to come any further.'

'Oh, come on,' she said softly, 'we have to learn to be friends.'

They walked on slowly. 'Was Rex drinking for long?' he asked.

'Yes. But it wasn't too bad. Clive was there.'

'Have you ever thought of leaving Rex?'

'Often. But I can't.'

'Why not?'

She hesitated. 'Apart from anything else, he's sixty, he has that disability, and he loves me.'

'A fine way of showing it.'

'I didn't expect you to say anything so stupid.'

'I'm sorry. I'm feeling sore. For a while, for weeks, I thought that at any time you would come to see me. I thought you wouldn't be able to help it. Don't say anything. Don't say you wanted to, or how hard it was not to. I know you won't say that, in case I start persuading you again. Not that I would, not that I would start persuading you again.'

She said nothing. They passed the place where the first sunken bench had stood before he burst out again. 'You always managed to leave me with some hope. You always managed to modify those firm decisions of yours.'

She turned up the palms of her hands. 'We must stop this. We must learn to be friends.'

'I've been seeing a woman I like,' said Owen.

'Good.' She turned aside to wave to a man with a black poodle, approaching across the grass. 'You're out nice and early,' she called. Owen also waved and smiled before he said, 'I like her very much. So now I can put you out of the picture, I guess that's the way it will be.'

'You need somebody, Owen.'

'And you and I, having learned to be friends, will attend the christening.'

'Yes.'

'I was trying to be funny. They won't have the baby christened.'

'Why ever not?'

'I know they've changed. But hardly that much.'

She was taking the tennis ball from her bag. 'Weren't your children christened?'

'That was Linda. Linda insisted. Here, let me throw it.'

She gave him the ball and snipped the leash from Gus's collar. Gus pranced backward and waited, in total concentration, but at last gave an agonized squeal of a bark. 'Throw it,' whispered Freda.

The dog's rush made a darker cleft in the soft grass. The ball went beyond the sunlit green and reached the shadow cast by the high wall of the yacht club. Gus had nearly reached it when a Doberman loped around the corner of the building from the road. Attracted by the last roll of the ball he snatched it into his mouth. Gus leapt straight at his throat.

Owen heard Freda's shocked gasps as she ran abreast of him across the grass. A very tall young man appeared at a leaping run round the corner of the building, carrying a leash. Gus and the Doberman were clamped together, a single threshing mass, no part discernible except the flash of a dark curved back, then the show of a white brittle hindleg. In a few great leaps the young man reached the dogs, plunged a hand straight in, and grasped the Doberman's collar.

'Good man!' shouted Owen.

'Don't pull,' shouted Freda.

Owen reached the dogs and swiftly bent in and grasped Gus's collar. Freda had fallen behind. 'Don't pull,' she cried again.

But the young man, ignorant or panicked, pulled as she spoke. In the Doberman's mouth hung part of Gus's face.

Gus's jaws held a little of the Doberman's breast. The young man stared for a moment, then put his tongue between his teeth and turned and ran away as fast as he could, his bloodied dog running with grace at his side.

Owen was appalled to see that the animal he held, this dog with the terribly mutilated head, was straining to follow. He held fast to the collar but looked wildly backwards for Freda. She was standing arrested, a forearm half-shielding her eyes, but as the dog's violent momentum occupied Owen again, she ran forward and knelt at his side.

'Down,' she said, in a sonorous voice of command. 'Down.'

'He won't,' said Owen.

'The other dog has gone. He will start to feel his injuries.'

And indeed she soon succeeded in laying the dog in the damp grass on his uninjured side. Owen stood up. 'His eye,' he said.

'The eye may be all right.'

He wanted to call her mad, to point out that only half the eye was in the socket. He thought her too calm. She was evenly, rhythmically stroking the dog's side. He said, 'I threw that damned ball too far.'

'Forget that,' she said, 'forget it.' He supposed she was speaking in that mesmerized voice so that she would not convey alarm to the animal. 'There's not much blood,' she said. 'I must get him to the vet.'

'Blanche has my car. I'll ring Rex if you like.'

She gave him a look of calculation, though she continued to stroke the dog, and her voice held its trance-like calm. 'It's the only thing to do.'

'Don't worry. I'll be careful.'

'The nearest phone is on the wharf,' she intoned. 'Ask whoever answers to ring the vet, then bring the car down here.'

She began to tell him the number, and when he curtly said he knew it, she said, 'Tell them to bring towels and a plastic sheet.'

Owen found no public phone on the wharf, but the boat agency was open. 'An emergency,' he said to the salesman. 'May I use your phone?'

The salesman indicated the phone with a nod. 'Someone injured?' he asked, as Owen waited for a reply. 'A dog,' said Owen. 'A dawg,' whispered the salesman. 'Rex or Clive Thewen, please,' said Owen into the phone.

'Clive here.'

'Mrs Thewen is in the park, behind the yacht club, with the dog. He's injured. She wants you to ring the vet, then bring the car down here.'

'How did it happen?'

Owen was relieved to be speaking to Clive instead of Rex. He said, 'A fight.'

'A fight, eh? What kind of dog was the other?'

'A Doberman. She would like you to hurry.'

'Gus wouldn't have had the height. How did he go?'

Owen reminded himself that a man who had lately driven round shooting his sheep would be unlikely to be moved by an injury to a disappointing dog. 'He went well enough,' he said. 'Please hurry. Oh, and will you bring towels and a plastic sheet.'

'That bad, eh? Well, old Gus, true to the breed after all. You don't see many good dog fights these days. Wait, here's Rex. Wants to speak to you.'

Rex said, 'Hello. There may be trouble getting hold of a vet. But tell my wife we'll be down as soon as we get one lined up. Who are you?'

Owen would never understand why he replied as he did, though he believed the abruptness of the question had something to do with it, as had the amused presence of the listening salesman. He said, 'I was just passing by.'

'Right. Thank you. Decent of you. Tell my wife we'll be as quick as we can.'

Owen felt the full extent of his own stupidity only as he was walking off the wharf. When he turned the corner into the park, and saw Freda crouched low over the dog, he began to run. Two young boys stood at a slight distance, in embarrassed or respectful attitudes. A woman passing on the path shielded her child's eyes with a handbag.

Freda no longer stroked the dog, though a hand still lay on his ribs. She was convulsively weeping, giving now and again a loud hiccupping sob. Blood poured from Gus's wound into grass and earth stained all around him. Seagulls wreathed above them. As Owen knelt at Freda's side, he saw that the animal was still breathing. He spoke close to Freda's ear.

'Freda, I called you Mrs Thewen to your brother-in-law. That didn't matter, I've never met him. But then Rex came on the line, and asked me who I was, and I said I was just a passer-by. *God* knows why. But it means I had better beat it, before they get here.'

Though she nodded, he was uncertain of her comprehension. He stood up and looked across the park. By the time the car arrived he would be over the bridge, on his own side of the park, perhaps on the stone steps, or quite out of sight. Yet he stood, hesitant and baffled. One of the boys came up and asked him if help was coming for the dog.

'They have to contact a vet first,' he told the boy, 'so that he'll be there as soon as they get the dog home.'

'Bad thinking,' said the boy. 'They should bring the vet here to give him a shot of something.'

The practical boy reminded Owen of Timothy at that age. 'Maybe they will,' he said with a sigh.

The boy returned to report quietly to his mate. Freda's weeping had become wilder. Owen knelt at her side. Weeping of this kind, this keening and choking and sobbing, had weakened and cajoled him so often that even though he knew her tears were not meant to command him, but were for the dog, he could not help but set himself against them. He said coolly, 'I'm going now, Freda.'

244

She nodded again. Conscious of the two boys, he put an arm lightly across her shoulders and kissed her cheek. Mingled with the familiar smell of her body were the the smells of blood, fresh grass, and damp earth. He pulled her towards him and spoke into her ear.

'Darling, my darling, I want to stay. I can't go, let me stay. What does it matter—'

And so he went on, almost incoherently, not noticing her struggles, until she moved her elbow up, and with a crude violent childish nudge, pushed him away.

At the moment of losing his balance he was instead able to spring to his feet. He heard one of the boys say quietly, 'He was kissing her.' He wanted to laugh, or cry, or pull her up and hit her, or do anything rather than walk away. And when he did start walking, he walked stiffly, and moved his upper body from side to side as if with indignation. The park was filling with people now, and on his side were many jubilant dogs, running free or with trailing leads. As he climbed the stone steps, he noticed grass stains on the knees of his trousers.

The phone was ringing when he got home. It was Blanche, to complain that his phone had been out of order, and to tell him about the baby. As he heard himself saying, 'That's great news, dear. That's splendid,' his voice sounded so hearty and false that he started to laugh. Blanche was ready to take offence, to believe he laughed because she and Justin had been so definite about wanting no children; but he managed to convince her that he was laughing with joy, about the baby.

He knew the dog must be dead, but had no confirmation of it until a week later, when Blanche and Justin came to return his car. Expecting the satisfaction and confidence they had displayed lately, he was surprised to see how subdued they both looked.

'We've just been over to see mum,' said Justin.

'How *are* your parents?'

'Freda's been sick,' said Blanche.

'She still is, really,' said Justin. 'Her dog got injured in the park. And you know what bloody Clive did? Brought down a gun, and when he saw there was no hope, shot him there and then. And dad let him.'

'Let him?' echoed Owen in wonder.

'He let him.'

'But if he was suffering—' said Owen.

'You don't shoot dogs in parks,' said Justin.

'We can't get over it,' said Blanche, her arms spread on either side of her, and her hands drooping over the arms of the chair.

Owen asked no more questions. They would meet again one day, as she had predicted. They would stand in a room, with other people, and talk to each other. He would be careful to talk also to Rex. It would not be soon. Perhaps, since she had thought a christening possible, they would meet for the first time at the christening of this baby. Linda would be there, and Timothy if he were home by then; Rex and Freda; his mother and himself. And Hester (Hester would be there somewhere). Blanche, in the centre, held the baby, and Justin smiled down at them both. There was always a photograph, a cluster in the porch of some church, or on the buffalo grass outside while the busy traffic slid by. Owen would slip the photograph from its envelope, take it to the light, and seek them out, face by face. And there they would be: the Thewens. By that time he would have learned more about her, and more about him, and about the conjunction would know less than before. He would never know what the Thewens were really like.

Also by Jessica Anderson

TIRRA LIRRA BY THE RIVER

A beautifully written novel of a woman's
seventy-year search to find a place where she truly
belongs.

For Nora Porteous, life is a series of escapes. To
escape her tightly knit small-town family, she
marries, only to find herself confined again, this
time in a stifling Sydney suburb with a selfish,
sanctimonious husband. With a courage born of
desperation and sustained by a spirited sense of
humor, Nora travels to London, and it is there that
she becomes the woman she wants to be. Or does
she?

'Finely honed structurally and tightly textured, it's
a wry, romantic story that should make Anderson's
American reputation and create a demand for her
other work.'
—The Washington Post

'There may be a better novel than *Tirra Lirra by
the River* this year, but I doubt it.'
—Cleveland Plain Dealer

'Subtle, rich and seductive, this beautifully written
novel casts a spell of delight upon the reader.'
—Library Journal

Winner of the Miles Franklin Award, Australia's
most prestigious literary prize.

DOWN BY THE DOCKSIDE

Griena Rohan

Eilishe Cahaleen Deirdre Flynn, otherwise known as
Lisha, is Australian by birth, Liverpool Irish in every
other respect. Raised by her grandmother, she grows
up in the tough slums of Port Melbourne during the
Depression.

Swept away by the excitement and sleaziness of
wartime Melbourne, Lisha marries a sailor at
seventeen. By eighteen she is a mother, by twenty-one
a widow. In desperation, she turns to the people of her
childhood. She sings in night clubs, teaches in
back-street dancing schools and associates with petty
criminals.

Down by the Dockside is a gutsy account of Australian
life in the 1930s and 40s by an author whose work has
long been unrecognised.

BLOOD IN THE RAIN

Margaret Barbalet

Blood in the Rain is about Jessie. Her life is, in many ways, ordinary — a young girl growing up and reaching for maturity in the Australia of the Great War and the Depression, as she moves from country town to country town and eventually to Adelaide. But Margaret Barbalet's evocative novel follows Jessie's odyssey to self-acceptance with a perception and compassion that reveals a person who is quite extraordinary.

'She writes with a delicate power of the elusive joys and the tangible pains of childhood until finally they become the shape of an adult.'

Helen Daniel

TILLY'S FORTUNES

Helen Asher

Tilly, the golden-eyed girl, becomes independent early in her life. With dreams that bear her beyond the drudgery of the chocolate factory, she has little trouble facing up to hardship.

Tilly decidees that to bear children is what she is cut out for. And the dream continues in an elated way as she gives birth to child after child. Can such tranquility last? She doesn't ask.